EVA
EVERGREEN
AND THE CURSED WITCH

EVA EVERGREEN
AND THE CURSED WITCH

JULIE ABE
ILLUSTRATED BY SHAN JIANG

LITTLE, BROWN AND COMPANY
New York   Boston

Copyright © 2021 by Julie Abe
Illustrations copyright © 2021 by Shan Jiang

Cover art copyright © 2021 by Shan Jiang. Cover design by Karina Granda.
Cover copyright © 2021 by Hachette Book Group, Inc.

Little, Brown and Company
Hachette Book Group
1290 Avenue of the Americas, New York, NY 10104
Visit us at LBYR.com

First Edition: August 2021

Little, Brown and Company is a division of Hachette Book Group, Inc.
The Little, Brown name and logo are trademarks of Hachette
Book Group, Inc.

The publisher is not responsible for websites (or their content)
that are not owned by the publisher.

Library of Congress Cataloging-in-Publication Data
Names: Abe, Julie, author. | Jiang, Shan, illustrator.
Title: Eva Evergreen and the cursed witch / Julie Abe ;
illustrated by Shan Jiang.
Description: First edition. | New York : Little, Brown and Company, 2021.
| Series: Eva Evergreen ; 2 | Summary: Young witch Eva Evergreen embarks
on a journey to find the source of the powerful magical storm
known as the Culling and put an end to it once and for all.
Identifiers: LCCN 2020028155 | ISBN 9780316493949 (v. 2 ; hardcover) |
ISBN 9780316493901 (ebook) | ISBN 9780316493925 (ebook other)
Subjects: CYAC: Witches—Fiction. | Magic—Fiction. | Adventure and
adventurers—Fiction. | Fantasy.
Classification: LCC PZ7.1.A162 Er 2021 | DDC [Fic]—dc23
LC record available at https://lccn.loc.gov/2020028155

ISBNs: 978-0-316-49394-9 (hardcover), 978-0-316-49390-1 (ebook)

Printed in the United States of America

LSC-C

Printing 1, 2021

THIS STORY IS FOR YOU, READER.

YOU SHINE WITH IMPOSSIBLE
POSSIBILITIES.

*

AND FOR EMILY—
WE LOVE YOU, FOREVER AND ALWAYS.

CONTENTS

PART ONE: THE CURSED WITCH

Chapter 1: The Crystal Castle 3

Chapter 2: The Secrets of the Crystal Castle 9

Chapter 3: The Confessing Map 21

Chapter 4: Twisted Lies, Twisted Enchantments 39

Chapter 5: Heartbeat 53

Chapter 6: Impossible Truths 61

PART TWO: THE FIGHT FOR THE FORGOTTEN

Chapter 7: A Call from Home 77

Chapter 8: Endless Gray 86

Chapter 9: A Loss Beyond Measure 97

Chapter 10: A Glimmer of Light 113

Chapter 11: The Forgotten Bookstore 128

Chapter 12: Rogue Magic 142

Chapter 13: The Start of a Journey 158

Chapter 14: The Elite Triplets 166

PART THREE: THE TWISTED FOREST

Chapter 15: The Hidden Camp...........................*175*

Chapter 16: The Mirage.............................*187*

Chapter 17: In the Shadows of the Twisted
Forest.................................*201*

Chapter 18: A Pocketful of Gold........................*214*

Chapter 19: The Cave of Secrets *228*

Chapter 20: Into the Belly of a Nightdragon.......*246*

Chapter 21: A Ghost from the Past *256*

Chapter 22: The Cavern of the Lost....................*269*

Chapter 23: Water and Fire................................*276*

Chapter 24: The Nest of a Monster *285*

Chapter 25: The Tomb of the Living..................*291*

Chapter 26: The Decision *299*

Chapter 27: Fighting for the Light......................*311*

Chapter 28: The Final Curse............................*319*

Chapter 29: Impossible Possibilities *331*

PART FOUR: THE BURNING FLAME

Epilogue: The Year-End Feast............................*349*

PART ONE

The Cursed Witch

CHAPTER 1

THE CRYSTAL CASTLE

Glimmering in the sky, the tips of the queen's crystal spires blazed like torches in the early-afternoon sun. But Mother and I flew low on our broomsticks through the side streets, swathed in the shadows of the magnificent castle.

"It would've been faster to fly overhead." Mother's eyes darted around as she nodded for us to turn left after a cobbler's shop. "Yet, if we tried that..."

"Grottel might see us," I whispered, fear lancing my heart. Mother nodded grimly. Her hair, the same inky black as mine, swirled around her shoulders in the chilling wind.

Even Ember, my flamefox, seemed wary as he stuck close to me, the warmth of his red-gold fur emanating through the canvas of my knapsack. He, too, understood the gravity of this mission. Just earlier today, after the ceremony where I'd received my rank as a Novice Witch—finally, I was an official member of the Council of Witches and Wizards—I'd managed to cast a spell on a map of the realm, searching for the source of the Culling. The last place I'd expected it to come from was Grand Master Hayato Grottel's tower.

And Grottel, the leader of our Council, was to be meeting with the queen any moment now. If he was the one who started the Culling, a strange, cursed force of nature...Each year, without a moment's notice, the Culling pelted the land with anything from a nearly unquenchable wildfire to the typhoon that had hit Rivelle's east coast, including Auteri, the town I'd sworn to protect. If Grottel was truly responsible for the Culling, the queen was not safe.

Mother and I looped around a family on a stroll and sped through the wide stone street needling through the wood buildings of Okayama, Rivelle Realm's capital city. Each sharp turn matched the pitter-pattering beat of my heart.

"There's a side street here." Mother nodded to the right. Her eyebrows were pinched with worry, which was strange on her usually serene face. "Takes us to a bridge, and—"

We flew around the corner, and I breathed in with delight.

The North Torido River rushed under a bridge, rippling playfully. Sunlight danced on the surface of the deep blue-black waters, a clashing, beautiful mixture of dark and light. On the water, a steamboat much like the one I'd taken to Auteri chugged along. The start of my Novice quest had been only a moon ago, but with everything that had happened since, it felt like a year. *Novice, Adept, Elite, Master, Grand Master.* There were five magical ranks, each more difficult to reach than the last, but joy still tingled through my veins: I'd managed to make my first step into the Council.

We swerved around a wood house, lines of laundry fluttering from the balcony, and then the street opened up to the castle, separated by only a moat. My boots skimmed the surface of the waterway, and a few floating birds rustled their wings, squawking loudly. We shot up a thin, rocky ridge snug against the castle. The thick crystal walls were opal-like, swirling white at the base, but without a door to be seen.

Mother pulled up her broom, gracefully landing on the stone ridge. I tugged up on the Fiery Phoenix, my broomstick, but it tilted to the right, as if it wanted to keep on flying.

"I'm going to turn you into firewood," I hissed, and half stopped, half fell when the Fiery Phoenix unceremoniously dumped me off. I stumbled to avoid hitting the patches of white flowers along the wall. Dusting off my skirt, my cheeks burned as Mother glanced at me. I quickly looked around at the sharp rocks leading back down to the moat and the thin line of dusty cliffside Mother and I were precariously perched on. "Um, where's the door?"

"Witches always have more than one entrance," Mother said, raising an eyebrow.

Ember jumped out of my knapsack and pawed the wall, but nothing happened. I looked closer and noticed etch marks in the crystal.

> FROM THIS DAY FORWARD, WE WILL BELIEVE IN THE IMPOSSIBLE.
>
> A CASTLE OF CRYSTAL, A DREAM OUT OF REACH.
>
> ALL CREATED BY TWO FRIENDS WHO WILL NEVER FALL APART.
>
> FROM THIS DAY FORWARD, THIS CASTLE WILL PROTECT THE TRUE RULER OF RIVELLE.
>
> *
>
> A.S. & N.E.

A.S., as in Queen Alliana Sakamaki? And N.E. as in...Nelalithimus...Evergreen? My eyes widened. I'd heard that the castle had turned from stone to crystal on the day Queen Alliana had stepped into power. I gaped at Mother. "Did you make this?"

The strain around my mother's eyes lessened, just a bit. "A story for another day. Watch carefully to see how to get in." She gestured her wand toward the patches of flowers at our feet.

"Do I need to pick the right flower?"

"Everyone thinks it's the flashy things, right?" Mother knelt down, the thick black cloth of her dress swirling, like the flowing currents of the Torido Rivers. "But it's the roots that matter. And all you need is a touch of magic."

I swallowed. A touch of magic *was* all I had.

Mother whispered to the roots, and I studied the swish of her wand, trying to understand how to cast enchantments like her, when a shock ran through my veins. Her hands were shaking. Ever so slightly, but they were shaking. She was far more worried about the queen than she would admit. *"We will believe in the impossible possibilities, a crystal castle, an underground escape, a choice we won't make."*

The ground rumbled underneath, and she waved. "Follow quickly, all right?"

"What if my spell doesn't work?"

A gaping hole opened underneath her feet. Mother firmly held on to her broomstick, flashing me a strained smile—

And the ground swallowed her up.

I stumbled back in surprise. There were only the crystal walls, the starburst white flowers shifting gently in the cool air, and me and Ember. My flamefox sniffed the ground, but not a trace of my mother remained. Ember and I were standing on the ridge next to the castle all by ourselves. Across the moat, the city folk strolled through the winding streets, oblivious in their own bubbles.

Follow quickly.

Ember pawed at me, and snuffled at the ground where my mother had disappeared, his pointy red-gold ears turning left to right.

There was no time to waste. I couldn't hold Mother back.

"*Do not glower, let me underneath these beautiful flowers.*" Light flashed from my wand, coating the blossoms with a warm glow. I blinked. The flowers waved happily in the breeze, their petals shimmering sunrise gold instead of white. Wonderful. I'd changed the way the flowers looked.

Knock, knock. I jumped. Below, Mother was likely wondering what in the realm had happened to me. I'd just passed my Novice quest. I had to show her I was stronger, especially after I'd fought the Culling in Auteri. Even though I was only twelve years and four moons old and didn't have the years of magical experience Mother had, surely I could manage an enchantment like this.

I squared my shoulders and pointed my wand at the patch of flowers where Mother had disappeared. "*I will not hide, let me inside.*"

Dirt rumbled, covering the tips of my boots. I was sinking. *Sinking* into the ground. Ember barked furiously at the ground shifting around us, and then jumped into my arms. Had . . . had my spell worked?

My stomach dropped as the world fell out from under me.

CHAPTER 2

The Secrets of the Crystal Castle

The ground twisted with the sharp scent of fresh dirt and swallowed us up. Ember and I fell through a tunnel, shock reverberating through my veins as I let out a cry of surprise. My knapsack cushioned my back as I tightly clutched my flamefox. Crystallized roots wove into a slide, sending me deep into the earth, curving left and right.

Just as suddenly as we'd fallen through the ground, we stopped, landing in a soft patch of vines, dotted with the same delicate white starbursts.

Ember leaped off my legs, shaking himself quickly. He indignantly eyed the slide. *I'm not sure if I want to try that again.*

"I agree," I muttered, grabbing my broomstick from

where it had tumbled to my feet. "But no time to worry about how we're getting out. Let's go."

I glanced around, and tingles ran up my skin in surprise.

The secret entrance had taken us to a tall, circular chamber of pure crystal that looked like it had been hewn from a single rock. The glowing torches on the wall made the room incandescent with light, every intricately carved edge sparkling like I stood within a treasure chest of jewels. Mother was nowhere to be seen, but there was only one way she could've gone—an alcove at the far end led to a ramp that spiraled up. I jumped onto the Fiery Phoenix, and Ember leaped onto my knee, to my shoulder, and then dove into my knapsack. I pushed off the ground, and my broomstick jolted forward, happy to be flying again.

The spiraling ramp looped and looped a dizzying number of times, like a tunnel leading me into the sky. As I went higher, the outside-facing walls showed slightly clear window-like spots here and there, revealing the city far below and the sky stretching around me. When I felt like I'd flown high enough to pierce the clouds, the ramp ended at a tapestry covering an opening. I slowed until I could dismount.

My heart thudding, I pulled back the edge of the tapestry and peeked out. From my knapsack, Ember sniffed at the air with curiosity. The secret entrance had led us to an empty hallway where everything was crystal: the white tiles underneath, the shimmering walls, the ceiling above. The corridor was as wide as the grandest room in Auteri's town hall, big enough to fit five sailing ships, but this tower stretched up so far into the sky that clouds drifted past the windows.

I stepped forward, and I gasped with realization: Ember and I were in one of the queen's famed crystal spires. Where Queen Alliana laid down the laws of the realm, where she met with her Advisors—the princesses and princes who served each region. I turned to see where I'd flown in from, but there was only the tapestry of gray rocks and blue sky, almost like a window to a different realm, and the statue of a phoenix, its wings stretched as if it was just about to take off, and a set of crystal stairs.

"Eva!" my mother whispered, from where she leaned against a tall white birch door, listening intently. I took one more look up and down the empty hallway and hurried to join her. Ember crawled out of the knapsack to lean against my boots, his pointed ears twitching as he kept a lookout for us, too.

Mother muttered a spell, and the door parted ever so slightly, soundlessly. She peered through the crack in the door. "The queen...the queen...Where is—"

Then my mother breathed out in relief. "Hayato isn't here yet." She nodded toward the white birch door. "Time for you to properly meet Queen Alliana and tell her what we saw on the map. The truth about the Culling."

"Right," I squeaked, plucking a spiderweb off

Ember's ear and brushing dust bunnies off my black skirt. "The queen. The map. The Culling."

My mother pushed open the doors and strode into the royal chamber, with me close at her heels.

I'd thought the town hall in Auteri was grand, with its five floors of marble staircases and gold doors. But the queen's chambers were extraordinary. Thick white crushed velvet runners lined the center of the room, and the crystal floor was inlaid with streaks of gold.

At the front, Queen Alliana sat on a gilded throne formed in the shape of the sun, with rays illuminating outward. Her crown rested on the dark hair, streaked with gray, flowing down over her shoulders, but her long, regal face looked like she was ready for war. Her pure white gown, laced with gold, glowed brighter than the sunrise. She was talking to a haughty-looking girl kneeling in front of her, adorned with the same thin circlet Princess Stella wore, marking her status as a princess and one of the Regional Advisors.

To our sides, Royal Guards were stationed all around the edges of the room, their hands on their long swords, but a nod from the queen eased the tightness in their shoulders.

"Alliana," Mother started. "Queen Alliana. May we see you—privately?"

"The queen has a meeting soon. Please state the manner of your business," said the princess, moving to the queen's side. The girl looked to be four or five years older than me, maybe sixteen or seventeen, with freckles smattered over the bridge of her nose and cheeks. I was sure I hadn't ever met her before, yet the way she carried herself reminded me of Princess Stella, the Advisor to Auteri.

Mother glanced at me pointedly, and I summoned the courage to speak. "It's...it's about the Culling."

The guards lining the room shifted, their metal plates clanking.

"We must speak to you alone," Mother insisted, staring deeply at Queen Alliana. "It's vital."

The queen pressed her lips together as she looked from Mother, to me trailing behind her, and then to the legions of Royal Guards all around. She rose from her throne. "Very well."

The girl followed in the queen's path to a side room. "And by alone, she means I'll join, too," the princess declared, in a voice that allowed no argument. Mother quirked her lips, but looked to the queen.

"Anri's right," the queen said. "She's my shadow, in the way your daughter is yours."

"Ah, Eva's no longer my shadow," Mother said. "She's a proper Novice Witch now."

"Well said." The queen turned to look over Mother's shoulder, her dark red lips curving up into a smile. "Novice Evergreen, I'm looking forward to hearing about your quests that are yet to come. I'm sure you will accomplish much for our realm, just like Nela."

"Thank you, Queen Alliana," I murmured breathlessly, dipping into a deep bow.

In a room crowded with plush chairs and shelves piled with dusty tomes, the queen walked to the window and stared out at the city. She gazed at the North Torido River running alongside the castle. "It's beautiful, isn't it? The waters flow through our realm like the blood of our land."

I remembered the common saying: "Our queen is the realm's heart; the Council is the realm's blood." Then I clapped my hand over my mouth.

"Well spoken, Novice Evergreen." The queen inclined her head.

My cheeks burned. Unintentionally, I'd blurted the proverb out in front of the very person it was about.

The queen added, "And I am lucky for such a faithful Council that serves me and the realm in these times of need."

My chest clenched. When we told her what I'd cast onto the map...what would she think of our Council then?

Mother carefully closed the door behind us and spun her wand in her hand. A white light flashed on the walls, and the queen smiled, her eyes soft with nostalgia.

"You haven't used a silencing enchantment in a long time," Queen Alliana said, tipping her head to the side. "Surely nothing warrants that?"

"We...we want to show you the source of the Culling," Mother said.

Princess Anri gasped, and the queen stiffened with shock. "The source? But the Council's been searching for eight years."

"Hayato's been searching." Mother crossed her arms. "I'd been staying out of his way, as he requested, until my own daughter had to fight the Culling."

The queen glanced at me. "I'm thankful for your help in Auteri."

Ember nudged me with his forehead, urging me to respond. I bowed, barely able to squeak out, "Glad to be of service, Queen Alliana." Memories of fighting the storm—the hopelessness that had swirled through me as the waves pounded the coast, and almost getting lost in the thick haze of rain—were so fresh in my mind. But against all chances, I'd used paper to fight water, and I'd managed to expand and waterproof a set of makeshift shields to protect Auteri from the worst of the storm. I shuddered, thankful for the summery warmth of the castle.

"It was frightening to have Auteri in the path of the Culling. Such a lovely town—and on the day of the Festival of Lights, too! But I heard Princess Stella and Mayor Taira's reports, and I'm very relieved you were there, Novice Evergreen. If you have any insight into the Culling, please share it with me."

"Watch this," Mother said, nodding toward me. I

pulled the map out of my knapsack, and Ember whimpered nervously.

Mother unfurled the thick paper, holding it out so the queen could see how the map displayed all of Rivelle Realm. "We cast a spell on this, so the paper would fuse with locks of hair from two children, Eva's friends from Auteri, whose parents are missing. This might give us insight into why Kaya disappeared, Alliana."

"Elite Kaya Ikko welcomed me to her bookstore with open arms when I first arrived in Okayama, even though I didn't have a spark of magic," Queen Alliana said. "Her book recommendations were always the best, almost enchanted. I was terribly worried when she disappeared, and not a clue was to be found about her whereabouts."

Murmurs of voices echoed through the walls, but no one drew near our room yet.

Princess Anri checked her pocket watch. "The meeting's set to start."

Queen Alliana smiled ruefully. "Oh, your spell was always so clever, Nela."

"They can't hear us, but we can hear them," Mother explained to my questioning glance.

"Shall we—may we cast the spell now?" I asked, glancing between Queen Alliana and Anri. The queen had to see this before she met with Grottel. "It's a simple spell, but shows the location of the three missing parents." Davy's mother had disappeared in a previous Culling, whereas

Charlotte's parents had been gone for so long that she had no recollection of them.

The queen nodded. "Certainly. If your enchantment can provide long-awaited answers about the Culling, my meeting can wait."

All four of us gathered around the map, and Mother said encouragingly, "Go on. You should cast the spell. It worked best with you."

Me? Just me?

I bit my lip. I couldn't possibly conjure up my magic in front of the queen.

But Mother nudged my shoulder, her dark brown eyes full of steadfast belief, and I swallowed. Stepping closer to the map, I tried to shutter all thoughts of the queen watching me, or the people outside waiting to meet with the queen. Ember pressed against my boots, giving all his support. I steeled myself and chanted, *"A search for two friends—"*

Outside, a man demanded loudly, "Why is Queen Alliana with the Evergreens?"

I could recognize that sharp, condescending voice anywhere. Grand Master Hayato Grottel.

A murmur from one of the Royal Guards answered him, and his voice rose. "The Evergreens are meeting with the queen about the *Culling*?"

A fist pounded on the door.

I tried to continue. *"C-close to my heart—"* Bronze light rippled over the map and faded as my voice cracked.

"Open up, Nela," Grottel growled. The door burst open, sending Mother's charm into a burst of white vapor. Her spell had only silenced our voices from being heard, not sealed the door.

And, in the opening, Grand Master Hayato Grottel stared down at us. His eyes were cold as they scanned me, Mother, Princess Anri, and then Queen Alliana. He was dressed in all black, with a heavy diamond ring on one finger marking his Grand Master rank. Grottel dipped into the slightest of bows toward the queen before eyeing the map.

"What. Is. *That*." His cold voice shook me to the bone.

Queen Alliana turned, quietly assessing the head of the Council. "It's a map of the realm," she said in a cool, light voice that didn't betray her thoughts. "But there's something very peculiar about it. Novice Evergreen ensorcelled the parchment to show a certain phenomenon I've wanted answers about, for many years."

Grottel froze, his dark, hooded eyes flicking between me and the glowing map, and scoffed. "What's this childish map supposed to prove?"

"The Evergreens are looking into the source of the Culling," the queen said. When Grottel's forehead pinched, she added, "At my command."

"The map shows the complete path of the Culling," Mother said. "And it's quite an...illuminating path, to say the least."

Grand Master Grottel froze, his face unreadable. I tried to study him, to see if there was some way it could be possible that the leader of our very Council was the one behind all the harm that had been done to the realm...but I couldn't sense a single trace of worry or surprise through his hard eyes. If anything, he looked *calculating*, but could that be just because Mother had finally gotten permission to look into the Culling without Grottel's say in the matter?

Grottel, after all, had been the one who'd taken over all efforts to find the source of the Culling. But after eight years, he'd been unsuccessful. Or, perhaps he *was* hiding something.

Mother crossed her arms, and Grottel raised a greasy eyebrow back. A slow anger simmered in my mother's eyes; Mother had fought each Culling, and had seen the destruction it wrecked across Rivelle, every year. She knew the terrible toll the Culling had extracted from the realm.

A head poked in from the main room. "Sir, Grand Master Grottel," Elite Norya Dowel, a perpetually nervous witch and Grottel's assistant, chimed. "We were hoping to begin the meeting, but the queen—"

Her eyes widened. "Oh, is that a charmed map?"

"It's nothing of significance," Grottel snapped. "*My* meeting is of utmost urgency." He sneered, looking between me and Mother. "I suppose it's convenient you are here, Nela. We have no time for this map or foolishness, not now. First, come, join us." He gestured back into the main room, the corner of his lip twisting up. "I'm sure you'll enjoy hearing what we have to discuss with the queen. Norya, it's time to discuss *that* matter."

His assistant squeaked in surprise. "But the merchant guild's requests—"

"*Now.* I will call the Inner Council." Grottel pulled a handful of black-tipped papers from his pocket, no bigger than the palm of his hand. With a few muttered words and a jab of his wand, the squares folded into birds with sharp wings and took off, soaring so fast that they were gone in the instant I blinked.

Mother and I glanced at each other in confusion. He was summoning the *Inner* Council? But—why?

Grottel bowed, motioning for Queen Alliana to exit the room ahead of him. After she passed, he straightened from his bow, looking down at Ember. "Is that a flamefox that doesn't light up? Does it even know how to breathe fire?" His lip curled derisively.

Ember let out a sad cry, and I took a step forward to defend him—

But before I could speak, Grottel spun on his heel, stalking into Queen Alliana's meeting room, his back already turned to us.

CHAPTER 3

THE CONFESSING MAP

Mother stopped in the doorway, and I looked up at her curiously. Her tanned skin bleached bone-white with shock.

"What is this?" she whispered, scanning the room. I craned to look around her.

I tried to muffle my gasp.

Earlier, the room had glimmered with light streaming through crystal windows, but now it seemed as if Grottel had dropped a cloak over the sun. The right side of the room had been thrown into darkness, with Queen Alliana's throne moved to the center. Nine tall-backed chairs surrounded the throne. All around, the Royal Guards stood watch, hands on their long swords. Princess Anri moved to the side, standing by the wall.

Grottel strode to the chair to the right of the queen's throne.

Mother started toward the chair to the left, but when Grottel settled into his chair, he raised a hand. "Oh, Nela," he said, shaking his head with fake pity. "I don't think there's a spot for you to sit, not right now."

The queen looked up from her throne. "Whatever do you mean, Grand Master Grottel? The agenda was merely about some inter-guild requests."

Grottel sneered, steepling his fingers.

"Ah, but I've invited the Inner Council, you see," he said as the door swung open. It creaked ominously as a hooded figure stepped inside and made their way to the nearest open chair. "All Inner Council members should be here soon...and what I have to share, well, it'll be worth the short wait."

෧෨

Less than a half hour later, the chairs for the Inner Council were filled. Except there was no seat for Mother—she'd had to charm up two chairs for me and her on her own. But judging by how they were hardwood and without a cushion for comfort, Mother was distracted. These chairs were nothing like the plush armchairs she would usually summon out of thin air.

Cloaks covered the nine members' clothes that might identify their ranks; deep hoods hid their faces. I'd tried guessing, many times over the years, who might be on the Inner Council, but even when I stood in front of them, their faces were too well concealed.

They lounged on their chairs almost as grand as thrones in the shadows of the room. The lanterns, enchanted with a flameless glow, didn't seem to be able to cut through the darkness.

I shivered as I looked around, trying to make sense of this. Mother was a member of the Inner Council. I'd known that nearly as long as I'd known about the Council of Witches and Wizards, though the identities of the Inner Council members were a secret, because her many days attending sudden and urgent Council meetings didn't match the once-a-moon cadence of the general Council. Once I'd started reading magical tomes about the history of the Council, I had pieced together her schedule with the passages about the Inner Council—books had always helped me find the right answer. And, with this information, I'd asked her directly, stating all the facts that I'd found in the magical tomes. She'd laughed, saying that it was impossible to keep a magical secret from me, and admitted she was part of the Inner Council.

Now, in this dark and forbidding atmosphere, her joyful laughter seemed like it was so far in the distant past that I might've imagined it.

The Inner Council was a secret group of ten witches and wizards, plucked from the general Council for their input on magical matters in the realm. Grand Master Grottel, as head of the Council, picked half the members, but the queen, who ruled over all of Rivelle, not just magic within the realm, selected the remaining five Inner Council members. I figured that she'd been the one to pick Mother.

"So, ah, I think we should start this meeting," Norya said. She hurriedly rearranged papers on her desk to the side and pulled out a stack of unfurled scrolls from a bag at her feet. "As it's a few minutes past the hour."

Mother and I stood, and our chairs vanished from behind us with a swish of her wand. My mother didn't want to cower in front of the Inner Council and I wouldn't, either. I wanted to stay by her side for whatever this strange, frightening meeting was.

"I understand this is an important discussion, but to bring in the Inner Council?" Queen Alliana asked.

"Oh, but we have much to share with you, Queen Alliana." Grottel sneered, looking at Mother.

"What is going on?" Queen Alliana said directly to Mother, who shook her head in confusion. The queen's forehead pinched.

Ember whimpered from beside me. All around, murmurs from the Inner Council seemed to bounce around the crystal walls. A bell tinkled, cutting through those whispers.

"Silence, please," Norya called nervously from behind her desk. Then Grottel's assistant turned to me, her eyes sympathetic. "I'm sorry, Novice Evergreen, but we must ask you to leave the room."

"Eva must be allowed to stay," Mother said firmly. "She's a proper Novice Witch."

My chest clenched. Did I truly belong at this meeting between the queen and the Inner Council?

"I'm so sorry." Norya's voice dipped softer. "You really shouldn't—not for this—"

"Let the girl stay, if she wants. Let her see the truth," Grottel sneered.

Norya's worried eyes studied me as I stuck close to Mother's side. Grottel's assistant looked like she wanted to help me, to save me from something—but what?

"Well, if you're done interrupting us," Grottel remarked disdainfully, tilting his nose up into the air as if I'd brought in the scent of something unpleasant. "I'd like to officially begin this meeting of the Inner Council."

My hands tightened around the map, my nails biting into my skin. My mother glanced at me briefly, a crease forming on her forehead. "There's something peculiar about all of this. . . . But stay to the side, and keep quiet, all right?"

Alone, she strode to the center of the room, her head held high as she stood on the cold crystal tiles, facing the Inner Council and the queen. I huddled near the wall with Ember, trying not to shiver when Grottel's gaze swept over me disapprovingly.

"It's a surprise seeing you like this, fellow Inner Council members," Mother said, her voice ringing out strong as ever. My heart bloomed with pride.

Grottel, from where he sat on the chair to the right of the queen, smiled coldly. "Yes, yes, well, this will be an illuminating meeting." His eyes studied Mother, as if looking for a crack, some weakness in her steady gaze.

"For what reason?" Mother parried his vague words. "Could it possibly be the reason that we were meeting with the queen? About the Culling?"

Norya dropped her wand to the ground, as if Mother's words had made her jump. She ducked under her small table to fish it off the crystal tiles.

Queen Alliana looked toward Grottel. "I, too, did not receive advance notice of this new agenda. Provide appropriate reasoning, or we'll go straight to the magic that Novice Evergreen was casting before you interrupted."

Grottel scowled, his sharp cheekbones darkening in an angry flush. "I'm positive that my meeting takes precedence." His hooded eyes narrowed at Mother. "After all, the Inner Council is calling upon the queen to charge Nelalithimus Evergreen for researching and drawing upon rogue magic. She is guilty as the instigator and creator of the Culling, harnessing the power of the land to transfer magic to her daughter, Evalithimus Evergreen."

I stumbled back against the crystal walls as shock rippled through my body. Ember leaned heavily on my legs, trying to give me any comfort he could offer, but I was frozen, unable to move.

Nelalithimus Evergreen…rogue magic…guilty as the instigator and creator of the Culling, harnessing the power of the land to transfer magic to her daughter, Evalithimus Evergreen.

Transfer magic? To me? But…*why?*

The silence burned, sharper than the scream that was trying to claw out of my throat.

Even Mother couldn't speak. Her eyes scanned the queen—she, too, had been shocked into silence—and the now-quiet, watchful Inner Council. I wondered if she felt like me, hoping that this was some awful nightmare, and that we'd all wake up in a few moments and laugh this off.

Last of all, she turned to look at me. A terrible foreboding filled my veins, turning my blood into molten fire. Could there really be a vein of truth in Grottel's accusations?

That strange stillness to her face, the way her lips pressed together…

Her silence…What did it mean?

Finally, the queen hissed, "Are you asking for a Grand Trial?"

Grottel's beady eyes gleamed as he said greasily, "Yes, my queen. I am calling for a Grand Trial."

"Was there a proper investigation?" the queen asked.

"Of course." Grottel sighed heavily, as if this was a horrid task for him, not one that had consequences for Mother. "The main pieces of evidence, please."

Norya scuttled to the front and handed over a stack of papers. "Nelalithimus Evergreen's requests at Okayama's main magic store, Good for Goods, sir."

"How did you get *that*?" Mother demanded.

I gaped. Our requests could be used against us? In a *trial*? I'd always believed my thoughts were safe and protected.

Good for Goods was a magic store in the heart of Okayama, across the street from Kaya's bookstore, with a scryer at the door who helped shoppers create lists of what they wanted and where they could find the enchanted items they needed. The clever part was that the scryer could tell exactly what one wanted, but that also meant if a shopper wanted a love potion or a life-extending charm, sometimes the wishes were left unfulfilled.

But for Mother's requests to be used against her...

"The store willingly provided them to us as a result of this inquiry," Norya explained, her eyes shifting away with sadness as I glared at her. Norya had always been so kind to me. But to see her take Grottel's side—for something like this...

From the corner of my eye, I could see Mother's hands shaking within the folds of her black skirt.

Grottel cleared his throat. "From eight years ago."

REQUESTS FROM GRAND MASTER
NELALITHIMUS EVERGREEN

- *Looking for magical baking supplies for a gift for my husband*
- *Is there any way for my daughter to get magic? Any way at all?*

"From six years ago."

REQUESTS FROM GRAND MASTER
NELALITHIMUS EVERGREEN

- *Childproof box for my wand*
- *Map of the realm*
- *Magic for my daughter*

"From two years ago. Coincidentally, before Novice Evergreen manifested."

REQUESTS FROM GRAND MASTER
NELALITHIMUS EVERGREEN

- *Supplies for a mission to the Sakuya Mountains*
- *My daughter needs magic. She needs magic before it's too late to manifest. I would do anything for her to have magic.*

Mother raised her eyes to meet Grottel's in a glare. "You cannot punish me for wishing for the best for my daughter. But I believe in her, and have always believed in her, that she is strong enough to overcome any obstacles in her way without me, without my intervention."

Grottel crooked a single finger, and Norya scurried over, lifting up a stack of papers. "All of these? All about her?"

The mountain of papers, as long as Grottel's smirking, awful face, rested below his hand.

Mother snapped back, eyes fiery, "Will you always be so angry and bitter to see that I care for someone? That I care for my daughter? That she is by my side? Do not take your pain out on me—"

"*Silence!*" he roared, but Mother shook her head again.

"I am *not* the reason for your troubles," she hissed. "There is no way that I am responsible for the Culling."

"Do you or do you not deny searching for ways to transfer powers to your daughter through rogue magic?"

She met Grottel's eyes, slowly, burning with anger.

I scoffed under my breath.

Of course Mother would never do such a thing. I'd manifested on my own.

Grottel smirked. "Go on, Nela. Tell us the truth."

Her voice was dry and lifeless, as if he'd drained away all her willpower. "It was all theoretical. There has to be a reason why some get magic, others don't. There—"

Grottel clenched his teeth. "By the power of the Council, give us a 'Yes' or give us a 'No.'"

The silence stretched out, Mother painfully quiet.

She stared at me for a long, long moment. I searched her eyes, wondering why, until she opened her mouth. "Yes."

A roar of wind and empty, broken sound filled my ears. Like I was being pulled out into the sky, tumbling down through clouds, battered by the weight of her words. It wasn't just me; the rest of the Inner Council had broken out in shocked exclamations. They'd spelled their voices for anonymity, but they clamored louder and louder, like clashing instruments. Their voices were skewed, a bit too echoey, as if time and space had distorted them, the peculiar sound ringing in my ears. Mother was shouting to be heard over the clamor, "It was purely theoretical! Research! There are famous, ancient magical tomes—like *Sorcery of the Lost Ones*—that reference the potential for an amulet or conduit to be used to collect magic from others, but not *attack* with something like the Culling. I never cast rogue magic, never—"

"SILENCE!" Grottel roared, and this time, Mother clamped her mouth shut. The Inner Council slowly settled down, but his flinty eyes were focused on Mother. "In a Grand Trial, you must follow the rules of the head of the Council, though, clearly, you've never cared to follow the rules of the Council before."

I cleared my throat. "Surely just her hopes for me to manifest with magic don't warrant this Grand Trial, it's—"

"I'll read a passage Nela wrote in an essay, back when

we were both studying to become Grand Masters. 'If I could tap into the magic of the land, if I could use it as my own, then I would. The realm itself might lose stability, though, and I'm not sure that would be worth it. Perhaps an item can be used as the focus of the magic, like a pool, to collect excess powers. Then I could use that for any moment of need or for a transfer to someone else.' "

Mother shook her head. "He's twisting my words, that was just pure theory, long before Eva was born—"

Norya pulled a stack of papers from deep within her bag and hurried to the front.

Grottel's lips twisted in a cruel mockery of a smile as he lifted sheet after sheet in Mother's smooth hand-writing. "Multiple. Each more specific than the next, detailing how, with the magic of the land, by using rogue magic, one might be able to transfer powers, whether for storage into this amulet idea of yours, or to other people. That was what you studied for your Grand Master work, part of what you used to show the strength of your magic. It was what you *specialized* in, Nela."

Cold horror raced through my body, numbing me and stealing away my voice.

"You cannot say that you were not interested in this power, too, Hayato. With your past, everything that has happened—"

"You misunderstand who is being tried here, Nela."

Norya flicked her wand toward the wall to the right.

"To *always be fair, to always be true, to initiate a Grand Trial, please count the view.*"

To my shock, an invisible finger traced the crystal wall, inking shimmering white letters that stayed solid, even as clouds brushed against the spire from outside.

THE GRAND TRIAL FOR GRAND MASTER NELALITHIMUS EVERGREEN

ACCUSATIONS: *Cast rogue magic to gather the power of the land, thereby creating the Culling that has devastated the realm. Transferred magic to her daughter, Novice Evalithimus Evergreen.*

EVIDENCE OF INNOCENCE: *Previous work completed on behalf of the realm.*

I waited for more, but the crystal stayed blank.

"That can't be all of her evidence!" I protested. "That's—"

Finally, more letters formed:

EVIDENCE OF GUILT: *More than one thousand requests for magic for her daughter noted by scryers at Good for Goods; a final letter from Elite Kaya Ikko stating Grand Master Evergreen as her kidnapper; research on the transfer of magic during her Grand Master quest . . .*

The list continued and continued.

I could barely breathe. Mother would never kidnap Kaya. Or, for that matter, be guilty of any of these horrid accusations.

"How—how is this *fair*?" Mother burst out. "I would never hurt Kaya. She's one of my closest friends. And look at this—'stealing from the village of Narashino'—I was eleven years old, and stealing a roll of bread so the current queen could *eat*! This is not a fair hearing!"

"As stated by the rules of the Grand Trial," Norya squeaked, her lips tugged down in sympathy, "the queen and a majority of the Inner Council must be in favor of the final decision."

"And what are the terms of the final decision?" Mother asked, her voice sharp.

Grottel sniffed, thrumming his stubby fingers on the side of his podium, eager to get to his anticipated result. "It will be only fair, for what you have taken. If guilty, I demand that Nelalithimus Evergreen lose her rights as a Grand Master, to become magicless for the rest of time."

I stared in disbelief. Mother, magicless?

The witch who had saved the realm time and time again? Now to take it all away?

"So, evidence on behalf of the accused party?"

Silence. A chair creaked, but no one spoke, and Mother's eyes—searching the Inner Council—switched to the floor, as if the crystal tiles could hurt less than flesh and blood, less than once-friends who were now silent.

But I wouldn't stand aside and just let this happen. "Mother has had no time to prepare evidence, especially for a Grand Trial—"

"A Grand Trial can be called at any time, Novice Evergreen," one of the members of the Inner Council intoned, their voice charmed to sound flat. "And the witch or wizard in question should be able to answer, not need time to gather excuses to prove themselves."

I stepped forward, quickly, before the queen and the Inner Council. "Then, if that's the case...Grand Master Nelalithimus Evergreen is renowned for her work to help all towns, not just the one she's been assigned to. Mother helped the queen get out of her horrid former life, Mother *saved* the farmlands years ago, when that nightdragon nearly burned down—"

"This is not evidence." Grottel smiled cruelly. "Simply a heavily biased personal reference. Stop. Your time is up."

I turned to the gathered witches and wizards of the Inner Council. Surely she had some allies, right? "Mother's friends, please. You know she would never do this. She wouldn't cast rogue magic to try to give me powers."

But...they only peered back, as if judging me, too. As if wondering whether Mother really had somehow transferred magic to me.

"Queen Alliana, please—"

The queen took a deep breath. "Novice Evergreen, these accusations...they cannot be taken lightly."

My chest clenched. I turned to Mother, my words bitter in my mouth. "I never wanted you to do this for me."

"Eva, you've got to understand." Mother shook her head slowly, eyes sad. "This isn't your fault. Not at all. It was just research...just trying to figure out what I could do, because I felt so helpless....But this was *never* your fault."

Tears burned in my eyes. This was all because of me, because I'd wished for magic like my mother. Grottel was taking my hopes and dreams and twisting them into ways to pin down Mother.

Grottel peered mockingly around the almost-empty room. "Anyone who has actual evidence on behalf of the party to be charged?"

I protested, but Norya, sending a pitying glance my way, spoke over me.

"Please raise your wands," she called. "Diamond light in favor of Nelalithimus Evergreen keeping her Grand Master status. Bronze light if she is guilty and should be limited as magicless for the rest of time."

Hands of the Inner Council rose. Sparks of bronze flickered, all around, and the horror seeping through my body was mirrored in my mother's eyes. Tick marks etched into the GUILTY side. It would have to be a majority, and there were already four marks decisively "Guilty."

Surely *someone* in the Inner Council believed in Mother?

Ember whined mournfully, as if trying to add his voice in support of my mother. I hastily lifted my wand up, and my heart pattered. *"Diamond light, diamond bright, for my mother who is always right."*

To my sick dismay, my wand light sputtered out. From the front, Grottel said mockingly, "Fitting. Absolutely fitting. Nela will become magicless and just as accomplished as her daughter."

I glared at Grottel as a spark flew onto his tunic, burning with fierce light.

He lifted his hand and ground it out with a finger, extinguishing the flame, but I evenly met his gaze. My vote would be shown.

"I'm sorry, but you can't vote," Norya said, her voice sad with a kindness that wounded me. Ember whimpered at my side. She paused, glancing away to watch the board. "Another few seconds for the last votes…Queen Alliana, we'll need you to provide your decision as well."

My heart thumped as I turned to the queen, who was studying my mother, as if she might see the truth somewhere in the worry pinching Mother's forehead or the stiffness of her shoulders. Then Queen Alliana gazed at me, as if asking what I had done to put Mother in this place, by my wishes to become a witch.

But…*because* I was now a witch, perhaps there was something that I could do.

"Wait!" I clutched the map in my hand. "I have evidence. You must postpone this vote until there is time for a *proper* investigation."

I just hoped that the map would work.

"A trivial map has no purpose in this meeting," Grottel growled.

"I…I believe my map will show that my mother *is* innocent." I looked over at Queen Alliana, hoping desperately she'd give me a chance, and even though I felt like quivering in my boots, I met Grand Master Grottel's angry gaze, trying to keep my voice steady. "The map… the map revealed a possible connection between the Culling and *you*, Grand Master Grottel."

The room went into an uproar.

CHAPTER 4

TWISTED LIES, TWISTED ENCHANTMENTS

Quiet, quiet!" Princess Anri demanded, over the shocked shouts of Grand Master Grottel and the Inner Council, and pounded her staff.

Queen Alliana gestured at two guards lining the walls. "Bring in a table for Novice Evergreen to lay out her map."

Grottel protested. "The vote, it's almost—"

"From what I saw displayed, there needs to be more evidence. *Real* evidence," the queen said coolly. "Requests from a general store are not enough to base a punishment on to this extent. I do believe that a Royal Investigation will be appropriate."

I gaped. A Royal Investigation was above the Council's

Grand Trial, a choice made by the queen. And once it was underway, Grottel wouldn't be able to stop it.

"A Royal Investigation isn't necessary; I've already done a proper review." Grottel's brow furrowed. "Each request from Good for Goods is signed by a Council-trained scryer—"

"Will you speak against the queen's word?" Princess Anri snapped, and Grottel irritably pressed his lips together. "If the queen wants to initiate a Royal Investigation, we *will* hold a Royal Investigation."

Still, despite the evidence I was trying to bring forward, doubtful whispers from the Inner Council echoed around us, spearing me with every harsh word.

Her daughter. Nearly magicless.

So that's why she did that, eh?

We should've known better. Her magic was always too peculiar, so late.

From the center of the room, Mother's eyes met mine firmly.

She'd believed that I would manifest with magic, and I had, all on my own.

Mother would never hurt the realm, hurt others, just for my magic.

My mother had more faith in me than that.

Guards spilled out into the hallway, propping the door wide open, and a familiar lean figure waiting outside spun around, all sharp angles and in all black, from his dirt-black hair to his leather boots.

Novice Conroy Nytta looked beyond the guards to see me, Mother, and most of all, Grottel looking like he was about to burst with anger.

"Uncle?" he said, striding inside. "What's going on?"

"You should wait outside," Grottel said stiffly.

Conroy turned to Norya, who relented and whispered, "Grand Master Nelalithimus Evergreen is being tried as the mastermind behind the Culling. But the Evergreen girl supposedly has evidence that your uncle was the instigator.... The queen is considering a Royal Investigation." With dead silence in the room, her voice echoed. "You need to stay out—"

Conroy's dark eyebrows slashed down. "No. I'll stay."

Some of the queen's guards shuffled back into the room, setting an oak table in front of me, and I spread out the parchment.

"Go outside, Conroy," Grottel snapped.

But my fellow Novice Wizard shook his head firmly. "If this has anything to do with you, Uncle, I need to be here."

His eyes met mine, and it was strange—the panic I'd felt about Mother being put on a Grand Trial was mirrored in his, except his eyes kept going to his uncle, as if searching for some way to help him. I'd known that

Conroy had apprenticed under his uncle from an early age, since he'd manifested so young and his own parents were non-magical. But I'd forgotten that, because of those years, Grottel was almost like a father to him. Still, he'd apprenticed under Mother as well—didn't he have some loyalty toward her, too?

"Let's proceed," Mother said firmly, and a quick nod from the queen sent nervous shivers down my spine.

I raised my voice, though I felt like a tiny breeze might push me off-balance. Ember huddled close at my boot, trying to support me. "Here's the most valid evidence the entire Council will have seen all day. A map showing the truth about the Culling."

"I can't believe we're looking at this," Grottel scoffed, but the members of the Inner Council, especially those who hadn't voted, leaned in to look, their cloaks still covering their faces.

"Grand Master Grottel is right. This is impossible," one Councilmember said. "All scryers have searched for the source of that freak of nature."

"Yes," Mother said. "That's true, but Eva had the clever idea of searching for something different." She gestured at me to explain.

I swallowed, trying to look at each person in the room in turn. The Inner Council, my mother, the queen, and even Conroy and Grottel. Whether a Councilmember or a non-magical inhabitant of Rivelle Realm, we'd all known someone who'd been lost to the Culling.

"Two of my best friends have had their parents disappear around the time of the Culling." My voice rang out loudly as I thought of Charlotte and Davy. This was an attempt to find the truth—but most of all, I wanted them to reunite with their parents. "My friends gave me locks of their hair to fuse with this map of Rivelle Realm, so I could use it to search for their parents' whereabouts."

Grottel sneered, "This has nothing to do with me—"

Queen Alliana raised her hand, cutting him off. "Novice Evergreen, please cast your enchantment."

I stared down at the sharp ink lines tracing the realm, showing cities and rivers and mountains. My magic wasn't always reliable—but I would use all my powers if that meant showing the truth and saving Mother from that terrible fate.

"*A search for two friends close to my heart*," I began to chant.

I poured all my love for Mother into my spell. The way that she'd believed in me from the very beginning, even when I didn't have a drop of magic.

I never thought, not for a moment, that she would've done anything to give me magic. Research it, maybe, but I knew she would believe in me and my future, whether

I had magic or—or even no magic at all. After all, when the Culling had hit Auteri, she'd known with all her heart that I would be able to help the town, though I hadn't been so sure myself.

And I poured in all my thoughts about my two best friends: when Davy looked out at the sea, wondering if his mother might come sailing in, or how Charlotte hoped she might get a letter, saying that her parents were alive.

"*Show their parents so they will never be apart*," I finished.

"Is anything supposed to happen?" Grottel sneered.

I tapped the map with the tip of my wand, and a light sparked, shimmering bright as the walls of the crystal castle. Air swirled around me, pushing my hair off my shoulders, as magic took hold of the map.

"Scarlet marks my friend Charlotte; the gold signifies Davy," I said loudly. Davy, my adventure-loving friend, and Charlotte, my prickly but pure-hearted friend, had both stuck by my side and helped me put in place the paper shields I'd used to protect Auteri from the Culling. I held up the map in front of me, following the inky markers through the thin paper, wishing my friends were next to me now. "Follow the path of these markers, please. It should be a familiar route."

From where she stood, surrounded by guards, Mother's eyes glittered back at me, full of pride, and I stood straighter. I'd...I'd managed to make the spell work.

Scarlet and gold circled over a dark tower in the Twisted Forest of the North. Then the bright marks surged like a rising storm, toward Okayama and then down to Auteri, where the ink stayed for a few seconds, growing brighter.

"Does that pattern seem familiar to anyone here?" I asked.

There was a moment of silence. Ember yapped at my feet, as if saying, *Isn't it obvious?*

One of the Inner Council members let out a gasp, the others turning with surprise.

"What is it?"

"What do you see?"

The Inner Council member traced one hand down, mimicking the path of the ink. "It goes...from Hayato's tower...then down the coast...the same path as the Culling that just hit, only days ago."

Everyone in the room stared at my map in stunned silence.

"This shows that there is absolutely a connection between Grand Master Hayato Grottel's tower and the Culling," I declared, my voice loud and clear. I felt like I was strong enough to cast a storm of my own. "I do not have all the answers yet, but I know that there must be some reason my friends' parents' life force can be seen at his tower *and* in the path of the Culling."

"Lies! Lies, all of it! The map must be a forgery!" Grottel simmered in anger, his eyes narrowing with disgust.

But the queen had begun nodding slowly, along with some of the members of the Inner Council, who had broken out into hushed, shocked conversations among one another.

"This is a *very* clever way to get around whatever magic is blocking our scryers," another member of the Inner Council said. "And I'm afraid of what this might mean if Novice Evergreen's map is true."

"Grand Master Grottel—your assistant, remind me of her name?" the queen said.

Norya scuttled to the front, bowing deeply. "Elite Norya Dowel, at your service, Queen Alliana."

With one motion from the queen, a guard stepped over to me, carefully lifting up the map, and brought it over to Norya.

"Elite Dowel, does this look like Grand Master Hayato Grottel's tower?" the queen asked.

Norya quivered under Grottel's intense glare. "It...it sort of looks like it...."

"Yes or no?"

Norya's eyes skimmed over the map, widening with horror as the path of the Culling began again, in the precise route of the past storm. "Yes, unfortunately, it does."

"And one more request," Queen Alliana said. "Could you please cast a spell to confirm that Novice Evergreen's map is not cursed? That it shows the truth?"

Norya glanced at Grottel nervously.

"Yes," Grottel sneered, staring down his assistant. "Go on, show them all. It's not me, is it, Norya?"

"*A truth for those who seek, find if this spell is too weak*," Norya chanted, waving her wand in a circle. Red-brown light poured out, like autumn leaves tumbling out of the sky, brushing against my map.

The light showing the path of the Culling shimmered, but it didn't break.

"The...the spell, it's real," Norya whispered.

Grottel's beady eyes bulged out of his face. "No! This cannot be."

Shocked whispers broke out. The Inner Council murmured to one another. From the other side of the room, Conroy swayed on his feet, as if I'd knocked the breath out of his lungs.

"The map has shown the truth." I turned to the queen, speaking over the buzzing crowd. "And if Grand Master Grottel played a part in harming the realm, are his accusations of my mother truly fair?"

"How *dare* you accuse me of such!" Grottel roared. "I did not earn my ranks nor get voted head of the Council for a simple-skilled Novice to usurp my role!"

"This claim that the head of the Council caused the Culling...," Queen Alliana spluttered. "What is this realm coming to?"

Grottel protested. "This is a setup. There—"

"There shall be a proper Royal Investigation," Queen

Alliana commanded, cutting him off sharply. "It does not matter if you are the head of the Council. I will not allow this to go unchecked."

Gasps echoed throughout the room. The Council and the queen hadn't been at odds in years. In fact, I couldn't remember it happening in my lifetime.

He spluttered. "No, I—"

"No? No, to me?" the queen snapped. Grottel paled completely. "You will temporarily step down from your role as Head of Council." She glanced around: at Mother, surrounded by guards, at Grottel quivering with disbelief and rage, and at the shocked Inner Council members. She shook her head, seemingly revulsed by the state of the Council.

"We shall continue this meeting tomorrow, at the crack of dawn, in my lower chambers. For a matter like this, the entire realm must be allowed to listen in. I do not allow subterfuge in my realm." Queen Alliana's eyes swept over us, fully expecting to see each of us early tomorrow.

Grottel objected. "But—"

"Grand Master Grottel," the queen said, her eyes narrowing. "Since you presume yourself to be innocent, you should be fine if I launch a Royal Investigation and have my guards visit your tower, yes? We would find you innocent, of course?"

He looked like a gasping fish, his greasy clump of hair

flopping on his head as he tried to speak. But it seemed like even he was out of words. His beady eyes flashed around the room, like he'd been cornered.

"Grand Master Grottel, Grand Master Evergreen," Princess Anri declared, "we will set aside rooms for you in the queen's castle where you can wait for tomorrow's session. Inner Council, the queen would also like to see you tomorrow." She pounded on the ground with her staff. "Meeting dismissed."

Guards swarmed Mother, their bootsteps heavy on the crystal tiles, and she flinched as they gestured her toward the doorway.

That movement curdled my blood. She was likely going to have someone watch her every step until tomorrow.

The Inner Council began standing, still cloaked, charming away their regal chairs into thin air.

A hand grabbed my shoulder, spinning me around. I wobbled for balance, and from my feet, Ember growled. Grottel towered over me. "You're making everyone twist my words."

"I—I didn't do anything like that," I stuttered with surprise, stepping away quickly. The furious black-rage look in his eyes made me uneasy.

From my right, Mother looked over worriedly.

"Hayato! Eva!" she called, trying to push through the guards, who grabbed her arms, pulling her back.

"You do not deserve your magic," Grottel hissed.

"You are a cursed witch. You are wrecking things you do not understand. I cannot be locked up like a common prisoner. This will mean harm to the entire realm."

"If you are even possibly to blame for the Culling, a Royal Investigation is the least of what you deserve," I snapped. "Hundreds, no, *thousands* of people have died. *Entire* cities have been wiped off the map—"

"How dare you accuse me of such things!" Grottel shouted. "After all the things I've done to protect you, and witches and wizards like you. I will *not* allow a person like you in my Council!"

"The Royal Investigation will prove to you and the rest of the realm that my mother *is* innocent." My hands shook with anger as I turned on my heel to walk back to Mother. Ember growled and followed me.

Grottel screeched furiously. "How dare you—don't you walk away from me like that!"

I felt a prickle on my neck. And Mother shouted, her voice edged with panic, "Eva! *Eva!*"

I spun around. Conroy, of all people, was running toward me, eyes glued to his uncle, full of panic, because—

Grottel—Grottel had his wand raised—at me.

A roar of sound came crashing over me, as if the Torido Rivers were shaking the castle with their power. In front of me, Ember's hackles raised, as he growled fiercely at the head of the Council, trying vainly to protect me, but he was small, far too small.

Grottel's breath was a hiss, the quiet before the storm. "For what you've done to me, for the ruin you are bringing to the *realm*."

I gasped. "What are you—"

"You will regret this day," Grottel thundered, "for the rest of your life."

From behind Grottel, Conroy shouted out, his voice tight with desperation, "Uncle, wait—"

That single moment somehow stretched out, burning in my memory instantly and for the rest of time....

Grottel sneered as he muttered under his breath, chanting something that sounded strange and twisted, though I couldn't hear the words. He raised his wand in the air, and the tip of it crackled with lightning, gathering in a fierce flow of light.

Mother, her scream piercing the room, broke away from the guards and sprinted toward me.

Her eyes met mine, briefly, teeming with things there was no time to explain. But love flowed from her eyes, gleaming, shining with warmth. And belief—a burning imprint of her faith in me, in my strength.

And as she dashed forward, she looked at me as though asking for forgiveness—but—I didn't understand why—

Grottel brought down his wand, and lightning radiated out like a snake striking, slamming directly into Mother's chest.

And she screamed, crumbling to the ground at my feet, as the diamond light burned painfully, and then faded into black.

CHAPTER 5

♀HEARTBEAT

My mother splayed out on the ground, clutching her chest.

I let out a scream. *What had Grottel done?* My heart pounded as I dropped to my knees, scraping them against the crystal tiles, sure to leave bruises later. "Mother? *Mother!*"

Her eyes were open, yet unseeing. Under her skin, her veins were turning gray, the pallor of a broken marble statue.

"Hayato Grottel!" the queen hissed. "*What* spell was that?"

Grottel backed up, step by step, eyes wide. "It wasn't meant for Nela!" he shouted wildly.

"Whatever that incantation was, it clearly should not have been cast," Queen Alliana said, anger threading through her voice. "Guards!"

The head of the Council spun on his heel, shoving his way through the shell-shocked onlookers to the door, as the queen's guards drew close. He pointed his wand threateningly at them. "Do not come near." Then he lifted his wand up. *"Darkness, found."* The glow from the lights burned out, and a veil of shadows covered the room. Inner Council members cried out in surprise.

"My spell—why won't it give light?"

"Why can't I see anything?"

I clutched Mother's cold body, her head cradled in my arms though I couldn't see her. "Ember," I cried out. "Please—"

There was a noise next to me; my flamefox snuffled, breathing in deep—

Then Ember howled, and his tail lit up, illuminating my mother.

I let out a cry as her head lolled back. I pressed my fingers to her neck, desperately searching for a sign of life.

A few long moments later, the other witches and wizards managed to chase away Grottel's curse for darkness. Queen Alliana thundered, "Inner Council! Chase him down!"

"Mother!" I cried out, searching for her pulse. Nothing. My world felt like it was crumbling down around me.

"Mother, please, *please*." Then the faintest beat throbbed under her skin, and I choked on my cry of relief. I looked up, eyes blurry with tears. *"What was that spell?"*

One of the Inner Council members said, their voice shaky, "That was a curse...a curse to take away magic."

The room went dead quiet. Then, suddenly, there was a roar, a roar of shouts, shock...

But I couldn't focus on anyone other than Grottel, who had disappeared in a flash of his black tunic through the door.

I ground my fist into the tiles. I couldn't leave Mother's side to chase after him.

"Novice Evergreen, we'll take care of your mother from here." A cloaked figure from the Inner Council knelt at my mother's side. "We've summoned healers."

It felt like hours, but what must've been moments later, footsteps hurried across the room, stopping at Mother's still body. An Elite Witch, with the white coat of a healer, swirled her wand, chanting steadily. *"In times of need, a carrier to proceed."* A stretcher, delicate as a spider's web, formed in the air.

"Faint pulse, but steady," she said, holding her fingers at Mother's neck like I had.

More white-coated healers gathered around my mother, trying to edge me out. But I refused to move away.

A Master nodded swiftly. "We'll take her to the infirmary downstairs. But we've got to move fast."

Ever so carefully, like holding broken glass, a few witches and wizards lifted Mother and set her onto the stretcher. Mother's head lolled to the side. They began moving away, and I quickly followed. But the witch who'd created the stretcher held her arm out. "You need to stay here, Novice Evergreen."

"I need to be at her side!" I cried out. "She's my mother! I can help—"

The pity in the witch's eyes stopped me in my tracks. She said softly, "The healers can't work on her properly if you're there."

The heavy doors slammed shut behind them, leaving a silence that burned my ears. I turned and turned, scanning the face of the queen, standing stock-still with her face ashen, and the remaining members of the Inner Council—witches and wizards I'd looked up to all my life—searching for an answer. "They'll...they'll get her magic back, right?"

They glanced at one another, at a loss for words.

"Right?"

No one answered. Only Norya reached out, to place her hand on my shoulder, soft and sympathetic. But her touch was no more comforting than the sad stares all around. I couldn't let this happen, I *wouldn't*.

I broke away, ignoring Norya's surprised shout, and dashed out the door, Ember at my heels, pounding down the steps to the infirmary. A sob choked my throat.

Just one moon ago, Grottel had tried to decree that the Council should take away my magic, that I wasn't powerful enough to go on my Novice quest.

If I'd listened then, would that have saved Mother's magic?

I burst through the doors of the infirmary. Mother lay on a cot in the center, her body small and fragile. The witches and wizards surrounding her looked up with surprise.

"Novice Evergreen," snapped a Master Wizard with a long nose and round glasses. "We already told you once—you're not allowed in here."

"But—but—what if I give up my magic?" I asked. "Can I—can I give it to her?"

"I—I don't know how to transfer magic," the Master stammered, flushing with shock. "No one does."

With a gasp, like she hadn't been breathing, my mother fluttered her eyes open.

"Mother!" I pushed to her side, grasping her clammy, cold hand. "Mother, please, tell me you'll be okay—"

The other healers spoke over me. "We need to stabilize her. She's—"

"Eva, stay away," Mother whispered. A ripple went through her body, and she let out a muffled scream. It felt like lightning bolts were ricocheting in my chest. She turned her face away, slightly. "Go find Father, send him here. But I don't... you don't need to see me like this."

I swallowed. "I can give you my magic, maybe—"

"No." Mother shook her head. "Go, Eva. Go— *please*."

My own mother didn't want me at her side. I muffled my cry and, unable to see past my tears, stumbled outside, to the hallway in one of the queen's famed crystal spires.

It was the same sparkling windows. The same city outside. The same Torido River, foaming and frothing as it went merrily on its own way...

But nothing was the same, nothing at all.

I stared at the blindingly bright glow of the windows, until the white light burned into my eyes and I could barely see as I wrote a letter out to Father, asking him to come urgently. My hands shook from the effort of casting the spell to send off the bird-letter.

Then I stood in the doorway of the queen's meeting room, watching as the queen and her guards interrogated Norya, Conroy, and the Inner Council members, searching for answers.

But there were none. To my surprise, even Conroy didn't have an idea what had happened, why Grottel had lashed out....Conroy admitted that he'd seen that spell before, years ago, when Grottel had been in a pinch with a witch who hadn't been able to control her magic, but as far as he knew, the Grand Master had never used it since....

And the rest of the witches and wizards of the Inner Council only knew the general basics of the spell, not how to reverse it. Nor did they have any more insight into why Grottel might be responsible for the Culling.

"It took me by surprise," one of the Inner Council members swore to the queen. "This meeting, urgent as the summons was, was just supposed to be about some inter-guild concerns Grand Master Grottel had…not… not about the *Culling*. It wasn't supposed to turn into this wreck."

The Inner Council kept looking over at me, shadowed in the doorway, my fists curled at my sides, trying desperately to wrap my mind around what had just happened.

My mother. My mother was the "wreck."

As the last of the interviews finished, the Inner Council's witches and wizards drifted to my side, but their words rushed over me like salty seawater, and I was drowning in their pity.

We're so sorry.

Terrible tragedy.

Do let us know if you need anything.

But, slowly, their patience waned, like a moon turning from a crescent into nothing but a dark sky, without a trace of light. As the day shifted to evening, they began to disappear to go home, back to their families, back to their lives.

They could leave, they could go home…but for me, home had changed. My home would never be the same.

I wished Mother would spring up from the cot, her eyes bright and sparkling. I wanted Charlotte and Davy to be at my side, holding my hands, reminding me I wasn't alone. Or Rin, my guardian from Auteri, encouraging me, telling me everything would work out. I hoped for Father to arrive quickly, so that I could return to Mother's side.

Numbly, I retraced my footsteps back to the infirmary and slumped on a bench outside, waiting. Ember crawled into my arms, shivering against my cold skin, but doing his best to warm me up. His tail had returned to its flameless state again, but he was still warm as ever, reminding me that there was still hope, that things could change. My flamefox coughed, as if something was caught in his throat, and my body ached, too; a scream lodged in my lungs I couldn't escape from.

Ember and I stared at the door leading to Mother, believing that something good might happen, that the healers would come out and announce Mother would be okay.

My heartbeat ached as hope and desperation warred inside me. Waiting, waiting, waiting.

CHAPTER 6
ＩMPOSSIBLE ＴRUTHS

I'm the head of the Council?" a voice squeaked. Norya stood in the middle of the hallway, hands clasped over her round cheeks, staring at Princess Anri. "But there are far more powerful Councilmembers—"

"Elite Dowel, the queen is asking you to serve as the interim head since you understand the Council so well. After all, you've taken care of it just as much as Hayato Grottel."

"Still…" Norya shook her head, looking terribly uncertain.

"Won't you serve until the Council has a new Grand Master? There's no one else who knows the Council like you do. The queen trusts you, especially after all you've just told her about your past. She understands you'd never jeopardize the realm in the way that Hayato Grottel has."

The queen and Anri were right. Norya had always been kind to me, even when I hadn't had a pinch of magic. My tightly wound shoulders eased slightly, despite my sorrow, to know she hadn't been involved in the Culling, too. That she would be able to lead the Council in a far better direction than Grottel.

"Oh, right, not permanent." Norya nodded with relief, her voice strengthening. "If that's the case, I should be able to manage."

The princess inclined her head. "Exactly; this will give the queen enough time to nominate a few replacements within the Council, for the witches and wizards to vote on, just like before." Her voice lowered. "Though her choices are slim…With Grand Master Grottel gone…and Grand Master Evergreen…in that state…" Anri shook her head sadly.

They glanced over at me, and I stared dully down at Ember. If Anri was here, where was the queen?

A figure settled on the bench next to me. "Novice Evergreen."

I blinked. Queen Alliana. I hadn't heard her footsteps. I moved sluggishly to get to my feet to bow. But with the folds of her gown shifting gently like falling snow, she raised one hand, motioning me to stay. "I just finished interviewing the last of the Councilmembers," she said. "Or else I would have come earlier."

"My mother, she—"

"I am terribly sorry, Novice Evergreen." The queen spoke softly and kindly, as though I were a broken animal, or hurt just as badly as my mother.

My heartbeat thundered in my chest. "Wait—is she—"

The queen breathed in deep. "I just heard from the healers. She's stable now. She's safe."

"But?" I sensed something else, something she was hesitant to say.

"She was cursed. The healers were able to lift the spell from causing further damage... but she has lost her magic."

The words echoed against the crystal walls, taunting and mocking.

Cursed. Cursed. Cursed.

It felt like thunder and lightning had filled my chest. "No, that can't be. Surely she has a pinch—"

The queen shook her head. "That spell—no, that *curse* Hayato Grottel cast was far too strong for the healers to fight off in time. The healers say that if she had been a lesser witch, she might not have survived. Nela... your mother... she's now magicless."

Ember whined from my lap, sensing my spike of sorrow, and I held him closer to my chest.

My voice was flat and lifeless, like pebbles falling onto rocks. "Well. Thank you for letting me know."

"Novice Evergreen," the queen continued, "I have

a request for you. I am asking as one of Nela's oldest friends, but also as queen."

A request? Or an order?

"It's for your safety, dear one," the queen said, as if she knew exactly what I was thinking. She placed a gentle hand on my arm, her skin surprisingly calloused. "Okay?"

"What is it?" I asked numbly.

"For your safety, you are banned from searching for Hayato Grottel, do you understand?" Queen Alliana's eyes were fierce. I understood that she was trying to protect me, but it hurt. It hurt so much. "Please promise me, Novice Evergreen, that you will not hunt for Grand Master Grottel."

"But—but—" I gasped out.

"I know how steadfast and loyal and wonderful your mother is. And I know you're cut from the same cloth. So, for your safety, I truly cannot permit you. I must have you swear to this."

I glanced toward the stairs, hopeful to make my way out before I had to promise. But Princess Anri seemed to sense my thoughts and shifted, standing between me and the exit.

"Novice Evergreen," the queen said, pressing her hand onto mine. "I will have the high-ranking members of the Council search; I will deploy my Royal Guards and Regional Advisors to investigate his tower. But I don't want you to search for him. Not for your mother's sake. She wouldn't want that at all. I can't have you both hurt."

My nails dug half-moon crescents into my palms. "I promise. I will not search for Hayato Grottel." I pressed my lips together tightly, compressing a scream.

"Thank you, Novice Evergreen," the queen said warmly. "This is what your mother would want—"

A black-tipped bird-letter fluttered down in front of me. The queen and I stared in surprise. Was it my first Novice mission, already? I'd only just been made a proper witch.

"Go ahead," the queen said, waving at me to open the summons. "It looks important."

URGENT NOVICE MISSION

Assigned to Evalithimus Evergreen

Requested by the scryers of the
Council of Witches and Wizards

Protect the farmlands
of Rivelle Realm.

We foresee the Culling will hit
in the next five hours.

I stared at the paper, just as footsteps clattered down the hallway. I looked up. Princess Stella, the Regional Advisor to Auteri, rushed toward us, running despite her heavy periwinkle gown. Her driving gloves dangled precariously from where they were hastily stuffed in her pocket. "Oh, Eva, Queen Alliana..."

"What is it?" The queen rose to her feet.

"The Culling." Princess Stella clenched the folds of her dress in her hands. "The scryers reached out to me as soon as they were able to foresee the path." She noticed the letter spread out in my hand. "Ah, you got summoned."

"This is impossible," the queen breathed out in horror. "No...Not again, so soon."

Princess Stella shook her head, her circlet sparking in the light. "I can't believe it, either, my queen. But it's true. The scryers have foreseen a Culling will hit the farmlands, tonight."

"It's been less than a week since the last Culling."

"Grand Master Grottel's gone." I spoke up. "If this isn't evidence of what he's done, what is?"

The queen pressed her hand to her mouth. "Stella, the farmlands are in your territory. Make sure there are enough emergency supplies routed to the area, enough Councilmembers on hand for immediate help. I'll deploy my Royal Guards. We cannot have another city destroyed or another person lost. Our realm must stay strong, no matter what."

Princess Stella nodded at me. "You should fly out soon. We'll need whatever help we can get."

I stood up, even if it felt like the world was spinning around me. "I'd like to see my mother first."

"I received word that your father was spotted entering the city," Princess Stella said. "He'll be here shortly, and then you'll be able to see both of your parents before this new…Culling." Her voice cracked with sorrow.

"Eva!" A familiar voice called my name, and my heart jumped.

Father burst out from a stairway, eyes wide with panic, and strode to my side. "I got your message and came as fast as I could. Where is she?"

I'd never seen Father so full of fear before, not even that time he'd nearly fallen off the roof of my parents' cottage. "Mother's here." I gestured at the door next to me. "She's stable. But she…she's lost her magic."

My father barely seemed to register that he stood before the queen and Princess Stella. "If you would excuse us—"

"Of course, Isao." The queen nodded, her fierce eyes burning like flames. "Take care, Novice Evergreen. Fight the Culling, for the realm, for those you love, and most of all, for your mother. She will be proud of you."

Father gripped my hand in his as we took leave of the queen, Ember pattering closely behind. Without a moment's hesitation, my father pushed the door open. A healer in white guided us to the bed in the middle.

Mother's thin frame lay under blankets, but as we strode closer, her eyelids fluttered open. Her skin looked so pale and sickly that she almost seemed like she'd been painted in shades of black and gray, missing her usual brightness. Still, she tried to move her lips into a smile.

"Mother," I whispered, my throat knotting up.

Father slipped into one of the two chairs that the healers summoned at the side of her cot, and rested a hand on her arm. "Nela."

"You're both here," she whispered, giving us another one of those faint smiles.

Father turned to look over his shoulder. "Can you tell us how she's doing? Her prognosis?"

"The curse has made her terribly weak," the healer said. "She'll need lots of rest at home to recuperate."

"We can do that," Father said. "I make a great bread bowl, filled with nutritious broth that's perfect for recovery from any cold or curse."

"But her magic?" I asked, scanning the Elite Wizard's face.

The healer's eyes shifted down, not meeting mine. Then he said, "I'm sorry, Novice Evergreen. Grand Master Grottel...took it all away."

"But what about Mother's research?" I whispered. "Since magic can be taken, that means it can also be *given*, can't it?"

"I don't—I don't know—" the healer stammered.

Mother took pity on him, waving the man away with

her hand. "It's all right, Elite Hahn. Would you mind if I spend some time with my family?"

Elite Hahn bowed, drifting back to the corner of the infirmary housing all sorts of jarred herbs and swirling, dark liquids.

I exhaled, and let out the words that had been captured in my chest, like butterflies itching to be let free. "I'm sorry, Mother, Father, I—This is all because of me—"

"*No*," Mother said sharply, then she let out a cough.

"Rest," Father told her. He turned to me, his dark eyes fastened to mine. "Whether we had known what the curse was or not, your mother would choose to do the same thing a thousand times again, as would I, because we believe in *you*. Because we know how much good you'll do for the realm, Eva."

Mother nodded, her eyes scanning my face. Her voice was faint, but rang with truth. "I would never regret this, ever. I'd give up all my magic for you, any day, just to know you'd be safe. You are our everything."

All the guilt that had weighed down my shoulders, burning away at my heart, eased, ever so slightly. "I *will* get your magic back, Mother."

She smiled gently. "I have you and Father, and that's all I need. Magic and all that is extra. And if I used my last drop of magic to protect you, then it's well spent."

Just then, a black-tipped bird-letter swooped through the doorway, pecking at me. It unfolded in my hand. Only one line was noted:

URGENT REMINDER:
YOUR PRESENCE IS REQUIRED IN THE
FARMLANDS TO FIGHT THE CULLING.

"Another Culling?" Mother's voice cracked. She shook her head. "Hayato's trying to cover his tracks...to get the Council to focus on something other than him—I think. But...why? Why would he do this?"

"I can't believe there's already another Culling," Father echoed, reading over my shoulder. "They had to send their best witches and wizards out there, didn't they?"

At first, I thought he was talking about Mother, and confusion battered me. But Mother's magic...Grottel had taken it all away—

Then I realized Father's eyes were focused on me.

"But—" I protested. "I want to stay at Mother's side."

Father frowned, deep grooves forming in his forehead as he ran his hand over his chin, thoughtfully. "Eva, I'm just a baker. I can take care of your mother." He pressed his hand to my cheek. "The realm needs you."

Still, worry pattered through my chest, my breaths drawing shallow.

Mother gathered my hands in hers and said fiercely, "No matter what anyone says, believe in yourself, your own powers. You can do that for me, right?" She looked at me, her dark hair falling over her tanned skin like thick clouds drifting over the light of the sun.

I wanted more than anything to see Mother's eyes brighten. "I'll...I'll always try my best. But I'm not very strong, not like Conroy or Grottel or anything like you."

Mother's voice was scratchy as she reached out to cup my chin. As she moved, the sleeve of her dress shimmered with her diamond status—everything I had ever wanted to be. "You don't quite see what I see when I look at you—not yet—but you will, someday. Believe in yourself, Eva. Believe in impossible possibilities. Can you promise that?"

Impossible possibilities. I swallowed. Because I couldn't swear to something I wasn't sure of. Ember pawed at my legs and I picked him up, holding him tightly to my chest.

Mother sighed, her gaze weighing down on me, but she didn't push further.

"Take good care of Eva, won't you?" Mother said, stroking the white star on my flamefox's forehead. Ember gave her wrist a hearty lick to give her warmth, and a smile cracked on her lips. "My daughter needs you."

"My magic, it's not enough," I blurted out, releasing a hint of the weight that pushed down my shoulders.

Searching for enough magic was like trying to hide from the summer heat when I was younger. As soon as I dipped my hands in the clear, cool waters of the stream near my parents' cottage, the back of my neck burned, itchy from the sun. And when I splashed water on my neck, it felt like the muggy summer air was turning the rest of my body aflame. The stream was just a thin, cool trickle in the valleys of Miyada, and it just wasn't deep enough to swim in.

My magic was like that stream. Compared to that of other witches and wizards, my magic was too weak.

My mother's magic was like an ocean compared to my trickling stream.

Or, at least, hours ago, her magic used to be like that.

Mother tipped my chin up. She pressed a kiss to my forehead, her lips cold yet solid with reassurance. "I know that you are my daughter. That you will do more than I have ever done. There is no greater contribution that I have made in my life than teaching you how to stand on your own. No crystal castle or other spell will ever compare. If anyone's going to find a way to help the realm, it'll be you, my dear Eva. No matter how strong or weak you think you are, you are full of infinite possibilities. It's why you've been a pain in Grottel's side ever since you manifested, but you're meant for more than helping just me. I know the realm needs you, and you need the realm, too. Magic is not enough to save this realm, no matter how powerful one may be."

I frowned. That couldn't be true.

"Simply having magic will not be enough to save us from the Culling," Mother whispered, sensing my doubts. "You've shown that time and time again. This is a time of darkness, but you are always my light. Go on, my dear witch."

My heart leaped and dove, swirling with the warmth of Mother's words. I nodded, my throat so tight I could barely speak. I embraced Mother and then Father, Ember curling around my feet, reminding me that I wasn't alone, that we all needed each other. Even Mother needed me.

I wasn't sure that I was strong enough, though. I didn't quite believe in impossible possibilities....

Still, looking at my mother, gazing firmly at me, a furious, roaring fire burned in my veins. At my side, Ember let out a long, fierce howl, sharp and keening.

I had promised Queen Alliana that I wouldn't look for Grand Master Grottel.

And I'd be busy fighting the Culling, or whatever missions the Council sent me on. But surely there would be moments in between, a chance for me to look for answers on my own. Reasons for what Grottel might be using the power gathered by the Culling for, answers that might help me find ways to return Mother's magic to her.

After all, I hadn't promised the queen that I wouldn't search for the truth behind the Culling.

No matter what, I would fight. I had to find some way to get Mother's magic back. Until she could smile again, like before. No matter if I would never be as strong as my mother, I would have to be strong enough to fight for her.

For my mother, to fix the realm, I would fight.

PART TWO

The Fight for the Forgotten

CHAPTER 7

A Call from Home

ONE MOON LATER

I stood in the town hall of Katsutadai, nestled in the foothills of the Sakuya Mountains, sipping at a tin mug of yuzu juice that the mayor had insisted I simply must try. After all, she'd said, the town had to thank me for the work I'd done, and their yuzu trees were legendary around Rivelle. All around, the townspeople leaned in, eagerly anticipating my reaction; my ears were turning crimson from all the watchful eyes.

The mayor, a wizened lady with her hair in braids gathered at her nape, much like my friend Charlotte, declared, "My, oh my, Katsutadai surely owes our gratitude to you and the Council. Please do send my thanks along to them for helping us with yet another Culling."

Yet another... My muscles ached, remembering all

the recent long days traveling around the realm. She was right. Now the Cullings were just as frequent as a rainstorm—though a thousand times more deadly.

"I will let Elite Norya Dowel, our head of the Council, know." I swept into a bow. My heart clenched whenever I spoke of the Council these days. It'd been tough enough proving my worth to them for my Novice quest, with Grand Master Grottel as its leader, but now...

Since Grottel had escaped the grips of the Council and the Queen's Guard one moon ago, our realm had been thrown into chaos.

This town was just one of many that had been hit by the Culling.

Katsutadai had been struck by a lightning storm. Not an ordinary lightning storm with rain and rumbling clouds. No, it was the Culling. According to the gray-faced, weary townspeople, it'd been all clear blue skies one moment, and then bright white light had pierced through the sky, scarring the dirt as it shot down.

Bolt after bolt struck the ground, the houses, the shops. Searing the wood-framed houses with flames. Igniting trees that were still wet with late summer dew. Wrecking their roads, the bridges leading over the slow, lazy river coursing through the middle of the village.

I hadn't received my summons until the damage had been done.

But like most of the realm, every town had prepared plans and supplies for nearly every kind of Culling imaginable. Even places like Katsutadai, landlocked except for their river, prepared for floods or blizzards. Wildfires or earthquakes. Nowadays, anything could happen without warning. Just two weeks ago, Charlotte and Davy had been caught in a sandstorm within the farmlands as they'd searched for clues about Grottel's whereabouts. Davy had included a sample of the sand in their latest letter, not realizing it'd blow straight into my face as I opened it, moments after facing down a windstorm in the northwest. It took a few tries to wash all the grit out of my hair.

The Council's scryers were exhausted in their constant searches, and more often than not, I was getting summoned after the Culling had swept through town after town, wrecking homes and stores through torrential rainstorms, merciless hail, or raging wildfires.

The Council was working on breaking down the enchantments sealing away Grottel's tower, but they hadn't gotten in yet. And the Queen's Guard had tried reviewing any locations or people associated with him, such as interviewing Conroy, but apparently even he didn't have a clue where Grottel had gone.

But I didn't believe that he had disappeared into thin air.

I still wanted to search Grottel's tower. I still wanted to look for the truth, and find a way to return Mother's magic to her. But...I had promised the queen that I'd keep fighting the Culling, not hunt down Grottel.

"Wonderful, wonderful," the mayor said, pulling me out of my thoughts. "Elite Dowel is just the temporary head of the Council, right? A girl named Norya once lived here; she went off to Okayama to work within the weavers' guild. Vicious girl, that Norya was. She would've skinned the hairs off a kitten if she'd been just a tad cold."

"It's a popular name, Norya." A woman nodded knowingly. "Why, there are three Noryas in our town now, remember?"

The mayor laughed. "So it is! My, you'd think with a town as small as this, we'd choose unique names. Well, have another cup of our honey yuzu juice, won't you?"

I glanced over my shoulder at the rising sun. I needed to get back to Auteri, to see Charlotte and Davy, to discuss our latest plans for finding clues about Grottel, and our search for the magical tome *Sorcery of the Lost Ones*, which we still hadn't been able to find. "I really must—"

"No, no, not until you refresh yourself with another sip of our honey yuzu juice. Citrusy and bright, just like drinking liquid sunshine, I tell you! And you *must* tell us how you enjoy it! It's exactly what you need after battling another Culling, I'm sure."

A shudder ran down my spine, filling me with a chill despite the warm day. *Another Culling*. But they were right. Every few days since Grottel had disappeared, I and each member of the Council had fought everything from dust storms threatening to destroy crops in the farmlands to fires sprouting at the border to Constancia. I had only been assigned to a small fraction of the Cullings that had hit the realm, each much sooner than the last. The Council was sending their black-tipped letters, summoning members to Cullings all around Rivelle, almost daily.

As the townspeople pushed trays of food and drink at me, they chattered happily.

"Thank you so much for your work, Novice Evergreen!"

"Now, you have to have more of our honey yuzu juice. Best in the realm, I promise you."

"Not another region has juicy yuzu like our dear trees."

The mayor prompted me, expectant for an answer. "Best in the realm, right?"

I glanced out the window as I thirstily drank up another cup of yuzu juice, the sweet and bright citrusy drink light on my tongue, and frowned. Marks in the orchard surrounding the town hall looked like scars on the land, showing where the lightning had struck. But the scars reminded me of the veins under my skin, carrying blood and magic from my beating heart down to the tingling tips of my fingers.

Or veins without magic...like Mother's.

My chest swelled up with a deep ache that always lingered whenever I thought of my mother, now magicless. Each time I'd visited Mother and Father back at their cottage, in the past moon since Mother had been cursed, it didn't feel the same. But then again, nothing was the same anymore.

Recently, I'd been splitting my time between Auteri, Miyada, and whichever town the Council sent me to. This past week alone, I'd been sent to five different towns, either to combat a Culling or to try to repair the wreckage of a past Culling, without a chance to see my parents or return to my seaside cottage. I missed Auteri; Rin, my guardian during my Novice quest, had recently sent me a letter with a one-way ticket back, offering a chance to ride on her boat whenever I needed a rest.

I wanted to rest, but I didn't have a spare moment.

"Look, look!" a little girl called, pointing at a spot outside the window, through the trees, and I was grateful for the distraction. It made me nervous to have the entire village watch my reaction to the juice. Until I heard her next words. "That magic bird, it's so beautiful!"

My heart pounded as I searched the skies.

The flutter of wings drifted on the air currents, the sound as soft as Ember's warm fur brushing against my legs.

But I stiffened.

Once, before I'd started on my first Novice Witch quest, I'd longed more than anything to see the fluttering wings of one of the Council's black-edged paper birds, like a sleek rockcrow, and that crescent-moon seal. Because, I believed, if I could get that one letter that would invite me to my Novice Witch quest, that would mean I was ready to become a witch. That I would finally become the person I'd always longed to be.

Through twisted, cursed fate, that first step toward me earning my rank as a witch was also the first step toward Mother losing her magic.

And now, only two moons after that first summons from the Council, yet another letter approached, soaring through the open window.

For a wild, hopeful moment, I thought it was summoning someone else to the Council. Maybe one of the children had manifested with magic. Maybe it wasn't for me. Maybe the mayor was receiving a message—

The bird fluttered straight toward me, flapping in a circle as it waited for a place to land. But I was frozen, even when Ember nudged at my boots.

The bird drifted closer, its long paper neck reaching out, and pecked me hard on the shoulder.

"Ouch!" Numbly, I held out my hand, and the bird landed neatly, its head raised up proudly.

Pulling my wand from my skirt pocket, I tapped it gently. *"Let the seal be broken, let this letter open."*

The paper unfurled, wing by wing, until the letter lay flat in my hand.

Somehow, as my eyes read the message, I couldn't make sense of it. Air disappeared from my lungs. I couldn't breathe.

This can't be. This can't be true—

I slid my drained mug onto an empty tray. I strode toward the door, picking up my broomstick. The Fiery Phoenix tugged up in my hands eagerly, probably bored from waiting around. Unhooking my knapsack from where it hung on the wall, I swung it on my shoulders and burst out the front door.

Above, the morning sky was a clear cornflower blue, with gentle winds swirling the tumbling late summer blossoms. Autumn was coming soon. Autumn, the season of things coming to an end. Only the weather was supposed to change, but why did it feel like the realm itself was crumbling into decay?

The townspeople hurried after me. "Wait, Novice Evergreen! Our celebration has only started!"

I mounted my broomstick, and Ember jumped up onto my knee, my shoulder, and then leaped neatly into my knapsack. My flamefox poked his red-gold head out just as I turned to look at him. "Ready to fly?"

"Novice Evergreen—where are you going?" one of the townspeople called, their brow furrowing.

"I'm sorry." I dipped my head, tugging on the brim of my pointy witch's hat. It fluttered in the gentle winds, waving its own farewell.

"But you've yet to try my yuzu scones! They're out-of-this-realm delicious, Novice Evergreen!"

I shook my head, a lump in my throat forming. "I would love to stay, if I could."

If only I could stay, and pretend that the realm isn't crumbling. If only I could enjoy this tiny moment of joy, untainted.

Yet there was no time. Not for me, not today.

"I must go." My heart clenched. "There's going to be another Culling."

I looked once more at the Council's letter, wrinkling in my sweaty hand, stuck it into my pocket, and kicked off.

URGENT NOVICE MISSION

Assigned to Evalithimus Evergreen

Requested by the scryers of the
Council of Witches and Wizards

Protect the town of Miyada.

We foresee the Culling will hit in
the next twelve hours.

Miyada. My parents' home and mine, too. I needed to fly back—fast.

CHAPTER 8
ENDLESS GRAY

The wind battered me as if Conroy Nytta was hidden by one of the dark clouds and using all the weather magic he had to delay me. Just in the same way he used to tease me when he was younger, apprenticed under Mother, claiming I'd never get magic.

With another swelling gust, the Fiery Phoenix dipped down toward the rocky foothills below.

"I'm going to fry you whole and serve you up to Ember if you don't fly straight," I warned. The broom-stick jumped, shooting up above the clouds, and then jetted straight toward Miyada—toward home.

"Here we go, Ember," I shouted over the billowing wind. My flamefox cuddled closer in response, his gentle heat radiating through the cloth of my knapsack.

From Katsutadai to Miyada, it would take nearly ten hours by automobile, but the direct route by broomstick should've been a three-hour flight.

Yet, four hours later, the winds still blew strongly straight in my face, and I struggled to fly forward. But the gusts only pummeled harder, keeping me from getting home.

"I'm going to have to detour," I called over my shoulder to Ember. I flew seaward, hugging the cliffs to stay out of the strongest winds.

The rocks had the faintest orange-purple shadows in the midmorning sun. Suddenly, the winds died as the cliffs opened up, leaving an eerie quiet, and I blinked, looking around at the desolation that surrounded me.

I screeched to a stop. Ember poked his head out of my knapsack and whined with confusion.

"We're..." My voice was scratchy, and it hurt to speak. "We're in Kelpern."

The city destroyed last year by the Culling.

Before, Kelpern was one of the most bustling ports on the eastern coast of the realm.

Now, though...

Buildings lay crumbled in the dirt, strewn with over-grown algae. The rotten stench of sulfurous dried kelp wafted up, and I gagged.

Kelpern looked like a sandcastle that someone had lovingly made and then kicked down, grinding it into oblivion with their heel and letting the ocean wash away the rest.

If I hadn't stopped the Culling, this is what Auteri could've become.

An empty, ruined sandcastle town.

I glanced to my left, where, far in the distance, the Sakuya Mountains lined the horizon. Miles and miles beyond, Grottel's tower stood in the North.

My heart beat quicker, like the pounding of drums, as I turned my broomstick northeast, toward Miyada, and into the wind. I had another hour or so to fly, so long as I could make it through the winds.

But I'd fly faster; I'd fly into the gusts that kept pushing me down.

Before long, Miyada appeared below the clouds, clustered among rolling green hills. I spied my parents' yellow house at the edge of the city.

Relief exhaled out of me in a huge breath that fogged in the cold air. It didn't look like the Culling—in whatever form it would come in—had hit yet. I'd have time to prepare.

During my Novice Witch quest, I'd had an entire moon to prepare just for the possibility of a storm hitting Auteri. Now I was grateful for a few hours.

My parents' cottage was just as I'd left it, weeks ago.

The two-story wood house stood tall next to a grassy knoll and surrounded by slender white birches. I spied my favorite cloudberry bushes in the sprawling garden, resilient and trying to bud during the late summer heat. I touched down in Mother's landing spot, the packed dirt area in front of the house.

Ember jumped out of my knapsack to my shoulder and bounded down. As soon as his paws hit the ground, he stretched out long, like a cat, and sniffled at the air. It'd been a long ride; even my graceful flamefox teetered as he found his footing.

"It's weird walking after flying for so long, isn't it?" I murmured.

I followed the stone path to the dark wood door and blinked. I stood even with the eyehole. I'd grown taller in the past moon. Throwing back my shoulders, I pushed open the door. "I'm home!"

My voice echoed on the high ceilings and dark wood floor, unanswered. Mother's magic books and scrolls were piled against the walls. Worse, the stacks were layered with thick dust, untouched.

Then I spied a set of papers that *weren't* dusty, laid out on a side table.

Mother's reports about rogue magic stared back up at me. Her looping, neat handwriting, the scrolls and scrolls of research she'd done...

I swallowed, wanting to read through it all, but

I didn't have time. Ember and I hurried through the kitchen and living room. Then I heard a sound from the backyard. A choked, strained laugh, like a flower that had long since withered. And a gentle, deep voice murmuring in response.

"Mother? Father?" I called, my heart thumping. Was Mother doing worse since I'd seen her last?

I burst through the back doors, into the garden.

For a split second, the aromatic scents of the late summer harvest gave me a moment's respite from worrying about the Council, Grottel, and the Culling. The nightmares I'd been having, more and more frequently, of the realm torn into disarray. Nightmares that Grottel had made good on his promise to ruin the realm, and had leached each drop of magic from the land and made it all his.

For a moment, all I felt were warm rays of sun, gentle on my face and soothing to my always cold blood. All I saw were the bright bursts of summer flowers in shimmering red and bold yellows, and I breathed in the warm scent of drying hay and sweet-sour cloudberries. And I believed, if I turned, I'd see Mother and Father laughing cheerily as they tended to the garden.

But wisps of clouds drifted over the sun, turning the world into gray-tinged hues. And I couldn't smell the late summer flowers anymore. When I looked around, I realized no autumn garden crops had been planted this year.

All I could see were the faded remains from over the summer, as if they, too, had been impacted by Mother losing her magic.

When I turned to my parents, my heart dropped further. Mother was sitting on the iron bench in the shadows of the house, thick blankets swaddling her thinned frame. She didn't wear her black witch's dress with a hint of a diamond shimmer. Instead, she was in a faded blue dress I'd never seen before. Father sat at her side, speaking earnestly, and the look in his eyes as he searched her face, trying his hardest to make her smile, cracked a fissure in my heart.

"Mother...," I whispered.

My mother looked up at me, eyes widening. "Eva!" A flash of her past self shone through her dark eyes, so similar to mine, and my heart leaped. Maybe, maybe it was possible to get her magic back. To make her smile like before. Maybe. "You're back!"

Father leaped to his feet and strode over, wrapping his sturdy arms around me in a steadying hug. I leaned in, pressing my forehead into his chest, wishing I could spend this afternoon helping him bake a new creation, maybe some cloudberry croissants, like I used to do. Ember twisted around our feet, as if he, too, wanted one of my father's hugs—truly among the best hugs in the realm.

"Go on, spend a few moments with your mother, would you?" my father murmured, his comforting scent of warm bread and buttery croissants wafting from the threads of his apron.

A protest was on my lips. *The Culling, I need to prepare the town, I—*

"Today's one of her good days."

I nodded, and he lovingly readjusted the slant of my hat.

Hurrying over to the bench, I leaned down to hug my mother. Her shoulder blades jutted out more than before, and my own shoulders ached, pulled down by an invisible weight.

"How's my favorite flamefox?" Mother smiled at Ember, who preened under her words. His tail swirled in the air, moving so fast little sparks flew. "Your tail's looking good these days. Are you breathing fire yet?"

Ember let out a little cough and then a frustrated growl.

"Do all flamefoxes breathe fire?" I asked.

Mother nodded. "I don't have any tomes on flamefoxes, but...ah, I wish Kaya's bookstore was still open. She'd have plenty to read."

My heart thumped. I missed the bookseller. Ever since Mother had been cursed, I'd looked for *Sorcery of the Lost Ones*, the book that had been mentioned in Mother's Grand Trial. But it was such an old magical book that I couldn't find it at Good for Goods, the general store, or any of the shops I'd passed through in the realm. I knew that kind Kaya, who always cheerily waved me in for a cup of tea and a good book, would've been able to find a copy for me with her bookish magic.

"There're some scrolls in your stacks that looked interesting," I said hesitantly. "Would you mind if I borrowed them?"

Mother blinked. "You're talking about my reports, aren't you?"

I bit my lip and then nodded.

She sighed, shaking her head. "I hope you know I have nothing to hide. Go on, read them. Maybe that'll give us some idea of what Hayato is doing, though I'm not sure it'll help."

My shoulders eased with relief, and I made a reminder to myself to stick the papers in my knapsack before I left.

Ember coughed again, and I pulled him into my lap, frowning at his muzzle. It looked like he'd smeared dirt on his face. "What's that?"

"He truly is trying to breathe fire," Mother said, reaching over and brushing off the dark speckles. "I think that's ash."

I scratched my flamefox's forehead and dipped down so just he could hear me. "Don't worry about pushing yourself to breathe fire, Ember. You're perfect just the way you are."

My flamefox blinked his dark eyes, and then licked me soundly on my nose. *But I want to try!*

Mother laughed as I scrubbed at my face. "Oh, I'm so glad you two have each other for your adventures. Back in my day, I had a snowcat accompany me; those times with her were some of my favorite quests. It's always nice to see the younger ranks with their pets. I wish more of you had companions."

Father drew up one of the garden chairs, all delicate yet sturdy swirls of iron, with patterns of spring flowers. Mother had made this years ago, and it'd stayed. Surely that meant Mother's magic wasn't gone forever, didn't it? He cleared his throat, looking at me expectantly. "So, what's the news, Eva?"

"Did something happen?" Mother asked worriedly. "Is it something with your friends? Charlotte and Davy, wasn't it?"

"They're fine....I..." My heart dropped, remembering the thin, black-tipped paper in my pocket. I swallowed. I needed to tell my parents, fast. As soon as I could, so I could go into town and begin preparations. Yet, somehow, with one glance at my mother, my idol, everything I had ever wanted to be, the words stuck in my throat. I wanted everything to be perfect for my mother. I didn't want her hair to turn white anymore. I didn't want her cheeks to be as gaunt as they were now.

Dreading every word, my hand drifted to my pocket. The edge of the summons stuck out, and I cursed my carelessness.

Immediately, Mother frowned. "I didn't get a summons—" She paused, staring down at her hands folded on the blanket. The words hung heavy in the empty air.

Mother hadn't been getting summonses. Not after...

I swallowed, looking at the strands of white in her hair.

Not after her magic had been taken away.

It'd been a full moon since she'd been cursed, but Mother had years of working for the Council, and it was a reflex she couldn't seem to suppress, not yet.

Father slid an arm around her shoulders, as if wanting to do anything to help keep her up. She cleared her throat and asked, "What does it say?"

I was too frozen. Words escaped me. Numbly, I passed the paper over to Mother, and my parents read it quickly.

"The Culling," Father gasped, his face turning pale. His eyes skimmed the garden, the gentle rolling hills and the thin, trickling stream leading toward town, and then the hint of gray starting to creep into the sky. "Here?"

"If the scryers say so, it must be so." Mother threw off her blanket. "I must—"

Her legs buckled under her, and I gasped, reaching out to grasp her arms and steady her. From her right side, Father had gotten to his feet, too, letting her weight press into his side.

"Maybe you should sit for a while longer," Father

said, his voice light and easy. But the growing darkness of the sky seemed to mirror the warring emotions on my mother's face. "The healers said you need to rest."

My mother grimaced. I'd heard the healers who flitted in and out of the house, and knew the truth: All the rest in the realm wouldn't get Mother's magic back. Hunting down Grottel and somehow getting him to reverse the spell might, though.

Mother's hands gripped the arm of the bench, still wavering. The tightness in my chest eased when she finally sat back down, but it swelled in anger toward Grottel. *How dare he do this to my mother?*

"Eva, go on to town," she said, looking up at me, eyes steadfast.

"But if the Culling is coming in, I need to cast spells on the house." Mother had certainly covered the house with protection charms, but I had to make sure they were secure.

"No." She shook her head. "Your father and I will be safe inside, don't you worry. Go on, my love."

I glanced over the hills, where the main town square of Miyada was likely still bustling, full of people who needed to stay safe in their homes.

"I'll go," I promised, "but I'll be back soon."

CHAPTER 9
A Loss Beyond Measure

As I hurried into Miyada, Ember close at my heels, rain splattered down like the sky had burst into tears. Thick clouds wept and wept, splashing heavy drops on the stone road to town, chilling the air.

With a swoop of black-tipped wings, another bird-letter from the Council confirmed my suspicions:

URGENT NOVICE MISSION

CRITICAL UPDATE FOR MIYADA

We foresee the Culling to be in the form
of a monsoon or other rain-related form.
Land may be impacted as well.

NOTE: An additional Councilmember may
be assigned—availability to be determined.

Grimly, I glanced back up at the pouring skies. I
wasn't a scryer and even I could tell that the Culling was
likely rain-related. Sometimes, the scryers of the Council
were a bit vague. But, I knew, it wasn't their fault. In the
same way I'd been casting spells day and night to protect
the realm, they were working around the clock to con-
tinually scry as much of the realm as possible.

And that last part about additional support...The
Council was spread so thin these days, I'd be surprised if
anyone showed up.

I was on my own.

I swallowed, turning around to look up at my dear
hometown. The wood-framed houses seemed frail
against the rain; I needed to secure the town, fast. Using
vial after vial of my waterproofing potion, which I could
never seem to make enough of these days, I coated most
of the houses, with the help of a few other kids in town.
Whenever I met someone on the narrow, soaked cobblestone streets, I asked them to stay on the second floor
of their buildings, or find a neighbor with open space.
Ember chased the cats off the streets, and whined at dogs
who came out with their tails wagging, looking to play;
he managed to send all the animals safely inside, too.

Others who offered to help I set to work packing sand-bags to shore up any cracks below their doors.

No more than an hour later, I had prepared the town for any sort of water damage.

Sandbags, done.

Waterproofing potion, done.

Warnings to townspeople, done.

Still, a strange feeling tugged at me, a haunting wisp of a worry I hadn't solved, as I looked around the empty town square that I'd always loved coming to. This was my hometown, where I'd grown up before I'd manifested. So why did this feel so off?

A shout from the far end of town caught my attention. "Eva!"

It was one of the grocers, Mister Hutoh, an older man who sold the best shiny, plump tomatoes every summer, perfect when chilled in the stream and then eaten in slices with a sprinkle of salt. He shuffled over, clutching the hood of his coat in the pouring rain, stumbling through a puddle to get to me, and I hurried his way.

"What is it, Mister Hutoh?"

"Eva," the man huffed, hands on his knees, trying to catch his breath. "There's something odd in the middle of my tomato patches. I know you're busy, but it seems almost sinister...."

My eyes widened and I nodded swiftly. The Culling

was cruel and twisted and *undeniably* sinister. I jumped onto my broomstick and kicked off, easy as walking.

"Wow," the old man said. "You've certainly become quite a witch, just like your mother...like your mother once was."

"We'll get her powers back. I'm sure of it," I reassured him. His eyes lit with that promise I didn't know if I could keep, but I wanted to believe it so much, more than anything. Those words—*like your mother*—danced in my heart. Yes, I *would* get Mother's magic back. Still, I didn't have time to chat.

The Fiery Phoenix seemed to leap forward, sensing my worry. Ember curled around my shoulders like a warm scarf. Jetting through the narrow, deserted alleyways, I twisted left and right, closer toward the edge of town, my heartbeat pattering faster with each turn. "Faster, faster."

A deep stretching sound echoed through town, and my blood stilled. It sounded like a band of rubber that was getting pulled far beyond its limits.

It did not belong here, not in my hometown.

The grocer's tomato patches were around the corner of the local sweets shop, the tawny, squat house straight ahead. I'd always walked by his tomato plots on my way into town. To me, it was one of the hallmarks of being home. And I couldn't let that change.

Whipping around the corner, I let out a shout, pulling my broomstick back.

I'd walked past Mister Hutoh's plots for so many years that I could almost see them in my mind: the way they were just outside the cluster of houses but close enough for the grocer to pick a fresh batch whenever he ran out at his stand, the trailing vines that crawled up Mister Hutoh's carefully handmade wood stakes, the low wire fence guarding them from troublemaking cats and dogs. The shoots he cared for in his greenhouse were likely budding with new growth, with delicate leaves reaching up toward the sun.

Those tomato plants—and the greenhouse itself—had disappeared.

An enormous gaping hole stretched where Mister Hutoh's garden had once been. The crater, as big as two sailing ships, stretched toward the edge of the trees and the rolling hills leading back toward my parents' house.

This hadn't been here when I'd flown over the town just a few hours before. On the hill closest to my parents' house, two figures stood frozen in horror, staring at the widening darkness steadily swallowing the town.

My parents.

My fingers tightened around my broomstick. I had to make them proud. I had to show Mother that I would help Miyada in her place.

That awful, inhuman stretching sound expanded again, pulling my attention away, and I gasped. It was like the ground was breathing in, pulling another set of the grocer's plots into the ground.

I nearly fell over from shock. How could something be there one moment and gone the next?

The unsettling emptiness, this terrifying sound, the dark pit: This was a sinkhole.

In all the times I'd fought against the Culling, I'd never seen one before. Worries bubbled up in me. How could I, a measly Novice Witch, fight against magic like this? Something that looked like it had no end to its fathomless chasm—it was as dark and deep as the abyss on the Constancia border.

I hovered over the sinkhole as it yawned, stretched, and pulled in more ground. Slowly, it was growing.

Inching toward the sweets shop.

A window flew open from the top floor. "Eva!" the old woman called. "What's happening?" Granny Ichaso made some of the best steamed cakes in all of Miyada. She and my father pretended to be rivals, but they always complimented each other's baked creations just as much as their own.

"Please," I called, gesturing toward the center of town. "Get away from this!"

The old woman set her chin in a stubborn pose. "Can't you stop it? I need to get my steamer and all my machinery out—"

"There's no time for that!"

"It's been in my family for generations!" Granny Ichaso put her hands to her forehead in horror. "I can't lose it; my ancestors would be ashamed of me!"

Moments later, I heard the old lady open her front door, dragging something terribly heavy. She was stubbornly trying to save her equipment.

My heart lurched as the sinkhole yawned again, pulling more ground into its gaping jaws. The foundation under Granny Ichaso's house crumbled, piece by piece.

I had to do something fast.

My wand trembled in my hand, slippery from the rain. I couldn't drop it. It'd fall in the pit; I'd never see it again.

I searched through the vials in my pockets. A waterproofing potion. Another sticky, sulfurous slime vial. A tiny jar of flamefox light from Vaud, the wild-animal caretaker. Nothing that could help me stop this sinkhole from spreading. From consuming my hometown. From consuming the realm itself.

Uncorking a vial of the waterproofing potion, I tossed it over the edge. The silvery blue potion spilled over the side of the sinkhole, and thick droplets of water rolled quickly down the side, but nothing else happened.

My mind raced, trying to think of possible solutions, but I could only see every way in which my so-called solutions wouldn't change a thing.

More and more townspeople darted out of their

houses, holding only a handful of mementos they'd been able to grab. A crowd gathered, voices rising in fear.

"Stop this terror that runs so deep, let this town earn its keep!" My spell was far from elegant, but the sink-hole stopped, momentarily, as if considering my pinch of magic.

But then it roared louder, like a hungry beast, and the speed of it eating the land only *increased*.

I froze, watching the wood-framed houses I'd known all my life waver like toothpicks at the precipice of the sinkhole....

Rich, dark dirt tumbled down into the darkness, never to be seen again....

The sinkhole swallowed more land, until Granny Ichaso's house teetered on the edge. It tipped over, pain-fully slow.

"Get out!" I shouted, and one of the townspeople pulled Granny Ichaso out of her shop as she clutched at an armful of supplies. The old lady burst into tears as her house trembled, slowly sliding down—

My icy-cold fingers slipped on my wand, sparks splut-tering from the tip. I tried chanting, with a sick feeling of knowing my magic wasn't enough, *"Save this town from the dangers underground!"*

The house paused, for a split second—

Until it slid down further, the growling, mangled

noises from the pit clashing with Granny Ichaso's sharp, keening cry—

Then there was a whoosh of a broom, a shadow passed overhead, and a voice roared, "*Windshield!*"

A burst of blissfully warm air beamed out from behind me, and dirt flew as a gust swirled under the house—

Holding it up.

I spun around as a lean figure stepped off his broom-stick, his dark eyes meeting mine through the pouring rain.

"Eva," Conroy Nytta, the biggest pain in the realm, greeted me coolly. "You're struggling here, obviously."

"So you're the backup the Council ordered, *Novice* Nytta?" I gripped my wand, pointedly using his proper title. The title that, still, was the same as mine. Neither of us had been able to even consider the set of quests to earn our Adept rank; until these Cullings were somehow stopped, the Council had put a halt to all rank changes. I threw a potion into the sinkhole, this one for gathering lost things. Maybe it would be able to pull the soil back together... though that wasn't likely.

Conroy's eyebrows furrowed in angry slashes, but he quickly returned to his stoic, proud face, like he'd managed an enchantment to hide his emotions. "I won't be a Novice for long." He glanced pointedly at Granny Ichaso's house, protected from falling into the sinkhole through his wind charm still swirling underneath. "You were doing well, were you?"

I bit my lip. "I was doing the best I could."

But those words echoed hollow and empty.

"Go on, then," he said. "Fix the town. We all know your magic won't be enough."

"You and your uncle always look down on me, no matter if I'm trying my best...." My heart ached. "Should I expect *you* to curse me, too?"

There was a flash of emotion on Conroy's face, like I'd suddenly cast a charm before he'd managed to throw up a defense. A split second of sadness—regret—no, *worry* darkened his eyes. "I...I still don't understand why my uncle cursed Grand Master Evergreen. But I had no hand in it, as I have told the queen and the Council, and they have fully accepted this."

To my surprise, so softly I almost couldn't hear it, Conroy added, "It's almost as if...as if he isn't acting like my uncle. Because Uncle Hayato wouldn't do that.... Not the uncle *I* know." Then he spun around, toward the other side of the sinkhole, and shouted, "*Windbeam!*"

A gray-faced townsperson, who had drawn far too close to the edge of the sinkhole, tumbled backward, buffeted by the wind. "I'm so sorry, I just wanted to see—"

"Get away unless you want to fall into the sinkhole," Conroy said scathingly. Ember launched from my side, herding the man back to safety. Then to me, my rival added, "I am *positive* that my uncle didn't cause the Culling."

But my map had to have shown the truth. His uncle *was* the reason for this sinkhole, wasn't he?

With the Council's teams breaking through Grottel's magical barriers and guards around that cursed tower, day by day, it wouldn't be long before he was stopped, before Conroy would have to face the truth about his uncle.

I turned away, unable to reassure him of Grottel's innocence. Instead, I dug through my potions. My fingers closed around a thin vial of sticking elixir; this might keep the dirt from eroding as fast. Quickly, I tried to think of a spell that would stop the sinkhole.

I tossed the potion directly under Granny Ichaso's house, and the wood beams stopped wavering so dangerously. Conroy raised one eyebrow in the slightest display of surprise before clamping down on his emotions.

Then a growling noise echoed through the clearing. The sinkhole yawned wider, dirt tumbling down the sides.

We were running out of time. I swallowed. If I couldn't figure out the right enchantment, this Culling was going to swallow up the town and wipe it off the map, just like Kelpern.

Conroy gripped his wand and called out, "*Windshield!*" Then to me, he added, "Do something *useful*, would you? Keeping this house up is taking all of my magic."

His sharp tone needled at me. For a second, I wanted

to tell him I had it handled, that I could take care of my hometown all by myself.

But another guttural growl from the sinkhole cut those thoughts off quickly. And Ember padded back to my side, reminding me of the way that my flamefox and I needed each other . . . in the same way that everyone in the realm needed one another—even me and Conroy.

I'd prove to Conroy that witches and wizards were *better* together. Not hurting each other, like Grottel had done. *Miyada* needed all the help it could get. As reluctant as I was to accept it, that meant Conroy's help, too. I couldn't let the townspeople suffer.

I needed a spell. A potion. Anything. But what could I do that was powerful enough?

"Well? Are you going to do something?" Conroy snapped. *"Windshield!"* He reapplied his spell, but this time I noticed his hand shook. Even if he wouldn't admit it, he was tiring, too.

"I'm trying to think of something!"

"Think faster," he shot back, like creating enchantments on the spot was easy. "Don't make me do this all alone."

My heart thumped, scanning the sinkhole. My fingers paused over a vial of sticky potion, and I blinked. I'd combined the vial and the spell to steady a bridge in Katsutadai, after a lightning storm from the Culling had corroded the foundation.

Maybe…maybe I could combine multiple potions to do something more for the sinkhole.

Another house teetered on the edge of the bottomless darkness. The townspeople screamed, backing away with terror etched in their faces. Grabbing my last vial of waterproofing potion and one of my slime potions, I threw them with all my might.

Memories filled me, as a spell formed in my mind.

Early morning walks into town with Father to pick up fresh ingredients for his latest baked goods.

Being Mother's shadow whenever she went from house to house, checking to see if anyone needed her help as Miyada's town witch.

Mister Hutoh hiding his smile when I'd passed his tomato garden, not realizing the grocer was tending to the plants inside, and I was chanting spells and waving a broken bit of branch as I pretended to be a witch, though it would be years before I manifested.

Running to Granny Ichaso's shop after school and picking up a few of Father's favorite brown-sugar steamed cakes, and imagining his wide smile when I brought them home.

This town had helped me grow into who I'd become. And I never wanted it to be hurt.

I brought down my wand, clenching it tight despite the fear and the cold making me tremble down to my bones. I shouted, *"Fill it from within, return and re-begin!"*

It was, by far, one of my less eloquent spells. But I channeled all my feelings for Miyada into each word, with pale purple light shining from the tip of my wand. Each townsperson, each house. Every bit of this town that I wanted to save. Every feeling of wanting to save the realm from the Culling—today, and every day that it might hit after this.

To prove to Conroy that we all needed each other, every one of us, whether magical, non-magical, or somewhere in between. That my pinch of magic *would* be able to help.

And wanting to stop Grottel from ever hurting Rivelle with his curses, ever again.

The two vials slammed into each other, and liquid poured out, like a river overflowing. My potion mixture swirled in the purple-tinged light, seemingly expanding and expanding, until it filled the cavernous hole with shimmering liquid.

And then, with a flash like lightning, the potions solidified, filling the sinkhole.

The earth stopped yawning, and the land stilled. My spell faded, leaving behind dark soil like a scar on the land, and when I brushed my fingers on the dirt, it had a slippery feel.

But it was solid ground.

I slipped to my knees, my body cold with exhaustion. I...had *stopped* the sinkhole.

All around, the townspeople cheered.

"You did it, Novices!"

"Three cheers for the Council!"

My rival knelt, crumbling grains of dirt between his fingers, probably expecting it to disappear in a shimmer of magic. Finally, Conroy said, "Well, I'm surprised your spell worked."

"Don't underestimate me." Determination beat through my veins as I raised an eyebrow. "When the Council is back to normal, after your uncle is caught, *I'll* rank up to Adept first."

His eyes narrowed in a glare. "We'll see about that."

Conroy spun on his heel, picking up his broomstick from where he'd dropped it on the dirt in his haste. "I'll take the east side of town and check all is well. You take the west." With a flash of his wand and a muttered spell—"*Windsweep*"—the grime slipped off the shiny wood, and he mounted his broomstick.

His tone clearly stated, *Stay away.* And, of course, *You'll never catch up to me.* He flew off, shooting charms here and there to clear out a clogged drain or dry out the clothes of a drenched townsperson.

I'll show you that the realm needs all of us, that we should never *have been divided by your uncle.* My heart thumped as Ember pawed at my boots. I rubbed behind his pointy ears, using the warmth to melt the coldness from my fingers. His nose snuffled at the drenched clothes that stuck to my skin and he coughed again, trying to breathe fire. But just his presence was enough to warm me, and I held my flamefox closer to my chest as I walked through town, checking over the foundation of the buildings, keeping my ears open for any sound of the sinkhole coming back.

My parents joined me, Father passing out baskets of freshly baked cloudberry croissants and Mother chatting with the townspeople, making them smile and easing their dark worries over the Culling. Whenever they were close, Father pushed a buttery, delicate croissant into my hands—perfectly hot thanks to a heating basket my mother had made for him years ago—and Mother pressed a soft kiss onto my forehead. Their steady presence felt like it was refilling my magic, giving me strength to continue on.

As I worked to fix my hometown, a thought burned in my heart, the determination of my resolution keeping me blazing warm despite the cold:

I'll stop Grottel, so he won't ever hurt our realm again.

CHAPTER 10

A GLIMMER OF LIGHT

The Council of Witches and Wizards convened in the stone-and-glass building on the outskirts of Okayama, Rivelle Realm's bustling capital city. The Torido Rivers rumbled and frothed around the Council Hall, splitting in two in front of the glass windows of the meeting room before heading out to sea in parallel, yet completely separate, paths.

Just two days ago, I'd fought the Culling in Miyada. Even now, as brisk early autumn air swirled inside as the door opened, the Council still held its normal once-a-moon meeting, as if nothing had changed over the past few moons, despite Cullings hitting the realm left and right.

I sat on a rickety oak seat at the front of the Council Hall, stealing a glance over my shoulder at the open door.

A team of five witches and wizards tromped through, their shoulders weary, their black clothes torn at the edges and stained with dirt.

Maybe, finally, there would be answers at this meeting.

A few witches and wizards tried speaking to them, but the group of five—all Masters by the look of their gold-hemmed cloaks—just shook their heads. Through the near-silence, everyone straining to hear them, I heard a clear, gruff reply from the short woman leading the group. "We'll report to Elite Dowel during the meeting. Too weary to repeat myself more than once." With that, she leaned back on her seat and promptly dropped off into an apparently far-overdue rest.

The Hall grew noisier with everyone whispering about what it might've been that the team had seen at Grottel's tower, but the five who actually could stop the rumors were clearly in no mood to chitchat.

"C'mon, when's the meeting going to start?" one of the Elites growled, running her hands through her short dark hair sticking up all over the place, nudging her Adept friend. "I want to hear Master Arata's report." She was maybe sixteen or so, a few years older than me, with pretty, thickly lashed eyes that sparked with energy. She noticed me looking over and winked roguishly. I blushed, returning to rubbing Ember's favorite spot on his shoulder. My flamefox curled in my lap, his eyes crinkling happily as I scratched his itch. *Now, this is the kind of treatment a flamefox deserves!*

Then a side door opened, and the murmurs quickly quieted, like a flame flickering out. Norya Dowel, the temporary head of the Council, shuffled inside. Her black witch's dress hung loosely on her frame, ill-fitting, but the dark red sleeves marked her Elite status.

She nodded at her new assistant, an Adept with a nearly gray face. He was probably breaking under the stress of possibly becoming the new Council head if something happened to Norya.

"The meeting shall commence," Norya said. "First, I would like to give an update on the Culling, as the queen and several other guilds have been inquiring. Please remember this and be able to provide this same update whenever you are asked."

Norya droned on and on, talking about all the places the realm had been hit by the ceaseless, recurrent Cullings and the countermeasures taken to ensure the safety of the townspeople. Her words were a constant hum, like a bee lazily searching for pollen. Mist from the Torido River splattered the window behind her, and I idly watched the droplets quickly slide off, the magic in the glass pushing it down and away. I wasn't good at memorizing things. There was no way I'd be able to list every excuse on how the Council had barely managed to save town after town.

Finally, she cleared her throat. "In summary, everyone

in this room is doing exactly what we need. That's the main message we must tell everyone. We've been making progress—"

"We need to take action on Grottel's tower," a sharp voice rang out. I nearly fell out of my seat with surprise and craned my head to look over my shoulder.

The Elite with the bright, energetic eyes raised her chin. "That's what they want to hear. Not that we're patching holes on a leaking boat. That we'll actually do something."

At the podium, Norya spluttered nervously. "It's far, far too dangerous. Our teams, led by Master Arata, are working day and night to break down Grottel's magical traps and enchantments, but it will still take time. With the Culling, we can't deploy more than we already have, Elite Ueda."

The name sounded familiar. Elite Ueda...I stared at the glass, with the water sliding down, and my eyes widened. The Elite triplets—Aurelia, Aurelis, Aureliette Ueda—they were the powerful trio that had magicked the windows of the Council Hall to stay clear and untouched by the foaming spray of the Torido Rivers. I had never known the Elite triplets by face; I hadn't known they were only a few years older than me.

"Team members are going missing, aren't they?" Elite Ueda said. "I can fill one of those spots, and find answers for the Council."

I gaped. A quick gaze around the hall confirmed what I hadn't noticed earlier—there were more empty seats than usual. I would have guessed it was from Council-members fighting the Culling, but was it because they'd gone missing at the tower?

"And we're running out of *time*," a voice called from the other side of the hall. Chair legs scraped on the stone floor as a girl with her hair pulled back in a long braid stood up. I blinked. Adept Akane, one of the witches who worked at Good for Goods, the magical shop in down-town Okayama. "The scryers of the Council cannot keep casting our magic endlessly like we have been; even our pool of magic has its limits."

The rest of the Council murmured in surprise.

"Adept Akane!" Norya gasped, scandalized. "The identities of the Council's scryers are a secret—"

"With all my respect, Elite Dowel, anyone who's shopped at Good for Goods knows I scry." Adept Akane raised her chin. "Besides, we're at the point of exhaus-tion. All of us scryers, we're working day and night, and the Culling isn't letting up. In the past moon, there've been forty-one Cullings in twenty-three days. We can't continue on at this pace."

Elite Ueda nodded. "Before we know it, Grand Mas-ter Grottel will take over the realm... because the Culling will have turned Rivelle into dust."

"Hayato Grottel cursed one of our own," Norya

hissed. "Are you saying that was acceptable? Because that goes against every rule I've ever tried to uphold. We need everyone's cooperation to fight the Culling, as they have been assigned, so the tower teams can focus on breaking into Grottel's tower. I think it's a fitting time now—Master Arata, can you please provide your report?"

Everyone turned to that last row of seats, where the five weary Master Witches and Wizards had roused themselves out of their naps. They all turned to the short woman in the center, with a long ponytail and short, chopped bangs. She had a sharpness to her eyes that reminded me of a rockcrow, the bird of prey from the North that was known for its cleverness.

Master Arata scanned the hall; it was the first time the tower forces had reported to the Council, and clearly, by the heavy silence filled with anticipation, all of us were hoping for good news.

"It's *going*—that's as much as I can say," she said shortly. "We haven't seen a trace of Grand Master Grottel, though. There're still layers of protections that we're breaking through, and each is stronger than the next. And more often than not, the charms leach magic from our teams, or members—like many have heard—are going missing. It's tough, but we're getting closer. Which brings me to my main reason for coming in today. My four team members here are being rotated out to get some rest, so I'm recruiting new members. Our caravan leaves tonight." Hands all around the hall raised eagerly, and she added, "Only four spots, and that's it."

"We want to go," Elite Ueda volunteered, standing quickly. At her side, a handful of Adepts and Elites also stood. Among them, a taller girl who looked quite like her and a slightly shorter, stocky boy who had the same short hair as Elite Ueda nodded firmly. The Ueda triplets. "I bet we can get into his tower and figure out what he's doing in there."

I curled my hands around my skirt. I wanted to volunteer, too. But would they accept a Novice like me? As one of the newest members of the Council, I felt so out of place standing up. Would I be able to combat any of the magical charms that Grottel had set up around his tower?

Then, in my mind, an image of my mother flickered. The gray paleness to her face after Grottel's curse; the way I'd promised to fight for her, until I got her magic back again.

I rose, slowly, feeling like a bird flying against the wind. "Elite Dowel, Master Arata, with all my respect... I would like to join the next team going to the tower, too."

I steadily met Norya's gaze; she was looking at me in the same way she had after Mother had been cursed, with pity filling her eyes.

"We can't use a Novice," Master Arata snapped.

"Novice Evergreen, you need to continue your work fighting the Culling," Norya said, shaking her head.

"Maybe I can work on a temporary basis; I can help relieve the team members by stopping by between fighting the Culling," I offered excitedly. "Then they can get some rest—"

"No." Norya shook her head, her eyes pitying. "We are very much in sympathy with your mother's plight, but we cannot expend underqualified witches and wizards to chase after a Grand Master."

I swallowed, a sour taste filling my mouth. I was only a Novice. She was right. What good could I do?

"What about me?" a sharp voice cut in. Conroy Nytta stood up from the other side of the hall, his dark eyes scanning Master Arata's face. "*I* know the tower well; I trained there as an Apprentice."

Some of the members of the Council stared at him with complete apprehension written all over their furrowed brows and thinned lips. For the first time, I realized the suspicion that I had felt toward Conroy, no matter that his name had been cleared by the queen's questioning, was something that other members in the Council felt, too.

And Conroy could sense their heavy misgivings all too well.

Master Arata let out a sharp laugh that echoed like a rockcrow's caw. "We don't need a Novice or Grand Master Grottel's closest family member."

I blinked. Conroy was Grottel's closest family member? I'd known Grottel had favored him—it'd been obvious from the moment I'd first seen Grottel and Conroy years ago, when the Grand Master had escorted his nephew to Mother, to be apprenticed. But his *closest?*

The witch next to me leaned in, taking pity on my confusion. Her nose wrinkled in distaste. "Grand Master Grottel lost his family many years ago; Conroy Nytta is just as much his son as one by birth, though Novice Nytta has a family of his own. Proper of Master Arata to deny this; just too close for comfort." She *tsk*ed under her breath disapprovingly.

Norya quickly added, "The maps you drew of the Twisted Forest and your uncle's tower have been very helpful. That's been very nice, and the most we can ask from you at this time, Novice Nytta."

Conroy bristled. "But—I know the tower so well. I can help dismantle some of the curses—"

"No. We all trusted Grand Master Grottel, and look where that got us," Master Arata snapped, her eyes sharp. "I won't put the lives of my team members in additional danger. Who knows what your uncle would do if he saw you in the Twisted Forest."

Her voice rang out so decisively—but with a scoffing tone that set Conroy's ears flaming red. For a moment, my heart leaped into my throat as he opened his mouth for some sort of rebuttal.

But, instead, he jerked his head down, away from the eyes of the Council, sitting roughly on his oak seat.

In all the years I'd known Conroy, I'd never felt pity for him. He cast a snowstorm the day he'd been born; he had far more powers than any other Novice.

But, as I caught another glimpse of his pale face through the crowd of Councilmembers, I'd never seen him as deflated and...*sad* as he was now.

Because, maybe for the first time ever, no one believed in him.

I'd grown up used to that over the years; no one other than my parents had thought I'd ever manifest.

But for him, this doubt, these misgivings...were all new.

Ember crawled into my lap. But his warmth wasn't enough compared to the cold drafts flowing through the hall.

Norya glanced over at Master Arata. "Pick your replacements, quickly now."

The Master Witch scanned her eyes over the standing Adepts, Elites, and one lone Master, a bald, round-faced man I didn't know by name.

"All right. I'll take the Elite triplets and Master Roone," she said without a moment's hesitation. "You four, find me after the meeting. We leave tonight."

The Elite triplets beamed, while the Councilmembers who hadn't been picked protested. "But—"

Even I tried, "I would really like to go—"

Master Arata shook her head decisively. "I've picked my team, and that's that. I need only the strongest and cleverest"—I winced from the weight of her words—"and the most faithful." Conroy ducked his head further down.

"We all have duties, and each of you need to stick to them," Norya declared, her voice ringing out through the protests of witches and wizards still vying for a role on the tower team. "The Inner Council, the teams that have *formally* been assigned to the tower, and I have Grottel under control. Everyone else is assigned to fighting the Culling. Meeting adjourned."

The sound of her words bounded through the hall in a dull echo.

Adjourned, adjourned, adjourned.

My stomach churned, like the Torido Rivers frothing outside the glass.

I was going to get sent to fight another Culling, chasing Grottel's cursed storms all around the realm.

But I couldn't do anything that might get answers for Mother. I couldn't actually find a way to get her magic back.

The Elite triplets and Master Roone hurried to Master Arata, their eyes bright with the focus of this new mission. I wished I could volunteer myself to do anything to go along—carry their brooms, polish their wands, *anything.*

My head spun as I called Ember, who was gingerly greeting another witch's companion, a sleek red-crowned hare, and stumbled out of the meeting room. I didn't know how I would manage this quite yet, but...

I *had* to find a way to get onto tonight's team.

My heart thumped as I burst out of the Council Hall. What could I do to win a spot? How could *I* do anything?

A group of witches and wizards strolled past, and murmurs of missing members floated on the wind. My stomach sank. I darted into the magical trees, the branches fluttering with markers showing each member of the Council. I walked through the trees, one by one. *Novice, Adept, Elite, Master...*

Grand Master.

The branches were empty. Mother's leaf had disappeared after Grottel had cursed her. And someone from the Council—perhaps Norya?—had forcibly removed Grottel's leaf.

Now there were no more markers on the Grand Master's tree.

The other trees tinkled behind me, but their sounds seemed subdued and sparse compared to before, without the top witch and wizard who had led our ranks.

Then another set of witches and wizards strode past, and my heart leaped.

Master Arata was gathering the four members she'd selected in the meeting. She looked around, but she didn't seem to see me in the midst of the Council trees.

"Ah, finally, a quiet place to talk. Master Roone, you've been to the tower before, so you know the drill," the short witch barked out, nodding at the bald man.

"But you triplets…here's the deal, and listen in because I won't repeat myself. One knapsack, max. I don't care what expanding spells you use on your stuff, so long as our trucks can cart you in through the mountains. No food needed, we've got that already at the campsite. Got it?"

"Understood!" her team said in unison.

Master Arata nodded grimly. "All right, scat. Get ready, and meet me back here an hour after sunset, tonight. Be ready to fight."

The tower team scattered, the Elite triplets and Master Roone hurrying off into town, probably to stock up on supplies from Good for Goods. Master Arata strolled through the iron gates and toward an inn down the road that often hosted the Councilmembers, to catch a few hours of sleep before her trip back to the tower.

Maybe…maybe there was something I could do to *earn* my place on the team.

I took a long look at the empty Grand Master tree. I stood taller. If I could get on the team, maybe I could find a way to get my mother's magic back.

A black-tipped bird-letter shot out of an opened glass window at the top of the Council Hall, circled once, and soared into the sky.

"More Cullings?" I whispered.

To answer, beating wings flapped above me. When I looked up, the sky was so full of the Council's paper birds that the sun was hidden from view, casting me in shadows.

Undeniably urgent missions, requests that any Council-member couldn't deny. These weren't simple inquiries requesting help with errant rockcrows attacking crops or the discovery of a nightdragon's slick, rounded scale that was actually just a shard of slate.

After the next Culling, there'd be another and then another....

I looked through the branches of the trees close to the Council Hall and stared out at Okayama. Gray clouds swirled low in the sky, smothering the capital city. Queen Alliana's crystal castle seemed like dull rock that had long since lost its shine. It almost seemed as if Grottel and the Culling were slowly taking over all of the realm.

Then one of the clouds shifted, with sunlight dancing across glass windows and curved roof tiles. A tall build-ing in the middle of town caught my eye and my heart leaped.

Enchanted Ink. Kaya's bookstore.

The book—*Sorcery of the Lost Ones*. The magical tome Mother had referenced in her research, the book that had been brought up in the trial. If I could find it, perhaps I could find clues as to how Grottel had used rogue magic to create the Culling. A clue as to what lay in wait *within* the tower.

Mother had said, moments after being cursed: *Simply*

having magic will not be enough to save us from the Culling. You've shown that time and time again. This is a time of darkness, but you are always my light.

Perhaps I could find answers. *If* I found answers, perhaps I could be allowed onto the tower team, too.

CHAPTER 11
The Forgotten Bookstore

Ember and I strode through the back alleys of Okayama. Here, the smooth cobblestone roads of the main streets split into narrow paths curving between spindly wood houses. I tensed each time a droplet of water fell off the curved vermilion roof tiles and plinked on the ground, echoing in the nearly empty roads. The sun was inching overhead, and the residential areas were cozily waking up, with the occasional homemaker pattering around on their balcony to hang up the day's laundry, hopeful for winds to blow away the clouds.

Since the Council meeting had ended before noon, I still had some time until the new tower team headed north to the Twisted Forest. A few more hours to prove my worth, that I *had* to join them. Hopefully, hopefully, Kaya had a copy of that elusive *Sorcery of the Lost Ones*.

At a fork between houses, I glanced down the empty paths and hurried to the left. The peaceful quiet of the side streets was comforting, slick rain-washed stones and all, reminding me that not every day with clouds meant that it might thunder or rain.

After another few twists and turns, the rumbling sounds of the main street grew louder beyond the row of buildings. With one last right turn, my breath caught. Enchanted Ink awaited me, its back door dusty and smothered in spiderwebs. There was a sad emptiness to the tall, two-story building; the rest of the shops were open for business and nearly glowing with energy and life, with workers carrying in hefty crates through the alleyway and happy chatter floating out the windows. Yet Kaya's bookstore was all heavy curtains and dust, a long-forgotten part of Okayama.

Ember stepped forward, but I grabbed him into my arms.

"Wait just a second. We need to sneak in when no one's looking," I murmured to my flamefox. Technically, no one was supposed to disturb Kaya's shop, not with her gone. Silence settled over the back alley as the last worker carried in a crate, and I gulped. "Now—"

Another worker hurried out from a nearby cafe, and Ember and I darted back into the shadows as the woman hurried down the street. My heart pounded unsteadily. That had been close.

As soon as the woman turned onto the main street, I dashed out onto the slick cobblestones, Ember close at my heels. Ducking under the thickest of the spiderwebs, I twisted the knob.

It was locked.

I needed some sort of spell. Maybe something like what I used for opening letters, but just a bit different—

From the store to the left, footsteps smacked against the stone, and my heart leaped into my throat. Ember and I would surely be spotted.

I could barely breathe. "*A book to learn, a book for Kaya's return,*" I chanted, in the faintest whisper. From inside, rumbling locks twisted, but the footsteps were growing louder and louder.

Just as the worker stepped into the alley, Ember and I tumbled into the pitch-black store, and I yanked the door closed, shutting us in.

My heart felt trapped in my throat as the footsteps got louder, walking toward us—and then, finally, the footsteps continued onward.

The darkness of the back room swarmed me, like a cloak over my eyes. Through the windows overhead, the ones that weren't covered in thick curtains, the faintest rays of light cut through the dusty air and the scent of something long forgotten.

I rummaged through my knapsack and pulled out my flamefox jar. Ember took one look at it and made a disgruntled noise, letting out that cough again. As though if he could breathe fire, or if he could always have his fur flicker with flames, then maybe I wouldn't need the jar. I knelt down, rubbing him behind his pointy ears, as I looked around.

We were in Kaya's tiny, cozy kitchen. My heart clenched when I saw her clay mug of tea. When I looked in the teacup, the leaves were still there, shriveled from moons of being forgotten. Gossamer-thin webs coated the top, and a tiny spider crawled along the threads.

Wherever Kaya was, she hadn't come back. I thought of the bespectacled bookseller, and the way she would always help me find just the book I needed, always at the perfect time. The books she found for me seemed to always spark joy in just the right way.

When Mother and I stopped by, she'd always invite us in for a cup of tea, too, and we'd sit around her table, Mother and Kaya chatting about the Council, while I pored over the latest book Kaya had found for me. Even the most seemingly unmagical of books had a special enchantment within their pages.

Nothing from her kitchen seemed to be particularly helpful. A few papers from the Council mentioning meetings and a summons to scry were stacked by her kettle. The clay bowls of shriveled summer garlic and potatoes, with sprouted roots that hung off the edges, were covered in thick dust. Piles of books rested along the windows, dark and curtained, and I itched to let in the light. It felt like these now-neglected books needed fresh air, in the way a plant grows toward the sun.

Or maybe the books needed a reader, but without Kaya to guide the books to someone who would love their pages like she had, they were lost.

There was a sense of quiet sadness, of infinite loss in these walls.

The same way I felt lost thinking about Mother without magic.

I quickly moved past the thin stairway that led up to her bedroom. Narrow as it was, she still had piled books along the steps, just like the kitchen. I pushed aside the thick blue curtain that separated Kaya's living quarters from her shop and stepped into the bookstore. My chest ached. Somehow, I'd hoped I'd see her, behind her circular counter in the center, beckoning me to look at the latest magical tome she'd acquired.

Just over two moons ago, she'd welcomed me into the bookstore, when I was barely an Apprentice Witch, full of hope for the future. Now, as a Council-acknowledged Novice, it felt like Kaya should be right at the corner of my vision, adjusting her glasses as she peered at her newest books.

The bookstore wasn't the same without Kaya. Despite all the magical tomes, shifting and fluttering their pages as I stepped into the center of Enchanted Ink, it felt like the store had lost its heart. More spiders spun webs over the books, making the curves of the spines into their home.

Laughter tinkled through the empty store, and I jolted in surprise. Kaya—Kaya's laugh—how could she—

Then, through the gauzy curtains, figures moved along the main street. My shoulders sank in disappointment, and Ember whined, curving between my legs.

I had to search for any clues fast, and then leave. I couldn't get caught; I'd definitely get in trouble with the Council, and then I'd have *no* way to make it to Grottel's tower.

Holding my wand out, I chanted, "Sorcery of the Lost Ones, *if you're around, please come out so you can be found.*" A warm, hazy light swirled from the tip of my wand, like a cloud searching for its home, and my blood pounded excitedly through my veins.

But the light flickered out, all too fast, and I was left in the half-lit store, empty-handed except for my wand.

"Well," I remarked to Ember, "I wonder if she's charmed the books so that only she can summon a certain tome? To avoid clients grabbing books from all over, perhaps?"

My flamefox sniffed at the air, trying to detect the book through the comforting scent of well-loved paper.

There had to be some other way to find the magical tome. At her counter, there were ledgers of books. I studied each pile of papers, each looking like a complete mess, but it seemed like Kaya had a system of organization that was all her own.

But if I could find *Sorcery of the Lost Ones*, somewhere here...

I found the ledger for books starting with *S*, and flipped through the worn pages, with ink marks showing books acquired and sold. The paper crinkled under my fingers as I squinted, the flamefox light illuminating the titles line by line.

Then, finally—

Sorcery of the Lost Ones. *Note: One magical tome available. Very rare. Likes to get lost, difficult to summon.*

Enchanted Ink had exactly one copy, somewhere within these walls. My blood thrummed with excitement as I spun around, trying to think of where she might have put it. Maybe in the magical history area? Or perhaps the section for reprinted books? Or—

Creak. Creak.

Was that footsteps from above? Or the back door opening?

Panic battered my chest, like the spiders had begun crawling over my skin. The slap of boots echoed against the floor, and Ember whined nervously.

I wasn't alone.

This wasn't the shoppers outside. It was coming

from the back—Kaya's kitchen. My escape out of the bookstore.

Had Grottel snuck into Okayama?

"We know you're in here," a muffled voice called out. Fear spiked in my blood, freezing me. I couldn't duel anyone. What would I do, throw my sticky potion and run away screaming?

Maybe—maybe it was just a ghost. Maybe Kaya had found the ghosts of the Twisted Forest and somehow managed to bring one into her shop, trapped in a book.

At my side, Ember growled fiercely. My heart pounded in my ears.

Then the curtain swished. It wasn't a ghost. I was no longer alone.

I whipped out my wand, bright sparks crackling from the tip. "Come any closer and you will regret your next steps."

At my side, Ember paused, his nose sniffing carefully.

"What is it?" I murmured, but he let out a half growl that sounded mildly confused.

From the darkness, something went *bump!* and then there was a loud "Ouch!"

"*Freeze with ease!*" I shouted, aiming my wand at the intruders. At the last second, my eyes flew open with horror, and I aimed the spray of white light toward a stack of books.

A startled cry rang out. "Whoa, whoa!"

Davy and Charlotte scrambled back, knocking over another pile of books and sending them cascading around their feet, like a mudslide of words. The frost quickly evaporated into thin air; it was too weak of a spell to really protect me—and thank goodness for that, because I didn't want my friends to get hurt.

"Charlotte! Davy!" I cried out. And then Ember and I ran forward, and I threw my arms around my two best friends, my flamefox dancing merrily around us, his tail glinting with the faintest sparks of light.

"Eva!" they cried out in unison. Davy slung his arm around my shoulders, and Charlotte assessed me from head to toe, as if having to check for herself that I was all in one piece. The sight of my two best friends was like a balm for my soul. After all that I'd gone through in the past moon, it was a relief to see they were still the same. A strand of Charlotte's wavy hair escaped the braid at the crown of her head, and dust from the books had smeared onto the side of her navy tunic and tan pants, but her gray eyes blazed at me as she, too, breathed out a sigh of relief.

"What are you two *doing* here?" I asked. "You scared me! I wouldn't have cast that spell if I'd known it was you two."

"Er, well...I thought you might be pleasantly surprised. So I was half-right!" Davy self-consciously rubbed a hand through his messy black hair, his light brown eyes sparkling at mine. He was wearing a new pair of dark green canvas overalls, with hand-sewn pockets stitched all over. "Like my pockets? I added them on by myself!"

"I told you we shouldn't sneak up on a witch. And no, she doesn't care about your pockets," Charlotte said crossly. She straightened to her full height, a few inches taller than me. "I know you're curious about magic, but being blasted into oblivion is a poor way to try it out."

"I thought Eva would be excited to see us. Is that so much to ask for?"

"Your last letter said you were wrapped up with trying to help Vaud when one of the Cullings hit the farmlands—how did you get here instead?" I asked, cutting through their bickering with a smile.

"Char sorted out Vaud's shelter in no time, so we took the early morning boat in with Rin," Davy said. "We guessed you might be in Okayama for the regular Council meeting. We couldn't find you at your Council Hall, so we decided to come here, because this is the only other place in the capital that you've mentioned."

"And Davy thought he heard some sounds inside, so we came around the back and found the door unlocked," Charlotte said. "We thought someone was breaking in, but, well, I guess that was you."

"We *had* to see you," Davy explained, scratching Ember behind his pointy ears. "It's been nearly *two* whole weeks since we've seen you last." Davy's eyes darted around at the tall piles of books, dark and looming, as if watching like furtive spies. "C'mon. Let's go back to the boat to talk."

I shook my head. "I've got to look around further. You two go on first."

"But are we allowed to be here, Eva? The shop doesn't exactly look like it's open," Charlotte said.

"I have to stay." I bit my lip. "I've got to find *Sorcery of the Lost Ones*, now."

Davy's eyes widened. "Elite Ikko has a copy? Really?"

I nodded eagerly. After Mother had been cursed, I'd filled in my friends on how the rare magical tome might have references to the rogue magic Grottel was using, but none of us had been able to find the book anywhere in the realm. Even Rin and my other friends in Auteri had tried to search for it.

"According to Kaya's records, she has exactly one copy. I tried summoning it, but it seems like the book is a little elusive. And I need to find answers by tonight," I said. Quickly, I explained to them about the group going to the tower and how I was trying to earn my spot on the team.

Davy's forehead furrowed as he looked toward the windows that faced the main street. "We'll help you. But let's get out of here, fast. I don't have 'getting caught breaking in' noted in my to-do list."

Charlotte jerked her head in a nod, her gray eyes

fierce as a storm. "Eva, look by her counter. Davy, go to the right side of the store, I'll go on the left."

My friends raced away, and I turned to Kaya's circular counter, muttering under my breath. "*Sorcery of the Lost Ones...Sorcery of the Lost Ones...*"

Davy rummaged through the shelves. "I don't see anything....Hey, here's a cool magical tome, *Travel Tales—*"

One pointed look from Charlotte silenced him immediately. He hastily returned to racing back up and down the aisles, scanning each of the spines embossed with gold and silver titles. "I swear I'm looking, Char!"

I studied the counter. If I was Kaya, where would I store my most important books? It had to be somewhere nearby, so they'd be close at hand. Ember whined, glancing toward the kitchen, where we'd come from.

Charlotte methodically walked through the magical history area. "Find anything yet?"

Davy poked his head out. "Nothing."

Thirty minutes later, we were covered in dust but empty-handed. Though Davy, unsurprisingly, had somehow managed to get spiderwebs tangled in his messy hair.

Charlotte muttered to herself, reading the titles. "Where are you? Where are you? *Sorcery of the Lost Ones...*"

Ember whined louder, catching my attention. My

flamefox took a step toward the curtained hallway, then circled back to me. What was he trying to say? That there might be more places Kaya would store books?

"The kitchen!" I cried out. "Or her stairway." How could I have forgotten? I'd passed stacks of books on my way in.

Ember sniffed like he was trying to say, *Took you long enough, my human.*

I grinned. "I owe you lots of mackerel, my dear flamefox."

His chest puffed up as we raced toward the back.

"I'll check the stairs," Davy said, and agilely took the steps two at a time, reading the titles under his breath.

Charlotte and I hurried into the kitchen. Here, too, books lined the curtained windows. She ran her finger over the spines, murmuring the titles. "Nothing, nothing yet."

An idea sparked in my mind. When Mother got lost in a book, she'd take it anywhere....I spun on my heel and strode to the pantry, pulling it open, scanning the narrow, thin shelves full of tins and glass jars.

It looked like Kaya had enough food to last for ten moons just in her pantry alone, but there were no books to be seen.

Then—as I was turning back toward the main room—

A slim dark green book caught my eye, set precariously on the edge of a tin box of cookies, and I snatched it up.

Sorcery of the Lost Ones flickered in gold embossed letters on the well-worn front, the edges of the leatherbound book soft from age. The dark green spine shifted in my hands, as if very determined to hide away and become lost, just like its title.

I'd finally found the magical tome.

"Look!" I cried out as I hurried back into the kitchen.

"How'd you know it was there?" Charlotte looked at me strangely, from where she was peeking out the curtains, checking the street in the back.

I grinned. "Mother and I read all the time when we're back home, and when she gets really into a book, she'll bring it wherever she goes." I gestured at the dried-out mug on the table. "Kaya was in the middle of a cup of tea. I figured she might've grabbed a snack to eat as well."

I glanced out the window at the golden late-afternoon light filtering through the grime. Hours had passed as we'd looked for the book. There wasn't much time until sunset, when Master Arata and the team would head out.

Now I just had to find reasons to convince Master Arata to let me join the team heading toward the tower.

CHAPTER 12

ℛogue ℳagic

In the kitchen, Charlotte, Davy, and I cleared off the circular oak table, wiping off the layer of dust, and I placed down *Sorcery of the Lost Ones*, keeping one eye on it. After having spent so long looking for this magical tome, with its shimmering gold letters that looked ready to disappear any second, I didn't want to let it out of my sight.

"So, what are our plans?" Davy asked excitedly, sitting down at the table across from me. Then he just as quickly stood up again, bustling over to the stove. "Elite Ikko wouldn't mind if I boiled up a pot of tea, right?"

"We shouldn't use the stove." Charlotte gestured up at the chimney. "Neighbors will wonder why an abandoned bookstore is all of a sudden making its own tea."

"Fair enough." Davy hurried over to two knapsacks

sitting by the door. "Then you'll just have to enjoy can-
teens of barley tea along with the sandwiches from
Edmund and Yuri. They even made a sandwich for
Ember!"

My heart panged with the memory of the two sugar
chefs at Seafoam Sweets Shoppe. Davy's family's candy
shop was one of the loveliest places in all of Auteri, filled
with the most delectable candies and delightful friends,
but also one of the saddest histories: Davy's mother, a
sailor, had disappeared on her ship during a Culling that
had hit the realm in the form of a blizzard, years ago.

I curled my fingers around my skirt. This was about
more than just Mother's magic. My friends—Davy, with
his mother missing, and Charlotte, whose long-lost parents' disappearance seemed to be somehow connected to
the Culling—and the *realm* needed answers.

"What's that glum look on your face for?" Davy
asked. "If it's because you're hungry, well, take a look
at these!" He piled three sandwiches, wrapped in crin-
kly wax paper, onto the table, and Charlotte pushed one
toward me.

I pulled back the tan paper to find a miniature wheatberry loaf as long as my hand. The crust crackled with
bits of crispy kernels, engulfing delicate swirls of bright
green herbs, roasted yellow peppers, and thick slices of
pale cheese. My stomach gurgled with delight, and Ember
whined hungrily next to me. Davy leaned down and gave

my flamefox his own tiny sandwich, made of smoked mackerel with roasted vegetables instead of bread.

"You know how to make us happy," I said with a laugh. We all took big bites, and chewed on the savory, herb-filled deliciousness.

"Mm, Edmund picked the perfect mix of cheese and herbs," Charlotte murmured. "And Yuri's outdone herself with this bread."

Davy nodded proudly; the two chefs were like an aunt and uncle to him. "Pa worries they'll start their own sandwich shop instead of working at Seafoam Sweets, but they've promised him that they never want to leave. I still understand why Pa would worry. These are so good I almost *want* them to make a sandwich shop."

As we polished off our lunch with icy swigs of roasted barley tea, I caught them up with everything that had happened at the latest Council meeting and the report back from the tower's team.

"I still can't believe they haven't been able to break through Grottel's defenses," Davy said, shaking his head. "They definitely need help." He set out a paper bag of pink-frosted cloudberry cookies in the center of the table and turned to me expectantly. Then Charlotte did, too, steepling her fingers and looking every bit the miniature of Auteri's mayor.

"Wh—what is it?" I asked, looking between the two of them in surprise.

"So, how are *we* going to get on the tower team?" Charlotte asked. "What's our plan?"

Were they really going to be by my side through this? I chewed on my lip. "Our plan…"

"You're not doing this alone," Davy said firmly.

The pinching sensation in my shoulders eased just a bit as my heart swelled with gratitude. When I was younger, the other kids in Miyada hadn't been interested in trying to become a witch like me, and when they went off to play pirates and guards, I'd surrounded myself with Mother's magical tomes, trying (futilely) to practice spells, hoping I might manifest.

Now I was so lucky to have friends who not only supported me as I chased my dreams of being a witch, but wanted to stick by my side, too.

"I got completely shut down when I tried to volunteer for the tower team," I explained. "So I need an *undeniable* reason for Master Arata to let me be on the team. The Council wants me to fight the Culling, and everyone who's on the tower team is an Elite or above."

"You're a Grand Master in my eyes," Charlotte said quietly. "What you did with the Culling back in Auteri… I'd never seen magic like that."

My heart, already so warm from being next to my two best friends, felt like it was bursting at the seams. I grinned back at her, but just as quickly, my smile drooped as I gestured at *Sorcery of the Lost Ones*. The gold font wavered in the light, as if getting ready to disappear. "The issue is...I need to find *answers*."

"But you have an idea of what you're looking for, don't you?" Charlotte smoothed out her braid, tucking in a stray strand.

I nodded, slowly. With hope fluttering in my chest, I said, "If I can find a way to fully explain Grottel's magic, how he used it to create the Culling, then I can find some way to stop him, right?" I pulled out Mother's scrolls from my knapsack, piling them next to the bag of cookies. "Maybe my mother's research will help get her magic back, too."

I cracked open the spine of *Sorcery of the Lost Ones*, and Charlotte and Davy leaned over to look.

Pages and pages were filled with small, cramped print. But when I blinked, the passages rearranged themselves, switching into a totally different order. On another page, text kept appearing and disappearing.

Davy frowned, tracing one finger against the smooth, worn page. "They weren't joking about lost. And what about those scrolls?"

"These are my mother's notes that she gathered during her Grand Master quest. I've combed through each page, but there's nothing that feels like anything that the tower team or the Council won't know about. But I feel like there's *something* I'm missing."

Charlotte pulled the scrolls toward her. "I'll go

through these again, see if there's anything that pops out."

"What about me?" Davy asked.

I nodded at the books piled precariously around us. "This shop is the perfect place to look for more information. Can you see if there's anything about breaking through magical protections, like what Grottel has set up around his tower? Or books about the Twisted Forest?"

Davy's light brown eyes glinted with joy. "Ah, a quest! I'm good at that!"

"Especially if it's about breaking things," Charlotte muttered under her breath, with a slight laugh.

He pushed away from the table, the chair bouncing against the tiles as he stood up. "A quest for our futures! Onward, then, mates!"

Charlotte rolled her eyes at me as Davy hurried to the books piled next to the sink, reading the titles and musing out loud about their use.

"Hmm, *Kettlecorn Recipes for All*...Sounds tasty... *Subtle Flavors to Curry Favors*...I don't think a cookbook will help us fight against Grottel, do you?"

After a pointed look from Charlotte, he quickly followed the trail of books back toward the store. "Onward!" he called to Ember, who had trailed after him in interest, probably from hearing Davy mention all sorts of delicious cookbook titles. "Let's find a way to crack those protections round that ol' man's tower!"

Charlotte shook her head with a quiet laugh, and started reading through the scrolls again. I returned to *Sorcery of the Lost Ones*, skimming the pages, flipping here and there.

Like Davy had said, the pages really did live up to the title; text and illustrations would be on one page, and when I turned back to look at them a moment later, they'd be gone. I'd read through plenty of magical tomes that showed just the right passage at just the right time, but this was a whole new level.

The information wasn't quite what I needed, either. The text illuminated the world of the seven realms back ages and ages ago, when magic flourished throughout the land, and everyone had at least a little bit of magic. I wanted to know about magic *now*, when there wasn't as much magic to be found.

When I turned the page, an illustration nearly made me jump. The figure of a girl, maybe a few years younger than me, stared, unblinking. The eerie look to her gloomy, dark eyes made me shiver, like she was haunting me from a long-ago past. Her inky hair swirled around her shoulders as the illustration moved, pushed by a strange wind I couldn't see.

There were no labels, descriptions, nothing.

But the illustration shifted as the girl lifted one hand, and her finger pointed straight at me.

I nearly choked on air.

Then the girl smiled, her lips parting to mouth something. Though she was just ink and paper, the razor-sharp look of her teeth and the shadowy darkness to her eyes made my throat dry. Quickly, I flipped the page.

Here, the pages were blank, but not completely empty—a scrap of folded paper was wedged into the spine. Carefully, I tugged it out, and blinked. It was a note in Kaya's looping handwriting, underlined. I read it out loud:

> *A rogue witch had, with one*
> *wayward spell, decimated an*
> *entire town.*

That was it, but still, a shudder ran through my body. What did that have to do with the Culling? Or the girl from the previous page? Sure, rogue magic was destructive, but I didn't see what one witch had to do with Grottel's storms hitting our coast or earthquakes that tore apart our farmlands.

Then I looked at the page and let out a gasp.

Somehow, after I'd read the note, thin, curling letters had begun to form on the page.

"What *is* that?" Charlotte asked from my left, leaning over to look.

"What's what?" Davy called, poking his head into

the kitchen, lugging a huge scroll. Then he hurried over to join us, setting the rolled-up parchment on the side of the table with surprising delicacy. "Ooh, this book *is* special."

ROGUE MAGIC

A branch of magic that has now been wiped out by the Council of Witches and Wizards, rogue magic is the practice of power exchanges between vessels.

Once upon a time, Rivelle Realm and its neighboring realms flourished with magic. But as power waned and slowly drained away, fewer and fewer witches and wizards were born with magic. Sometimes, those without magic wished for powers. Rogue magic started as a way to store magic; precious heirlooms were imbued with powers that could be called upon by descendants. Over time, transfers were discovered and used to fulfill this need. More and more people began selling off their magic for worldly favors like gold. However, this imbalance led to a sharp decrease in innate magic users.

In addition, for a successful transfer, a conduit was needed between vessels. Without a strong connection between the two power sources, it is impossible to swap magic. A proper conduit oftentimes must be kept underground, and in the form of an amulet or some sort of metal object, as the power exchanges are volatile and deep earth helps prevent wayward magic from harming anyone nearby, as there is a chance of leaks into the surrounding area.

Those practicing this branch of magic found its name : rogue magic.

Over time, the deep stores of magic were used for once-impossible deeds : to bring life to the dead, to raise cities out of dust.... To avoid misuse of these powers, the knowledge of rogue magic was banned from Rivelle Realm, with all writings removed from existence. This is the last passage that will be kept on rogue magic ; hopefully, this twisted magic will never resurface again. However, in times of trouble, remember this : The destruction of a conduit will revert the flow, and return magic to its original sources.

> Therefore, if you are reading this, please protect the realm. The power of rogue magic was once used for good, but now, it has only led to evil.
>
> Rogue magic *must* be stopped, before it leads to the end of the realm, the end to all magic as we know it.

Charlotte, Davy, and I stared at one another in shock.

"This is it," I whispered, my eyes skimming the wrinkled page again. "This *has* to be what Grottel is doing. He's gathering everyone's powers for himself."

"Rogue magic." Charlotte shook her head, her gray eyes dark. "But how does this tie into the tower? Is the tower this conduit that the passage is talking about?"

"It must be hidden in the tower! If we can destroy the conduit, we can return magic to the people it was taken from! Including my mother!" Hope unfurled in my chest, like spring buds after a long winter.

"Underground...," Davy muttered, repeating the book. "Underground..." Slowly, as if in a trance, he picked up the scroll that he'd brought into the room. "I didn't know if this would be helpful, but I thought, considering the magic you'd done before...I found this hidden by the register," Davy explained as he unfurled it across the table. "I was thinking that maybe Elite Ikko might have a safe or something like that hidden around the store. And Ember kept going back to the register, as if he wanted me to take a look, so I finally crawled around. There was a strange sort of latch *under* the counter, this really complicated sort of lock." Then his eyes sparkled as he pulled a brass ring out of one of his many overall pockets. Keys and wires twisted into all sorts of shapes dangled from a brass ring. "I fiddled with my all-in-one lock opener until there was a popping sound and then this rolled out."

I scratched Ember on his forehead. "Clever flamefox."

"And clever boy?" Davy asked, grinning.

Charlotte mussed his hair. "Here, I'll give you a pat, too." Davy laughed, batting her hand away.

My flamefox's eyes brightened, too, preening under my praise. But then he looked down at his tail and let out another little cough.

"I've got to take you to Vaud; he'd know what to do about your cough," I said worriedly. But my flamefox nudged my hand away and toward the scroll.

I studied the map that Davy had found. The Twisted Forest smothered the North, cut off from the rest of the realm by the Sakuya Mountains. This map focused just on the forest, featuring waterways and even rocky cliffs throughout the land.

Most of all, it showed Grottel's tower, nestled by a small lake and village.

I rolled up my sleeves. "Char, Davy... I want to try that spell again. This map is so detailed, it'll be able to show far more. Would you mind—"

Charlotte pulled out the blade she used for her messenger work, and with a flash of metal, she sliced off a dangling strand from her braid. She passed it over to Davy, who chopped off one of his curls. Without a word, they placed their locks onto the map, eyes trusting me.

There wasn't a moment to waste. Pulling my wand from my pocket, I chanted, "*A search for two friends close to my heart, show their parents so they will never be apart.*"

The tip of my wand glowed, shimmering bright as if it had been carved from crystal. Despite the closed windows and doors, a draft ruffled my hair playfully as magic leached from my blood, channeling through my wand.

Scarlet and gold ink marks gathered on the map.

"Look! It's not quite coming from the tower!" Charlotte cried.

Davy squinted, his nose nearly squashed into the parchment as he pointed at a formation of rocks and a waterway enclosed between the cliffs. "But it's coming from right *next* to the tower... this waterfall... why?"

But before we could wonder any further, the splotches shot out from the waterfall area in four directions. If it'd been a clock, it would've been right at the three, six, nine, and twelve o'clock markers. And then the light gathered as it swirled south, past the Sakuya Mountains, and then slammed into a familiar place in a burst of light.

Miyada, the spot of the latest Culling. I swallowed, remembering the way I'd had to fight alongside Conroy to save my town from the sinkhole.

That attack *had* been Grottel's doing.

As the inky glows faded away, I stared between the three things we had gathered around us: my mother's papers, *Sorcery of the Lost Ones*, and now this, the map.

Why did it seem so familiar? What was it that I was missing?

"He's not storing his magic in the tower," I whispered, the pieces finally clicking. "The passage said, 'Deep earth helps prevent wayward magic from harming anyone nearby.'...I think the conduit is *underground*. It's not in the tower. The Council's team is trying to break into the wrong place."

Charlotte put her hand over my trembling fingers; her skin was cool to the touch. "But—wait—I think there's still more to this...."

"What is it?" Davy asked, squinting at the map.

Charlotte turned to me, her gray eyes wide. "Your mother's papers...She would've never done something like this to you, because it says rogue magic like this can't be trusted, that it can *harm* people."

I needed more...more answers to get me onto the tower team....It felt like I was *so* close to finding the missing pieces of this strange puzzle.

In her research, Mother had noted that this type of rogue magic was volatile, that it couldn't be trusted... that it was dangerous in the wrong hands. But how did the new Cullings connect to the disappearing tower team members? A cold sweat coated my palms as I tried to summon up the right words. "I have to check something...."

I pointed my wand at the map again. *"A search for two friends close to my heart, show their parents so they will never be apart."* I added, *"Show me over time the future I need to divine."*

My head spun as magic poured out of my blood. My wand flashed with sparks of white light, like sand pouring down in an hourglass—sparkling, trickling time.

Again, scarlet and gold lights flickered, swirling around that waterfall.

But this time, the spots had shifted, like the hands of a clock slowly churning, and the lights glowed ominously from their new spots, each slightly shifted to the right.

"The magic...the path of the Culling, it *changes*," I gasped, watching as the ink shot out toward the Walking Cliffs on the east coast of Rivelle Realm.

We stared at one another, eyes wide.

Davy was as pale as the parchment. "But if the

Council's tower team chooses the wrong path to try to get close to the conduit by the waterfall…"

"They'll never make it to the source," I whispered. "The Culling will sweep them away. The magical shields and curses on Grottel's tower are actually *saving* them right now. But not if they really do break through… They're going to unleash the full strength of Grottel's curses onto the entire Twisted Forest. The entire realm."

"It…isn't too late, is it?" Charlotte pointed out the window; through the cracks between the curtains, I saw the sky had faded to a purple-orange. The sun was slowly setting. Time had seemingly flown like the sands of a broken hourglass, pouring out.

"The team *needs* to know this. The tower is a trap," I said with a gasp. "We need to get back to the Council Hall, fast."

CHAPTER 13

THE START OF A JOURNEY

With bounding steps, Ember led the way through the streets winding back to the Council Hall. Charlotte, Davy, and I raced to keep up. My heart pounded in my chest. *Please, let the tower team still be there, please....*

When we turned the corner and onto the path leading to the Council Hall, hope swelled in me. Five bulky trucks were parked outside the iron gates, their coats of white paint shining under the moonlight. Workers buzzed here and there, loading in boxes and parcels. A pair of women were wrestling down the canvas tarp for one of the trucks jammed with goods. These were the kind of trucks used to transport supplies across the realm, anything from crops to passengers. The canvas-covered backs were filled with all sorts of boxes and supplies, tied down, but there were some spots here and there that looked like they were set aside for people.

This *had* to mean they hadn't left yet.

I sprinted the last few steps into the courtyard of the Council Hall.

Ember stood in front of a group of five witches and wizards, his legs firmly set in the ground. Every time one of the witches or wizards tried to move forward, he growled, his tail sparking. Intermittently, he let out flameless coughs, as if his attempts at breathing fire might keep them back.

"Call off your flamefox, would you?" the shortest of the witches snapped, with a sharpness to her voice that reminded me of a cawing rockcrow. "We haven't got time to lollygag."

I blinked. It was Master Arata, her face nearly hidden in the shadows of her pointy witch's hat.

Trying to catch my breath, I tipped my hat at her and swept into a quick bow. I gasped out, "Please—I *need* to be part of the team."

"Ahem," Master Roone coughed, his round face pinching up. "Master Arata has confirmed she will not take Novices. It's far too dangerous, anyway."

From behind the two Masters, the Elite triplets shifted, adjusting the heavy knapsacks on their backs and glancing at one another, their lips tugged down. Couldn't I trade places with one of them? I wished I could be an

Elite or Master, so they *would* consider letting me go with them.

"Novice Evergreen, I respect your mother enough not to just walk past you," Master Arata said. "But what's with the Novices this year, persistent as nightdragons? First Novice Nytta wouldn't leave me alone when I was trying to get some rest, then you." Her eyes flashed. "It wasn't a joke when I said team members go missing. When they disappear, they *don't* come back. I don't have a good feeling about this. I'm not going to let that happen to a Novice, not on my watch."

The gravel crunched as Master Arata strolled on by, not giving me a second look. The rest of the team—the Elite triplets and the other Master—followed in her wake. The three Uedas gave me pitying looks.

But I wasn't here for pity. I was here because I was trying to fight for my mother. Because I wanted to believe in impossible possibilities.

"Master Arata, please! I can help stop your team members from disappearing!"

She stopped.

"I know a way to get directly to the conduit." I clenched my skirt in my damp fingers. Hoping, hoping...

Slowly, Master Arata turned around, her eyes narrowed. "Explain."

"Whatever Grottel's doing, it's not actually in the tower. That's a decoy—but if you keep breaking down the defenses surrounding the tower, your team might get hit by the brunt of the Culling! *This* just might be why the team members are disappearing!"

"His magic...his amulet...it's *not* in the tower? That's ridiculous—there's no basis for that."

"Look at this," I said quickly, before she could turn away again. Charlotte pushed *Sorcery of the Lost Ones* into my hands, and I offered it out to the witch, showing the passage that shimmered under the moonlight. "Because of the strength of the magic, the conduit is likely kept underground."

"That's good to know," she said, scanning the page. My throat tightened at the sharpness of her tone—it was a dismissal.

"And," I added, my eyes burning bright, "thankfully, I've memorized the layout of the Twisted Forest. I've found a path that might lead us to Grottel's conduit, without having to rely on the tower itself. A route that will keep us safe from the magical guards and away from the strange magic Grottel is raising."

The other Master cleared his throat. "That...that would help. That would stop us from losing teammates, if it is true. Master Arata, it's worth a shot."

But Master Arata simply narrowed her lips and extended her hand. "Then write that spot down and give the scroll to me. Thank you for your work, Novice Evergreen."

I swallowed. She wouldn't understand the buzzing in

my chest whenever I thought of Mother, the way I needed to do something to get her magic back. Or—I glanced between Charlotte and Davy, staunchly standing at my side through the fierce glares of the tower team—my friends who needed their parents back, too.

"Your team needs me." I gestured at the swirling ink dots on the map. "I've cast a spell to check the path over time. It changes depending on where magic is leaking from Grottel's conduit, and believe me, we don't want to get in its way."

Master Arata frowned. "Fine, then. Give me the map."

"But—"

The woman poked her wand at the parchment and declared, "*Show me the path to take, so my team shall not break.*" A gray flash covered the map, and then just as suddenly disappeared.

Master Roone cleared his throat, rubbing his bald head. "Ahem. I think it's already charmed to Novice Evergreen's spell. It's like trying to reuse someone else's spell. I'm not sure that your charm will work, Junko."

"I know how magic works!" Master Arata growled. "Novice Evergreen, should I really trust your word? What if this is all a hoax?"

"You can send me home, instantly," I promised, though my gut churned from those words. "I'll keep fighting the Culling, like the Council requests."

"And you'll never ask me again?" Master Arata raised her eyebrow.

I swallowed, my heart heavy. That meant I only had one chance. What if I got assigned to a Culling before I could get close to Grottel's conduit?

Possible...Possibilities...

Maybe this was an impossible possibility. But if I could figure it out, unlikely as it seemed, then...

"Well?" Master Arata snapped, cutting off my train of thought.

"Yes," I said. "Just this once, I promise. I'll do anything to get us to the conduit before I get called to another Culling. I...I believe it's possible."

Her eyes glittered. "Fine. Join us, if you must. But *stay* out of the way. I'm not having Grand Master Evergreen cursing me to the end of the seven realms for putting her only daughter in danger."

My heart leaped and flew, like the Fiery Phoenix had taken me up to soar among the stars.

The Elite triplets raised their eyebrows in unison. The girl who'd spoken up at the meeting earlier, with the spiky hair, grinned. "You're more like your mother than I expected."

"No time for niceties," Master Arata barked. "Get in the trucks before I change my mind."

The willowy Ueda triplet turned toward her. "Truck,

ma'am? I thought we'd go by broomstick and leave the trucks for supplies?"

"It's the best way to travel to the Twisted Forest," Master Roone explained. "Flying over the Sakuya Mountains gets us there, but then we'd be too weary to fight Grottel's curses. So going by truck means we'll be able to sleep as the non-magical drivers do their work."

"And in the morning, we'll arrive at the edge of the Twisted Forest." Master Arata's lip curled up in a half smile. "And if you don't sleep while on the trucks, well, after a day in the forest...let's just say it's a *little* difficult to get a good rest."

With that, Master Arata spun on her heel and stalked out the gates, the rest of the team following.

Charlotte and Davy grinned at me. "You did it!" Charlotte breathed out in relief, her eyes sparkling.

"Oh, no! I need to ask her about you two, too," I said, appalled. I turned to look for Master Arata; she was already jumping into the back of the first truck, along with Master Roone. "Let me see if—"

Charlotte nudged me with her elbow. "Don't worry about us," she said quietly.

"But—"

"We've got our own ways to get there." Davy winked. "Go on, before they leave you in the dust."

I tried protesting, but my two friends spun me around,

put their hands on my shoulders, and firmly started pushing me toward the gate.

The driver for the first truck let out a shout. "All aboard!" Then the engine turned on, coughing out a puff of pale white smoke. Within moments, it jetted off, the glowing headlights moving through the darkness, taking Master Arata with it.

"Trust us," Charlotte whispered. "Now run to the next truck, before you get left behind."

The Elite triplets were clambering into the third truck. The girl with the spiky hair poked her head out of the opening in the canvas tarp. "Are you coming or what?"

"Take care of yourself, and trust us," Davy said, patting me on the shoulder. From outside the gates, the driver of the second truck started the engine, the car rumbling through the quiet night.

With that, Ember and I dashed toward the third truck. I scooped up my flamefox, and Elite Ueda reached out her hand, pulling us in.

CHAPTER 14
ᴛHE ᴇLITE ᴛRIPLETS

The Elite triplets studied me in the faint glow of the overhead light swaying as the truck churned over the bumpy gravel road.

It felt like they were examining every bit of me, from my pointy black witch's hat to the chain of my bronze hourglass disappearing under my gray blouse—even my black skirt and leggings, laced with a bit of Novice bronze. I swallowed, my back flush against a pile of boxes, somehow feeling like, though I'd made it onto the truck, I hadn't quite made the cut. After all, I was nothing like the three of them, lined up on the other side of the truck. They were about sixteen, four years older than me. And every fiber of them oozed with strength, with magical power, as evident by the stripes of silver marking their Elite status, hemmed around the collars and sleeves of their loose black shirts and pants. Even their cloaks had a small, bright strip of silver that sparked in the faint light, constantly reminding me of how much more powerful they were. In short, the Ueda triplets were *intimidating*.

To the far right, the willowy, graceful witch stared at me from over the opened pages of a book. "So, Novice Evergreen. Welcome. I'm Aurelia, the eldest of us three, and I prefer knowledge magic."

I blinked with surprise. Knowledge magic was rare in the realm: the power to recall long-ago read passages with startling accuracy, or to create unique kinds of spells that had never been fathomed before. Knowledge magic users were often innovators, working hand-in-hand with creation witches and wizards to advance the realm's technology and medical care. Many knowledge witches and wizards also excelled at scrying, for their knowledge of the past sometimes helped them foresee the future.

"A pleasure to meet you, Elite Ueda," I said, and Ember snuffed in agreement.

"Please, call me Lia." She inclined her head gracefully. "It's the only way we're able to tell which of us you're referring to."

In the middle, the boy with wide shoulders nodded at me. He had a broad forehead and thick eyebrows that reminded me of furrowed carvings in the bark of a tree. "I'm Aurelis. I go by Rel." His voice was deep, like stones slamming together. "My go-to is repair magic. Mostly because I'm always cleaning up after this one." He poked the girl on the left, the one who'd spoken up at the Council meeting.

She flashed a sharp smile, running a hand through her short, spiky hair. "And I'm Ettie, short for Aureliette. I prefer things shorter—whether hair, wands, or knives." She winked, her hand sliding down to her belt, where a short dagger hung, with an intricate hilt that looked like it was made of three strips of braided metal.

"Knives?" I echoed. Ember pawed at the dagger and then gnawed on my wrist with his teeth, reminding me he was just as good as any old knife.

Ettie grinned, running her fingers along the braided hilt. "If Grand Master Grottel's trying to keep us out with magical protections, sometimes you need unmagical devices to get out of a pinch. Hence Barty, my steel dagger."

"I still don't know why it has to have a name," Rel groaned, shaking his head. "Barty? Really?"

"Well, it's better than—"

Lia cut in smoothly, seemingly unfazed by their bickering. "Let's make this truck a little more comfortable so we can sleep, shall we?" She gestured around at our rectangular area among the creaking towers of supplies. It wasn't a big stretch of space; if we laid down, we'd have to be pretty close, side by side.

"I guess," Ettie said. "I'd be fine with just the wood floor. So long as we get some sleep."

"Yeah, but we need enough rest for what we're going to face," Rel insisted, his voice low and deep. "I agree with Lia, I'd prefer if we magicked this so it's decently comfortable."

"What *is* it like in the Twisted Forest? With Grottel's traps?" I asked.

Ettie's eyes glittered. "We've heard witches and wizards are grouped together, each team assigned with breaking down a certain area of Grottel's traps. It's kind of like rings of traps and magical layers...and if you turn your back on your teammate...or on the tower itself...likely your teammate will have disappeared or the protection curses might hurt you, too."

I gaped at Ettie. "People disappear that frequently?"

"Don't scare her!" Lia scolded her sister.

"But that's what it's really like," Ettie insisted. "That's why Master Arata really had no choice but to bring you along, because any chance of saving a teammate is worth it, even if it comes from a Novice—she had to be sensible about this. Ranks don't matter. Results do."

I looked between the two of them, Ettie with her eyebrow raised at her sister.

Then Lia sighed, her darkly lashed eyes flicking over to me. "To be honest, it's worse. Stay with your group, no matter what happens. Guard their backs, and they'll guard yours. But we can't have more witches and wizards disappearing. Anyway, let's sleep, so we *can* fight whatever comes our way."

"Ettie?" Rel said.

The short-haired girl sighed dramatically. "Fine, fine. But you two better help this time."

"Can I do something?" I asked.

"Nah, don't worry about it," Ettie said. "We're used to setting up camp together, whether by the abyss on the southern border, at the edge of the Walking Cliffs, or in a truck. I'll get it up in no time. Just enjoy my creation magic."

The girl pulled her wand out of her pants pocket, spinning it in the air with a grin. When she caught it, she swished it down, chanting, *"Beds for each of us, all at once."*

Cream-white futons—soft, plush mattresses meant for sleeping directly on the floor—unfurled out of thin air; I sank into the silky futon, feeling like I'd just landed in a cloud. With another twist of her wand and a quick chant—*"And blankets abound, so we'll sleep sound"*— Ettie created puffy blankets that settled on our legs, the pale color of freshly whipped cream, enough to chase away the cold of the night air.

Rel added in a growl, *"Dim the lights, till we see starry nights."*

The swinging overhead light burst and I gasped, expecting glass to shatter over us. Instead, the little dots of light spread out over the canvas tarp, like Rel had painted the night sky with his wand. A starry sky glowed softly above us, enough light so we didn't feel like we were falling asleep in a pitch-black cave, but not so much brightness that we might wake.

And Lia, in her gentle, delicate voice, chimed in, "*Worries abide, just for this time. Let dreams take us away, and return rest for the next day.*"

A sense of softness settled around me; the air was perfumed with the faint sweetness of lavender and vanilla. Some of the tension in my shoulders eased away, and I took in a deep, calming breath.

"Well, let's get some sleep," Rel said from the other side of the four futons. The fabric rustled as he pulled his blanket up. "G'night."

"Good night, all," Lia chimed.

"Good night," Ettie and I echoed back, getting into our futons. Ember crawled under the cloud-soft blanket with me, wiggling into my arms.

Ettie shifted, so she was facing me. "So, are you ready for the Twisted Forest?" she whispered. The outline of her sharp cheekbones and dark eyes was barely visible under the stars Rel had charmed.

"I don't know," I stammered.

"No matter what, it's ready for us," she quipped. "Lia and Rel are right: Sleep while you can. I'll wake you once we arrive at the camp; it's at the edge of the Twisted Forest. Or if we get caught in a trap, then you'll *definitely* wake up from that."

I swallowed nervously.

"Unless the traps get you first," she chuckled. Under the starlight, her teeth flashed in a grin. "Well, then, sweet dreams."

Before long, the gentle murmurs of the Elite triplets, snoozing restfully, filled the truck. But I couldn't quite fall asleep; as soon as the rocking lull of the truck started pulling me asleep, worries about tomorrow kept tugging me awake. I missed Charlotte and Davy, wishing they were at my side. The Elite triplets had each other; I wanted my best friends.

But as time stretched, I knew I had to sleep to get some rest before tomorrow...before the fight to get into Grottel's hideout truly started.

And I had to prove my worth, or else Master Arata would send me away from the Twisted Forest at the slightest of mistakes.

Ember snuggled closer in my arms, his heat keeping me warm as cold breezes whistled ominously outside.

PART THREE

THE
TWISTED
FOREST

CHAPTER 15

THE HIDDEN CAMP

I knew I was in a dream, but I didn't want to wake. I was back in my cozy cottage on the cliffs of Auteri, polishing off a platter of roasted mackerel with Charlotte and Davy and Rin. We were celebrating my ascension into becoming an Adept Witch, and Charlotte was nearly bursting at the seams to tell us some good news, but right as she opened her mouth—

"Eva…" A faint, haunting voice, light as chimes, broke into my dream. I rolled over, trying to cover my ears from that strange, hollow-sounding call. *"Eva… Please…"*

Then a cold hand shook my shoulder. "Wake up, Novice Evergreen. But be quiet."

A hot, wet snout smeared against my cheek, and I spluttered awake.

Quickly, Ettie—I sleepily realized—murmured, "*Shh.*"

It was early morning, and I was still in the rattling truck with the Elite triplets. My heart tightened. My best friends weren't with me, not anymore. But while I was still bundled in my cream-colored puffy blanket, with Ember snuggled close, the triplets were crouched at the end of the truck, scanning the snowy ridges around us.

"We're just about to descend into the Twisted Forest," Ettie whispered when I joined her. "And it's time for all of us to be on alert."

"Alert?" I echoed.

"You can feel it, can't you?" Lia whispered, as pine trees appeared along the cliffs.

I scanned the Sakuya Mountains looming over us, the rocky precipices getting smaller and smaller as more pine trees closed in, like the forest was swallowing us up. There was a strange sense of heaviness in the air, biting sharper than the cold. I shifted uneasily as Ember pressed against my leg.

"This is a strange place," I murmured.

"Strange is an understatement." Ettie scowled. "This place reeks of rogue magic. Grand Master Grottel's put up a few defenses since he escaped from the clutches of the Council and the queen."

Rel shook his head, trying to clear out the heaviness of the air, and then passed a small bundle over to me. "Eat this. We've got extra."

I opened a small tin box filled with three different rice balls, the grains glistening in the early morning light, and a warm-to-the-touch canteen. Ettie was also munching down a rice ball covered in salty dried seaweed.

"This looks delicious," I exclaimed, but then quickly lowered my voice. "Thank you, Elite Ueda—er, Rel."

He nodded, his eyes still scanning the area. "Eat fast. The driver said we're nearing camp soon."

Ember happily chewed on one rice ball while I polished off the remaining two. I took swigs of the roasted green tea, and fed Ember some water from my own canteen. But all the while as I ate, I studied the Twisted Forest, wondering if I could spot the magical traps Grottel had set up.

It was a peculiar place. Birds didn't sing; bugs didn't chirp. Nothing felt alive. The silence felt wrong in the faint daylight, almost like the heaviness in the air that had begun creeping onto us throughout the ride was beginning to smother my breath and the life of everything in the forest. Even the water, tinkling in a stream that ran alongside the road, sounded peculiar, like echoes of a voice trying to catch my attention, trying to call my name. "*Eva...*"

I frowned, rubbing my ears. This place was making me hear things.

"How do we know there won't be any traps?" I asked.

Lia's smooth face rippled in a grimace. "We don't.

Grand Master Grottel made sure of that. Look over there." She pointed at the trees closest to us.

I gasped. The dark wood had *eyes* carved into the bark, open and staring at us.

"I'd heard rumors about this, but it's the first time seeing it for myself," Lia whispered. "Those are sentry trees that Grottel charmed when he escaped to his tower; he twisted nature to protect him—until our teams came in and dismantled those curses. But not without losses..."

"Then it's safe?" I ventured.

"These trees alone triggered some sort of vapor that burns lungs. Master Kaki—one of the other team leaders—he barely managed to protect the first set of trucks that came in. Between this and the other traps we're dismantling, there are still seven witches and wizards recovering in the Council's infirmary; another dozen are still missing....The Twisted Forest is anything but safe."

Ettie added, "The teams that set up the camp made sure this road is clear, and Master Arata and Master Roone continue to watch over our path. That's why they took the first truck." Ettie polished her dagger as she glanced around. "But Lia's right. We don't know for certain. Just lay low, and have your wand by you at all times. Now and for the rest of the time you're in the Twisted Forest."

I swallowed, my sweaty fingers curling around my wand, the other hand pulling Ember close to me as I scanned the thick trees, wondering what lay ahead.

Somehow, the forest felt like a whole new realm, something beyond the world I'd always known.

Around thirty minutes later, as the sun crept into the sky in streaks of caramel and cardinal red, I pointed down the road at a strange golden bubble ahead of the trucks. "What's that?"

Rel grinned. "Welcome to the Council's camp in the Twisted Forest, protected by some of the best in the realm. That's a protection spell, so Grottel or any of his curses can't get in. Without it, no one would be able to sleep. And the good news is, we've finally made it!"

With a faint *pop!* we entered the shield. The truck pulled up into a clearing filled with half a dozen cabins, and Rel leaped out of the truck. "Time to break down Grottel's barriers!"

Lia gracefully jumped out, grabbing her knapsack and heading to one of the smaller cabins. Ettie clambered to the ground, giving me and Ember a hand. Master Arata was already meeting with four other Master Witches and Wizards, their heads bowed together; Master Roone was chatting with the non-magical truck drivers, and overseeing the unloading of the trucks.

Wait—non-magical—?

I spun around, studying each of the non-magical workers who jumped out of the trucks, all with gray caps

and billowy gray tunics and pants. Surely—possibly—
Charlotte and Davy *had* said not to worry about them
making it here—maybe—

But the workers lined up, efficiently carting the crates
over to the cabins, and my heart sank. My best friends
were nowhere to be seen.

"What're you in a daze for?" a voice barked, and I
jumped.

Master Arata glared down; though she was only a
few inches taller, it felt like she stretched as high as the
Sakuya Mountains, and I was a measly tree stump.

"I, um, I'm just studying the charm used for protection," I said, gesturing quickly at the golden sheen of the
bubble. "It's a very strong enchantment; isn't something
similar used for the barrier at the southern abyss? With
a spell this sturdy, it looks like it could deflect anything
from a wayward spell to a nightdragon trying to burn the
camp down."

Master Arata's narrow eyes glimmered, and to my
surprise, her lip twisted up in a half smile. "You are your
mother's daughter; she was always good at analyzing
enchantments." Then her eyes dropped to my hand clutching my wand. "Though, I must say, she was much stronger
at *casting* spells when I met her. She was only one year my
senior, but I was a Novice when she was an Elite."

I blinked; that was the same rank gap between me

and the Ueda triplets. But my mother had been much, much younger.

"Stay out of the way, okay?" Master Arata said, and let out a surprisingly soft sigh. "I respect your mother far too much to let you get hurt. If something happens to the rest of us, get *out*. Don't you dare try fighting Grottel or any of his traps alone. You're just not strong enough."

Indignation rose up in me. She'd been a Novice once, looking up to my Elite mother, just as I looked up to the Elite triplets. Plus, I'd spent the past two moons fighting the *Culling*, the twisted force of nature created by Grottel himself.

But then I remembered the dark look of the Grand Master's eyes, and the way his curse had struck Mother down; she hadn't had a chance to defend herself... because she was protecting me. Maybe Master Arata was right.

She pointed at the cabin closest to us with a stubby finger. "You're in that one with me, Master Roone, and the triplets. But I want to see you *stay* there. Don't go out past the protection shield—unless it's to go back home in a truck. For the next few days, your life stays within this bubble. You can give us the information from here, and *you are not allowed to leave*."

All around, the workers glanced up at her stern tone. From the doorway of the cabin, I could even see the Elite triplets, watching me with pitying looks.

I spluttered. "But I can help with Grottel's traps, I can—"

Master Arata's eyes were as fierce as a storm. "I will not be the one who has to go to your mother and explain that Grottel managed to hurt you. *No.* You are staying inside. Now go."

My head drooped down as I followed her demand and hurried into the tiny cabin.

I'd made it to the Twisted Forest, closer to finding answers for Mother and for Charlotte's and Davy's parents...but I was *stuck*.

∞

The cabin where I was supposed to spend the next few days was no more than a glorified place to sleep, tinier than my cottage back in Auteri. Though a team member had managed to create a solid four walls and roof, they hadn't bothered with any frills. It was a plain square of dirt, with three sets of rickety bunk beds and a tiny, high-up window cut out of the planks.

Ettie frowned as she threw herself on the upper bed; Ember and I had the bottom bunk. Her fingers twitched around her wand, but Lia spun around.

"Don't think about it," Lia warned. "We've got to save our magic, now that we're finally in the Twisted Forest."

"I know, I know, but it's *miserable* here. Thank

goodness we'll get out. I'd rather duel Grottel himself than be stuck in this—" Ettie cut off, looking down at me.

I tried to summon up a smile. "Don't worry about me." I gestured at the map. "I've got plenty to do here— I'll be busy."

The door screeched open and Master Arata stomped inside, Master Roone trailing behind her. "Where's my team?" she snapped. "We've got to get a move on while there's daylight. I'm not letting my team stay out when it's dark."

The Elite triplets rolled out of their beds and jumped into a line, bobbing into quick bows. "Ready for our mission, Master Arata."

The Master Witch only nodded. Then she turned to me. "Novice Evergreen?"

My heart leaped as I scrambled upright, nearly falling as I stumbled out of the bed. "Yes?"

Was—was she going to let me go along with them? As a guide?

"Give us the latest coordinates on the map," Master Arata snapped.

Hope stirred in me as I pulled out the scroll, smoothing it out over the thick blanket of the bottom bunk bed.

The team *needed* this spell to stay safe. And even if Master Arata was persnickety, I didn't want her to get hurt.

I breathed in deep, calling on my magic for the spell. The faces of my friends flashed in my mind—steadfast, strong Charlotte and cheery, troublemaking Davy. I chanted, *"A search for two friends close to my heart, show their parents so they will never be apart. Show me over time, the future I need to divine."*

The map flickered gold and scarlet next to that waterfall maybe half a mile from Grottel's tower, shooting out from the north and south ends of the tumbling waters. "Here's the concentration of magic," I said, studying the shifting ink marks. "And...ah, fairly soon, it looks like the powers of the Culling will start shifting to the northeast and southeast."

"It's quite like scrying, really, what you're doing there," Lia murmured, her dark hair falling over her face as she studied the map. "Impressive. Have you ever considered you might have an affinity for knowledge magic or scrying?"

A thrill of excitement rushed through my blood. An *Elite* with knowledge magic was praising me for her very own affinity?

"Oh!" I said. "I'm not sure I'd be able to manage proper scrying; my magic is mostly good for repairs and potions...."

"Still," Lia said, "I think—"

Then Master Arata cut through my swirling joy. "Lia. Memorize that."

But the girl paused, her smooth brow creasing. "If we can have Novice Evergreen join us, we'll have accurate updates—"

"No." Master Arata's voice chopped through the air like an axe falling onto wood. "I'm not letting a Novice get hurt on my watch. Master Roone, you too. See how it matches up with your map."

Lia pressed her lips together as she scanned the map one more time. But I couldn't miss the way her eyes flicked toward mine, apologetic. "Okay. Memorized, Master Arata. I'm ready."

Master Roone looked between the map in his hands to mine, his brow creased. "Ready."

"Let's go." Master Arata spun on her heel, hurrying out the door. "We need to make the most of the daylight."

"Ah, here we go," Master Roone muttered, his face turning gray. "Back to the Twisted Forest I go. . . . Another day of seeing someone disappear from my map. . . . Hopefully we'll see you later, Novice Evergreen. Though each trip into the forest seems more perilous than the last." The wizard shook his head, trying to clear his dark thoughts, a small parchment map clutched in his hand, and quickly followed Master Arata.

The triplets pulled on their knapsacks. At the doorway, though, they looked over their shoulders. I could almost see myself mirrored in their eyes: looking small and tiny, helplessly clutching my map, stuck inside the confines of the camp.

"We'll tell you all about what it's like out there, so it's like you're with us!" Ettie whispered gently. Rel and Lia nodded, giving me overly bright and kind smiles and quick waves.

Then the door slammed shut, leaving me nearly in the dark.

I slumped onto the edge of the bed. Ember whined, crawling into my lap. He let out a sad, wretched cough and started chewing anxiously on his unlit tail.

My heart tightened. He and I were the same: a weak witch, a flameless flamefox.

"Don't worry," I whispered, smoothing down his fur, trying desperately to believe my own words. "You don't need to breathe fire to be a flamefox. You already *are* one. And I'm a witch, too. I'll show them somehow. My rank as a Novice isn't what matters. It's what I *do* with my magic that does. Mother is right. It may seem impossible, but I'll show them I *am* an impossible possibility."

CHAPTER 16
THE MIRAGE

Master Arata had declared I couldn't leave the protection shield, but that meant I could still look around the camp, right?

Hesitantly, I poked my head out of the cabin door. No alarms went off. Half a dozen non-magical workers, in the same gray caps and clothes of the truck drivers, were busily hurrying around the camp, doing everything from cutting up wood for the fires to kneading plump rounds of dough.

The camp filled the small, cozy clearing, closed in by thick trees and the shield. But it was a comfortable place, with sunlight streaming through the leaves and a gentle breeze swirling around inside the golden, bubble-like shield, carrying the smoky-sweet scent of the camp-fires. There were six cabins total, three on each side of the center filled with crackling firepits and long tables with oak stumps as seats, and a seventh building that looked like it housed several washrooms.

A strange sound tugged at me, pulling me past the sparking fires and toward the cluster of three cabins on the other side of the fires and tables. It sounded so familiar, like someone was calling my name from far, far away.

There *were* whispers that I was aware of—the workers were murmuring to one another.

Why isn't that witch out with them?

That's Grand Master Evergreen's daughter. You know, the one who got cursed by Grottel.

Ah, so that's why she can't go out there? Or is it because she's weak?

Their murmurs flew around like pesky flies, but I tried to keep my head steady. I'd heard worse before. People would say whatever they wanted, but I didn't need to prove myself to them. As long as I did enough to make *myself* proud of what I was doing...

The gilded shimmer of the shield flashed and my shoulders drooped. Ember whined reassuringly at my side. *Don't listen to them.*

But those whispers...they were right. I looked longingly at the world outside, the sweeping pine trees and giant boulders, covered in moss and tangled in vines. I was still so far from reaching my goals.

Instead of walking back through the camp, I followed

the strange bubbling sounds behind a cabin. As soon as I turned the corner, I breathed easier, not feeling the weight of everyone's eyes on me.

But the peculiar buzzing only grew louder. It almost felt like the winds were calling my name.

"Eva..."

I jolted upright. The workers continued chopping wood or tending to the fires, completely unbothered.

But someone *definitely* had called my name.

"Do you hear that?" I asked Ember, who padded alongside me. His ears were turned toward a stream that slipped through the bubble of the protection spell, and then went out the other way. By the looks of the heavily trodden ground, this seemed to be the camp's water source.

"Eva..."

It almost...it almost sounded like a *voice* calling out from the water.

But that was impossible.

I clambered over the small rocks and knelt down. Sunlight poured through the overhead oak trees, hitting the stream. I shielded my eyes from the bright rays, studying the shallows that looked no deeper than the height of my hand. Speckled gray rocks, polished smooth by the running water, lined the bottom. It was as innocuous and gentle as the stream that wove by my parents' house.

I had to just be hearing the call of some strange bird,

or a new creature that was only in the Twisted Forest. That had to be why I'd heard those odd sounds. I just wasn't used to the forest.

"*Eva...*" There it was, again. That faint whisper. "*Help...*"

But water didn't talk, water didn't—

Movement from within the shallow depths caught my eye. Was it a golden trout?

A glimpse of sharp, dark eyes stared back at me, surrounded by pale skin and inky-black hair rippling with the currents. "*Please...save me.*"

I bit down a scream.

There was a girl staring out of the bubbling waters.

Her eyes widened as they met mine.

"*I'm Maika....Please, get me out of this place.*" She reached out her hand, as if she could reach straight out of the water—

But Ember let out a yelp and pounced, straight onto her.

The surface broke, her image disappearing in a flash. Wet and with his fur soaked, Ember turned left and right, like the girl was a fish he wanted to catch.

Maika—the girl—she was gone...but she'd definitely been there.

I sat back on the rocks, stunned, scanning the stream.

But she didn't appear again, even as I waited with my hand on my wand, goosebumps prickling all over my skin.

Was this one of Grottel's traps? It seemed different

from the eyes on the trees or spells that might make witches and wizards disappear.... Had he found a way through the protection shield?

But why would he send a sad-faced girl like that, asking for help?

The Grand Master Grottel I knew didn't ask *anyone* for favors. Mother had always alluded to stories back in the day when she'd tried to help him, but he'd get upset, saying he was fine on his own.

I backed away from the stream. The waters bubbled as cheerily as before, but that mysterious girl was gone.

Maybe I was safer closer to the other workers. This was my first up-close taste of the peculiarities of the Twisted Forest, and I wasn't liking it one bit.

Rubbing the goosebumps on my arms, I hurried back to the clearing.

I turned the corner around the cabin. Ember scampered toward the old man kneading rounds of dough; my flamefox was following his stomach to safety.

When I reached them, the man had fished out a shred of dried sweet potato, and was grinning back at my flamefox.

"Mind if I give him a bite to eat?" the baker asked.

"Oh, go for it." I laughed, my shoulders easing. Talking to someone who wasn't submerged in water—or a strange mirage—made me feel a little better about being in the forest. "But don't be surprised if he won't leave your side."

"With a creature as cute and clever as this, I don't think I'd mind," the old man admitted, kneeling down to give Ember the treat.

My flamefox gingerly took the slice of sweet potato from the man's wrinkled hand, and then swallowed it all in one gulp. The old man chuckled, a deep belly laugh.

Ember's tail flickered, shooting with sparks of light, as he pranced around my legs with joy. And then he let out another little cough with a splutter of ash, and my chest squeezed.

"Is he all right?" The man frowned.

"He's trying to breathe out fire," I explained, biting my lip. "But he's different from most flamefoxes.... He was the runt of his litter, so I think it'll just take him more time than most."

"Nothing wrong with that," the man said with a nod. "All of us, we have to go at our own pace. Shoot for the stars, y'know, but we all gotta take our own paths to the stars that shine brightest to us."

Then the man hurried to one of his shelves and brought back a small silver can. "Mind if I feed your flamefox this? It's a bit of mackerel. The oils might be nice for his throat. I'd say it'd help his coat, but he's already beautiful."

Ember preened under the praise, but when the man

cranked open the can and offered it on his large hand, my flamefox looked up at me with wide eyes.

"Go on, Ember," I said.

He didn't need to be told twice; in a flash, my flamefox polished the metal tin clean and gave the man a lick on his hand.

The man laughed. "Ah, that tickles. But he's so warm. What a treat for me, to meet an actual flamefox."

"I've got quite some time before Master Arata needs my help again," I said. "Is there anything I can do to repay you for Ember's food?"

"Is Master Arata all right with that?" the man asked.

"Oh, she's fine," I said. "So long as I help them figure out safe paths before they head out. It's a spell on a scroll, you see."

"That's grand work you're doing," the man said, nodding approvingly. The other workers nearby nodded, eyes wide.

I smiled at them, a sudden shyness overcoming me. "What can I help with?"

The older man looked around. "Well, if you don't mind, Ralvern over there could use a hand with the laundry, I'm sure. He's got piles to work through."

I squinted at the older boy on the other side of the clearing, up to his elbows in a tub of water, scars ringing his arms. He had a shock of black hair covering his scarred face, and the thinness of his arms and his sloped shoulders reminded me of a scarecrow. A gray cap was pulled low, protecting him from the sun. Still, somehow, he looked familiar.

I stepped closer to him. "Excuse me?"

He jolted upright. "Ah, a witch." Wiping his forehead, he squinted his round eyes. "Anything I can do for you, miss?"

"The baker over there, he said I could help you with the wash?" I gestured to the soapy water. "I'm afraid I'm not particularly good at laundry charms; most of the spells I try end up with shrunken clothes, so I usually do my laundry by hand, too."

"Any help would be great, magical or not," Ralvern said, nodding toward a machine next to him. "Can you crank them through that to wring out the cloths? Pile the laundry in that bamboo basket, and then we can hang them up to dry."

We set to work in a comfortable silence, the boy handing over towels and washcloths as soon as he scrubbed them down.

But I kept stealing glances over at the boy, who was determinedly rubbing a stain out of a dirty tablecloth. There was something so familiar about his scarecrow hair; I was *certain* I'd seen him before. "I was wondering...have we met?"

He grinned sheepishly, revealing a flash of a charming smile. "Most witches and wizards here, they tend not to remember us non-magicals." Then he widened his eyes as he stammered, "Not to be rude. You all are so busy, what with your work helping the realm. But you were something else, the way you helped Auteri with that Culling. I was mighty grateful for that."

I let out a gasp. Suddenly, I remembered where I'd seen him before. He'd been one of the folks in the town hall who'd folded the paper shields to protect Auteri. "You're one of Davy's friends! I thought you were a sailor?"

"I guess so, oftentimes, I'm a sailor," Ralvern said with a grin. "But I take what odd jobs I can, because whatever pays is what I need to help my younger brother."

"Oh! Is he in Auteri?"

The boy nodded, his hair flopping over his eyes again. "He's in the orphanage. I want to save up enough money so that he'll always have enough to eat, especially when he gets older. Maybe you remember him? He won't stop talking about you, and he treasures that paper dolphin you charmed for him. His name's Hikaru, a tiny load of trouble but—"

"I know him!" I said excitedly. No wonder Ralvern looked so familiar—Hikaru was the little boy who'd gone into Trixie's corn shop with Mayor Taira, and he'd kept the mayor from noticing me, which had been particularly helpful since I hadn't quite been on her good side then.

"I'm glad for the steady pay," he said, but then he waved one scarred hand out toward the trees. "But I don't like what's out there. I'm glad you don't have to go out into the forest like the rest of them."

"Not many volunteered for this, then?" I asked.

The boy grinned. "Nah, hence the good pay."

"I want to be out there, though," I said with a sigh. "I can't do as much from here. I *want* to see what's out there."

"But, Novice Evergreen...it's safer here," he said, looking down. "With or without magic, whatever Grottel's doing...it's not safe if you're not in one of those protected trucks or this bubble...."

"What do you mean?" I asked.

He glanced around, his eyes shifting around the camp. "Here," he muttered quietly. "Follow me. Let me show you round the site, and a few other things, too. Something you might find of interest."

Ralvern limped over to a tray filled with freshly baked bread, picking up a roll and waving at me to take one. I picked out a crusty round with cheese baked into the center and bit into it with relish. The rice balls I'd eaten during the ride felt like they'd been years ago.

The boy walked me around the campsite, showing me the long tables that everyone ate at, and introduced me to the rest of the non-magical workers, all ten of them. Their jobs ranged from the chef I'd met earlier who had been baking bread, to medics that supported the Council's healers and were working on restocking non-magical elixirs, to drivers like Ralvern who helped out with odd jobs like laundry.

"There's always someone awake and about among us workers," he explained. "Safer if we stay on alert and let the witches and wizards know if there's anything odd going on."

Shivers ran up my arms. I'd have to tell Master Arata about that strange mirage of the girl in the water when the team got back.

"There are five teams of witches and wizards, right?" I asked.

He nodded. "A total of twenty-five. Well, twenty-six including you. Or, at least there *should* be..."

I blinked. "What do you mean?"

Ralvern jerked his head toward a tree next to the cabin I was staying in. A paper scroll was tacked into the bark. "That's the current count of everyone here, all the teams, magical and non-magical."

I stared at the list. It was sorted into cabins, six different groups. The non-magical cabin was at full capacity, with ten workers. But it was the magical cabins that caught my eye.

Names were crossed off, one after another, and new members were crammed into the margins.

"What...what's happened?" I asked.

"The names that are scribbled out...those are the ones who didn't make it back. Or if they managed to return, they got sent to the capital for urgent medical care," Ralvern said, his voice low.

Shock pounded through my veins. Even the cabin I was in...ghosts of names filled the roster.

CABIN FIVE

MASTER RINA ARATA

MASTER JUNKO ARATA

MASTER EUNICE SHERN

MASTER CHIKA BERRY

ELITE AOI NAKANO

ELITE TARA RITTA

ELITE SAKI BERRY

ELITE CHIYO KAGEYAMA

MASTER S. T. ROONE

ELITE AURELIETTE UEDA

ELITE AURELIS UEDA

NOVICE EVALITHIMUS EVERGREEN

ELITE AURELIA UEDA

"There was another Master Arata?" I asked.

Ralvern nodded grimly. "Master Junko Arata—the one leading the teams now—she used to be second-in-command to her partner. Now Master Roone's the one who watches the coordinates of the team through his map. He's the one who has to watch his teammates disappear."

My throat went dry. No wonder both of their eyes had looked so dark when Master Arata had spoken of the losses in the Twisted Forest. Seven Masters and Elites were either missing or had to return to the capital for treatment from Grottel's curses.

Then there was a shout from outside the shield. I spun around, scanning the periphery. Was it the girl in the water?

But Ralvern made a strangled noise. "Look." He pointed at a pair of Councilmembers rushing between a set of trees, a stretcher floating between them.

They hit the bubble, and after a second, the shield rippled to let them through.

As they passed through the protection spell, I recognized the figures.

Ettie and Rel stumbled to a stop, their faces bleached from shock. Ettie bowed over the stretcher, checking on their charge, as Rel sank to his knees, breathing heavily. "We brought her as fast as we could."

The non-magicals beelined over, crowding the stretcher. Then one of them split off, calling over her shoulder, "I'll start up the truck! Healers, jump in!"

Through the workers, I could see a girl on the stretcher, curled on her side and clutching at her arms. She let out a hiss. "This pain, it won't let up!"

The buzz of chatter swelled. Ember let out a piercing whine and I cried out, "What happened?"

Ettie's wild, shocked eyes met mine through the crowd. "It's Lia," she gasped out. "Grand Master Grottel...He was there, in the spot you'd found for us. I don't think he'd realized we'd figured out his real hideout is by the waterfall. But the moment he saw us, he cursed Lia."

CHAPTER 17

In the Shadows of the Twisted Forest

The camp workers stood alert as the truck rattled down the winding path back to Okayama. As it turned around a set of trees, everyone—magical and non-magical alike—bowed, sending our best of wishes to Lia.

In the Twisted Forest, though, there was no time to dawdle. Master Arata, Master Sato—a scryer, apparently—Master Kaki, who had an affinity for protection spells, and a few other team leaders met in one of the cabins to discuss this new development of seeing Grottel for the very first time.

The mood inside the bubble was grim. The witches and wizards who had just filtered in looked particularly on edge, and they studied the bronze shine of my Novice rank when they caught sight of me. Most of them wearily

limped over to the medics' tent to heal up the various cuts
and wounds they'd gotten through their latest foray fighting Grottel's magical protections, though some lined up
for bowls of hearty brown curry and freshly baked bread.

"We're hitting a new low," one of the wizards muttered to his friend. "A Novice?"

"That's Grand Master Evergreen's daughter." His
friend shrugged. "I heard that Novice Evergreen's got
some scrying map that's supposed to help us find the conduit faster. But I guess Grottel takes that path, too."

"Elite Ueda got *cursed*. I've never heard of a spell like
that—to make the body feel like it's been stung? How's
that progress for us?"

Before I could hear an answer, Ember pawed at my
boots, and we hurried back into the cabin. I had to look
over my map. The wizard was right; I had to find some
way to help Master Arata more. Even if I couldn't go
out into the field, I had to be able to tell Master Arata and
the rest of the teams the best ways to avoid Grottel's traps.

∽

The next few days passed in a haze of worry and uncer-
tainty, each dawning more formidable than the next.
Every morning, I'd give Master Arata and the other teams
an update on the constantly changing paths of danger
and safety, after a night of casting and casting the spell,
trying to track the currents of magic as accurately as

possible. Every morning, the teams would bicker about whether I should go, or why they were trusting the word of a Novice, or even arguing that we were running out of time.

But on the day after Lia's curse, a team that didn't follow my guidance stumbled into the brunt of Grottel's magical curses, and an Elite Wizard fell down a rocky pit, breaking his leg and getting bitten by a strange poisonous spider. He got sent back on yet another truck. On the second, another team lost an Elite Witch completely—her partner said she'd been there one moment and then vanished the next. And like the marks on the roster showed, she hadn't been the only one.

The mood in the camp was uncertain and somber, and when I wasn't scrying the map, I spent time with Ralvern or Ettie and Rel, away from the piercing gazes of the rest of the witches and wizards.

On one morning, before the crack of dawn, I summoned up the courage to tell Ettie and Rel about the whispering waters.

"Could I talk to you for a few minutes?" I asked. Rel and Ettie stopped where they stood in the door, about to follow Master Arata and Master Roone out to breakfast.

Rel sat back down on his bunk bed, his broad forehead pinched. "What is it, Novice Evergreen?" He was constantly on edge these days.

"I saw something strange in the stream that goes

through the campsite....I was wondering if you'd ever seen anything like it before," I said.

"It's got loads of protection spells on it," Ettie reassured me, from where she sat next to Rel, her head leaning on his shoulder. "Grottel can't poison it or anything like that. We're sure of it."

"Er...then..."

Ettie waved at me. "Spit it out, Novice."

"Can he send mirages through the water?"

Rel and Ettie stared at each other. "*Mirages?*" they said in unison.

"The...the day I arrived, I heard someone calling my name. I followed it to the stream...and there was a girl in the water, trying to talk to me. Ember jumped in, and the image scattered. I haven't seen her since, but sometimes...I swear I hear her voice on the wind."

I looked nervously between Rel and Ettie, my palms damp, wondering if they'd believe me. Rel's square face was quiet, unreadable. But Ettie chewed her lip, pulling out her dagger, rubbing a cloth along the blade, and pushing it back into the leather sheath.

"I've never heard of anything like that before." Ettie stood up, and horror twisted through me. Maybe she'd recommend Master Arata to send me back to Okayama. Then she said, "But let's go take a look."

Rel and Ettie paced the length of the stream. Rel muttered spell after spell under his breath, his wand flashing with sparks of colors. Ettie silently checked the areas where the stream bubbled through the shield, shaking her head.

The water was clear, without a strange sound to be heard. My stomach clenched as they finally straightened and turned to me.

"Nothing," Rel said.

My shoulders drooped. "I *swear*, I heard a voice....I saw her...."

"We don't doubt you," Ettie said firmly.

"What?" I blinked.

Rel's pinched forehead smoothed. "Novice Evergreen, you helped our sister. We all would've been in a far worse state if you hadn't given her a heads-up of what to expect. Because of you, she was aware that Grottel's curses might come from the northeast. But it was only due to Master Arata not letting you come along that we didn't have enough accurate information."

My throat was dry. They *did* believe in me.

Then Rel frowned again. "Still, if you've heard something...it's best to stay away from the water. Grottel never cared much for your mother, not with her being the only other Councilmember with the same level of powers as him."

Ettie nodded. "I don't want him to target you. Stay near us."

"But you're gone for most of the day," I said.

Ettie and Rel glanced at each other, somehow communicating in that single gaze. Ettie nodded and turned to me.

"It's time we talk to Master Arata," she said, her eyes set. "Let's meet her after breakfast. Don't pack your knapsack—just keep everything in your pockets, so you can travel light. You'll need to be mobile."

"Pack? Travel light?" I echoed, my eyes widening.

Rel crossed his arms. "Master Arata needs to see the truth. You're the only reason why we haven't lost more people these past few days. Three Councilmembers is a lot, but it was nearly twice that number before you came here with your map. If we can get you in the field with us, we'll actually have a chance of breaking into Grottel's hideout."

◌◌

Rel, Ettie, and I found Master Arata back in the cabin, doing one last check of her knapsack. "Canteen, check. Wheatberry bars, check. Rope, check."

Ettie cleared her throat. "Master Arata, permission to speak?"

The leader of our team looked up and noticed me behind the two Uedas. "Oh, not this again."

From where he sat on his bunk checking over his supplies, too, Master Roone shoved a towel into his knapsack and then set his bag aside, listening in.

"We'd like permission to bring Novice Evergreen with us," Ettie started.

"No," Master Arata snapped. "I told her the only way she was coming to the forest was if she stayed in the protection of the camp. She agreed. She is *staying*."

I swallowed. I had agreed. But that was before Lia had gotten cursed. Before someone else had gotten nearly fatally hurt, before another wizard disappeared into thin air. Before I'd really known the extent of what the tower teams were facing...before I'd realized how much they needed me to keep them safe.

Master Roone drew upright, rubbing his bald head. "They're right, Junko. You know this. We all know this."

"It is too dangerous!" Master Arata shot back.

"We can't keep wandering blindly! *That* is too dangerous—we're going to lose more people this way!" Master Roone said. "By the time we make it through the curses that Grottel casts in our path, we've missed our window to follow Novice Evergreen's instructions!"

"I can't lose a Novice to Grand Master Grottel!" Master Arata spluttered, her eyes wild. "Especially not Grand Master Evergreen's daughter. She'd never forgive me!"

"Mother misses her magic," I said, staring straight at Master Arata. "If we can get into Grottel's hideout and destroy the conduit, the amulet, whatever he's using to gather his power, then we can return the magic to the land, to people like my mother. And even find our missing team members, too."

I gestured out at the campsite. "We're missing ten, no, *eleven* people, including Lia." A truck was coming in later today *because* our numbers had dwindled. Between the injured getting shuttled back to the capital for treatment and the vanishing witches and wizards, the magical teams fit in three cabins instead of the usual five.

Master Arata growled under her breath. "I don't like the idea of missing team members, either." Then she snapped, "Give me that map."

The Master snatched up my scroll. Ember let out a yelp of surprise, but I held him to my chest. "If others could've cast the spell, I would have gladly let you take this map, Master Arata."

"*Let me see the path he'll take, let me see a haven of safety for my team's sake!*" Master Arata roared, her wand slashing down on the map.

The parchment fluttered, but the inky lines stayed the same. She jabbed her wand at the drawn tower, scratching at the waterfall and the endless miniature trees.

Nothing.

"It's Novice Evergreen's connection to her friends whose parents are somehow involved in the Culling," Master Roone said.

"I know. I *know*." Master Arata covered her face with her hands. "But is it so wrong for me to want to keep *someone* from getting hurt? The moment Novice Evergreen steps out of the shield, there's no guarantee of what might happen. Nelalithimus Evergreen was always my idol as I pushed through the ranks of the Council. How can I look her in the eye if Novice Evergreen gets hurt?"

"But countless people continue to suffer," I said. "Lia...the other witches and wizards...and every person in Rivelle Realm who's lost someone to the Culling. I want to help. I want to do something to stop all of this. And if it's going along with you, then I want to do that. Can you look my mother in the eyes and really say you did everything in your power, if you don't let me go out into the forest?"

Master Arata was quiet for a long, long stretch of time, her eyes closed in thought.

Finally, the witch cracked open one eye and sighed, crossing her arms. "Allow me to cast protective charms on you. Only then will I consider it."

"What...oh!" A tingle of excitement swirled through me. That meant—that was a *yes*. Even Master Roone had his eyebrows raised in surprise. But then what she was saying tamped down on my shock. "But—everyone should have those charms, not just me."

"If we had endless magic, yes. But we've got to save powers when we can. Plus, you were the initial focus of Grottel's curse that hit your mother. So you need a little more than the rest."

The sting of those words burned. Finally, I nodded. *Cast any protective charms you want, so long as I can go with you.*

Master Arata gestured at Master Roone. "I'm thinking of one spell each. Not too much magic depletion, but enough to curb this bad feeling I have."

Together, the two Masters swirled their wands, chanting quickly.

"Protect her from sight, so she can fight."

"Willful travel, do not let her path unravel. Hide her steps, for easy rest."

Sparks tingled along my arms as their magic settled over me. When I blinked, it felt like my skin was slightly flushed, a little warmer with their extra protections. Ember's fur shimmered slightly, too; it seemed they'd included my flamefox.

Rel deciphered the spells. "The first one's a charm to make it harder for Grottel, or any foes, really, to see you. You'll appear a little faint to them—it'll give you time to run if you need it. That's clever; I've never thought of that one before. It does take quite a lot of magic and practice to get something of that level right. And that second one is for safe travels, so you can't be tracked by your footsteps; they won't imprint on the ground. Better so that Grottel can't find you."

"And we won't have safe travels if we dawdle," Master Arata snapped, her charm complete. "Let's go." She took one long look at me. "I expect to see us all back here in the camp, all in one piece, at sunset. Stay close to the Uedas. And if you see a curse headed your way, block it. If the situation gets too much, get back here to safety. If I disappear, get back. If Master Roone disappears, get back. If the Elites disappear—"

"Get back," I finished, with a nod.

Master Arata spun around. "Let's go. Toward the tower, then curve around the cliffs so we get closer to the waterfall. As we approach, keep us on the right path, Novice Evergreen."

"Understood," I said, but the Master was already at the door of the cabin, calling for the other teams to start heading out.

Ettie and Rel walked alongside me as we stepped out of the bubble, the protection shield shimmering over our skin, stretching like a too-tight sweater—

Then there was a soft *pop!* and we were in the thick of the Twisted Forest. The air was heavy, as if imbued with a strange curse. Ahead, the two other teams were striding through the forest, their wands at ready, then stopping every hundred feet, until Master Arata gave them the affirmative to walk onward.

I looked over my shoulder, at the camp, at safety. From inside the golden bubble, Ralvern waved at me.

Ettie nudged me along. "C'mon, we can't get left behind."

Quickly, we wove through the gigantic boulders, covered in vines, following in Master Arata and Master Roone's footsteps. As we turned the corner, the path opened up through the trees, and a cold wind whistled through, shaking the thick leaves with a skittering, strange sound. The two teams up ahead were barely visible through a mist that wove through the boulders and trees.

"There it is," Ettie whispered.

A tall tower rose over the cliffs. The wind snapped with a cold bite, warning me off. My skin prickled. But I'd fought for my place to be here, and there was no way I'd let myself get scared off.

I studied Grottel's tower. The rectangular rocks at the base jutted out strangely, like it'd been broken and resurrected, but it somehow wasn't quite the same as before.

Rel leaned in and explained, "The waterfall is on the other side, so we have to skirt well around the tower to avoid the traps." I nodded; I'd studied the map countless times and knew the tower lay between us and the waterfall, where it seemed that Grottel was hiding the conduit somewhere nearby, underground.

But even though I'd seen it in ink, staring at the tower and the Twisted Forest head-on felt startlingly scary.

"I can do this," I whispered, though a bitterly icy breeze tore the words from my lips as soon as I spoke. Even if I couldn't hear myself, I wanted to say it. I needed to believe in myself.

On the horizon, hills met tall, blocky rocks, blending in and out of the thick fog, and the faint splashes of a stream tinkled. Next to the tower, on the other side of a thicket of trees, a handful of broken, long-since abandoned houses lined the shores of a small lake. The sharp scent of pine needles wafted through the misty air.

Ember stayed close to my side, his pointy ears shifting left and right, but he stood tall, reminding me that I always had him by my side. My heart pounded, nearly about to jump out of my chest. I clutched my sweaty palms around my wand and narrowed my eyes. The brim of my witch's hat rippled as I took a big step into the Twisted Forest: one step closer to stopping Grottel once and for all.

CHAPTER 18

A Pocketful of Gold

The wind whispered of mysteries and secrets, swirling through the vines and curving around boulders. In this wild land, everything felt strange. The trees grew thicker as we moved closer to Grottel's tower, stretching up like monsters. The path brought us through tangled vines wrapped between gigantic boulders, and we had to crawl our way through. The scent of fresh pine and sap, oozing from the bark, wafted through the air, flowing with the mist that rose from the mossy ground. When I brushed against a tree with low branches, water droplets rolled off with a splash, making Ember jump back with surprise.

Though the forest seemed empty, I felt like I might see a ghost around any corner, like one of the haunting stories Mother used to tell me when we'd been cozy around the fire on summer nights.

A voice, light as chimes, whispered, *"Eva ... Running out of time ..."*

I froze, and Ettie bumped into me. "What is it?"

Carefully, I listened to the forest. Again, absolute quiet. "Nothing."

Nothing, I hoped.

Rel glanced around at the thick mist clinging to our clothes, and unfurling along the ground. "This place is as creepy as ever, but this fog doesn't help. I've never seen it this thick before."

Through the white mist, Master Arata waved at us to join her on the path between two boulders. The three of us, with Ember bounding in our wake, hurried to meet her and Master Roone, who was leaning against the rock to the right, consulting his map to check on the locations of Master Kaki's and Sato's teams.

"Ready for your map," Master Roone said.

I was already casting the spell. With a familiar scarlet and gold glow, the ink marks swirled on the map. "East and west of the waterfall," I said.

Master Roone scratched out a big X on the east and west sides of the waterfall.

"It communicates with the maps carried by the other team leaders," Ettie quickly explained to my questioning gaze. "So we can get instant updates. Master Arata reviews our positioning and decides the strategy, and Master Roone shares that with the teams."

Master Arata cleared her throat, her eyes still scanning the periphery. "We're all approaching from the south, so this should be perfect timing. Good. Keep an eye on your map for any changes, Novice. Keep casting your spell regularly. We're getting close to the waterfall. Closer than we've ever been before."

We strode forward, our wands out and ready. The other two teams were up ahead; they'd advanced through a path that led through a set of boulders and into a clearing, edged in on all sides by tall cliffs.

As we turned the corner, the sound of the waterfall bubbled, breaking through the heavy quiet. Rel shot me a grin. "We're closer!"

The cliffs of the waterfall stretched as high as Auteri's town hall, towering above us; we couldn't see the waterfall through the fog, but the rumbling, pounding water grew louder as we walked forward. White pine trees filled the clearings between the cliffs, swaying in the breeze. The spray misted our face, rinsing away the sweat from the hike.

When we made our way through the boulders marking the path leading to the waterfall, I swallowed. Thick mist rolled over the soft, tall grass, and we couldn't see the other teams.

"Stay close," I told Ember; he was already sticking to my boots, his ears warily flicking from left to right.

There was a strangeness to this place that made me

feel uneasy. Glancing back down at my map, I muttered the spell again: "*A search for two friends close to my heart, show their parents so they will never be apart. Show me over time, the future I need to divine.*"

"Any changes?" Ettie asked, leaning over to look.

"Nothing," I confirmed. Grottel's rogue magic was still concentrated on the east and the west, the gold and scarlet marks surprisingly steady.

There was a noise from our right, like a crack of a branch, and we jolted up, peering around. But the fog kept swirling, white and thick, showing no more than the occasional tree or the black cliffs edging us in. Then, through the fog, the outline of a figure darkened—

And then disappeared.

"Did you see that?" I whispered.

"See what?" Rel asked.

I swallowed. "I thought I saw someone...."

Ettie nodded. "I saw it, too." She raised her voice. "Master Arata. Master Roone."

The witch and wizard paused, retracing their steps back to us.

"What is it?" Master Arata said, her voice low.

"Eva and I saw something, over there," Ettie said, pointing to our right. "Maybe it was just a tree in the mist, but..."

The other teams were in the second clearing up ahead; it should've just been our team in this area. So what had *that* been?

The ink spots on my map swirled gold and scarlet, churning like a pan full of mercurial potion. I let out a gasp, my hands shaking. "The map, it's changing.... We're in the path of his rogue magic. Tell the teams to come back south!"

Master Roone swiped his wand at the map, desperately trying to communicate the warning. There was a sudden shout from the clearing ahead, then—

Silence.

Master Roone stared down at his map. "Gone. Master Kaki's team is *gone.*" An involuntary shudder shook his body. "And...no...Master Sato's team, too?" He looked up wildly at Master Arata, who'd started studying the shifting marks on my map, her face bleached of all color. "I swear, they were here, I don't know what happened—"

Rel, Ettie, and Master Roone hurried toward the next clearing, toward the other teams—or where they'd been.

Master Arata was pale. "I said I had a bad feeling about this...." The witch shoved me behind the closest tree. Ember let out a cry and wove around my boots. "Stay hidden," she hissed, low. She spun around, racing after Master Roone, Rel, and Ettie. "Stop! Wait! It's coming down this way, you'll get caught—"

A laugh sounded from the mist, and a figure loomed over Master Roone. In a mocking tone, a man in all gray and black said, "Caught? Like this?"

Rel spat out, "Grottel hired mercenaries."

Nearly two dozen figures loomed out of the thickening fog, spinning daggers in their hands, their faces twisted into cruel smiles.

Without warning, one of the men threw his blade. Master Roone buckled over with a cry, clutching at his leg, and a sudden bloom of red stained the grass below his feet.

I clutched my hand to my mouth, trembling, as I backed away. No. *No.* My map was supposed to stop this.

"If you run, we'll catch you," the tall man in the center called, in a singsong voice.

"We have to get away," Master Arata shouted. "Retreat, team!"

"We're so close, though," Ettie cried out. "We didn't come all this way to slink back. We've got magic—"

"We didn't come all this way to show up on Grottel's doorstep and serve ourselves to him," Master Arata shot back. *"A screen not to be seen, let us leave."*

Black mist shot out of her wand, gathering in the air like a shimmer of silk, hiding us from view of the mercenaries. Figures slammed into the shield, and the sound of a piercing crack shot through the clearing as daggers hacked at the spell.

"Let's go!" Master Arata shouted. "My spell won't last forever."

Grimly, Ettie bowed her head as she and Rel ran to Master Roone, hefting him between the two of them.

They started coming back toward me and Ember, and I was about to step out of the cover of the tree trunk and run with them when Master Arata's spell shattered, like a thousand pieces of crystal, and then vaporized.

As if it had never existed.

In its place, a shadowy figure stood in the center of the clearing, the mercenaries surrounding him, their daggers clanking.

I huddled against the tree. My heart pounded so loud in my ears, it felt like it echoed through the mists. *No, no, no.*

Grand Master Grottel glared at my team, studying each of them in turn.

Ettie and Rel, holding up Master Roone. Master Arata with her feet planted firmly in the dewy grass, as if she was about to challenge Grottel to a duel, her wand out.

He still wore the same black tunic, lined with that diamond shimmer, marking his status as a Grand Master.

But his eyes were bloodshot and cold, his skin pale. There was a recklessness to his thin lips, curled up at the corner.

"So," he drawled. "We finally meet again, Junko. I've been wondering why so many people have been scuttling around my lands."

"Stop raising the Culling and the Council will stop 'scuttling' around," Master Arata shot back.

"Ah, yes, this new Council. I'll bet Norya simply loves dancing to the queen's commands," Grottel sneered. "She never was good for much.... It was only fitting I left when I did."

How could Grottel be so cruel, even to Norya, who had supported him all these years?

"Well, I'm 'dancing' to Elite Dowel's and the queen's commands," Master Arata snapped. "And I'm going to return you to the capital for justice, to put an end to all the evil you've created."

"Sweet sentiments, but you're outnumbered," Grottel drawled, as a terrifying grin spread over his face. "Lay your wands down."

"We're not—"

Another dozen figures in gray-black rose from the mists. More mercenaries. Their belts, with gold-filled pouches, jangled ominously as they closed in, with sharp daggers at the ready.

"We won't give in," Master Arata growled. "Ever—"

A scream sounded through the clearing, and a pair of mercenaries dragged over a wizard.

Master Kaki's gold-rimmed glasses dangled from one ear. He shouted and cursed as his knees bounced against the ground.

The taller of the two mercenaries smiled unpleasantly at Master Arata. "Well, well. You wouldn't mind missing this comrade, would you?"

Master Kaki spluttered, eyes wide when he caught sight of my team—surrounded but not yet captured. "Junko! You've got to tell the queen! Elite Dowel! Grottel is going to raise the last Culling tonight—"

With a thump of the base of his dagger, the tall, bearded mercenary knocked him out. Master Kaki's head lolled to the side, his glasses falling into the grass.

The mercenary dropped Master Kaki's arm, his comrade kneeling to wrap the wizard's hands in rope. Leering, he dangled the blade over Master Kaki's neck. "Do you want his blood on your hands? If not, put down your wands."

Master Arata's shoulders tightened as she looked left and right. And, for an instant, I could see what she saw: Master Roone was barely standing; Rel and Ettie wouldn't be able to escape with him. Master Arata herself was so weary that she swayed in place, drained from her spells, trying vainly to protect the team.

No...don't give up, no! I wanted to scream; I wanted to step out of the cover of the tree to fight.... But Master Arata had tried to keep me safe; I'd be ruining all her efforts.

Slowly, she set down her wand on the grass. "Just don't hurt him, please."

The instant the wood touched the ground, one of the mercenaries slammed his boot down. Master Arata flinched as her wand snapped into two.

A faint vapor, like the wand had breathed out a final sigh, floated out. Then the wand looked dried and as plain as any broken branch.

"Go on, do the same," Master Arata called to Rel, Ettie, and Master Roone. "I refuse to have the blood of a fellow Councilmember on our conscience." She stared up at Grottel. "Let him carry the weight of these betrayals."

Grottel merely sneered and flicked his fingers toward them. A dozen mercenaries swarmed out of the mists, grabbing the rest of my team, tying their hands in ropes, and breaking their wands.

Each snap of their wands resonated in the clearing with a haunting, ear-aching sound. Ember pressed against my legs, shuddering.

Too soon, my team was bound by ropes around their hands and waists, their wands no more than scattered remains.

I wanted desperately to help somehow. Ember shivered at my side as I took a step forward, inching out of the cover of the tree, hesitantly.

But Master Arata looked over her shoulder, for a split second, and her eyes glowered. *Remember what you promised. You said you'd stay out of the way.*

And then Grottel flicked his wand, and the consciousness slid out of her eyes as her head lolled forward. I bit down a scream, trying my hardest to suppress the urge to jump out and help her. Somehow, though, she remained standing, fully entranced.

Grottel's spells were far more powerful than anything I'd ever seen. After all, even though Mother had also been a Grand Master, she'd never cursed anyone.

A pair of mercenaries led them away. The line of witches and wizards, in that strange sleeplike state from Grottel's curse, followed obediently, moving with each tug, stopping when the mercenaries stopped.

"Is this all of them?" Grottel snapped to the tall, bearded mercenary.

"Five per team, max, and you already cursed the third Elite on this team, sir. Gotta love how reliable they are, this Council."

Grottel merely stared at the man, but his eyes were piercingly cold.

The man quickly added, his voice slick as oil, "Er, sorry, sir. Nothing against witches and wizards. We are here to serve."

"Fulfill your service and then you'll get your full reward," Grottel said. "And if I hear anyone, and I mean *anyone*, magical or not, escapes and warns the queen, I'll have their head, and you, unfortunately, won't have any gold."

"We got them all, I swear!"

Grottel shook his head dismissively and muttered, "Thankfully, I don't have to rely on your middling skills much longer. Now that I've got these extra witches and wizards, by midnight, it'll all be over. Finally, I'll have the power I need for the conduit. And then, at last, all will be right for the realm. Keep up your end of the bargain until then, or you'll be paying *me*."

My heart thumped in my chest, so loud I was sure Grottel would be able to hear it. Midnight…as in… *tonight*? What was going to happen to Master Arata… the Elite triplets…all of the witches and wizards that Grottel had entranced? Was he going to take all their powers for the conduit, too?

"We understand completely," the leader said. "We are here to serve you, Grand Master Grottel."

Grottel peered once more at the man, perhaps thinking otherwise, but the mercenary stayed steady, meeting the Grand Master's gaze. Finally, Grottel spun on his heel, disappearing into the mist.

When the outline of his figure had faded out of sight, one of the other mercenaries sneered, " 'Here to serve you'? You sound *so* sweet."

"Here to serve your gold-lined pockets," the man who'd spoken to Grottel smoothly finished, stroking his beard with satisfaction. "But shut up. We can't risk him overhearing."

Then the leader swiveled around, peering through the mist. "We need to sweep the area. Grottel's not going to pay us the bounty if we've let someone go free."

Oh, no.

Ember and I backed away slowly, thanking Master Roone for the spell that hid our footsteps.

But the mercenaries were so close; how would we be able to get away?

"Ha. We've got their camp locked down. There's no chance of that."

Locked down? Had they found the campsite, too? But Ralvern, all the non-magical workers...

"Sweep this place, from cliff to cliff. If this confounded mist is hiding just one person we've missed, we're going to have the life squeezed out of us, like those witches and wizards and non-magicals we've been capturing. Do you want that? Want me to recommend you as an appetizer?"

What? The life squeezed out—

My back slammed against something hard. I looked up, and terror filled me. I was flush against a rocky cliff, the back side of the waterfall. I'd hit a dead end.

"*Eva...*" I jolted up, looking all around. That soft, whispering voice, delicate as wind rustling through leaves—it was the girl from the water...but how was she *here*?

"Yessir," the men intoned, saluting the leader. "We'll sweep."

Somehow, no one else, not even my flamefox, seemed to hear her. Ember sniffed at the rock, desperately searching for a way out. But no matter where we looked, it was absolutely solid. No spell could make me blast through this rock, and I didn't have my Fiery Phoenix to fly up and out of sight....

The footsteps grew louder. I looked over my shoulder and turned toward the mercenaries, wand at the ready.

"*Eva...*"

They stomped into sight—

"Eva!" A hissed, rough whisper came from the rocks *behind* me.

I started—was it the girl from the waters?

I spun around to stare at an arm snaking out of a crack in the rocks, a hand that was scarred and calloused from work. And again, that voice: "Eva, hide here!"

The hand grabbed me by the wrist and pulled me into the darkness of a crevice.

CHAPTER 19

The Cave of Secrets

I stumbled into a dark crack within the cliffs, my heart pounding. What had just happened?

"Shh!" a boy urgently whispered through the dark, before I could speak.

My sudden fear melted, just a bit. Why was that raspy, sharp-as-nails voice so familiar? In the shadows, Ember brushed against my leg. He let out a quiet noise of confusion, but he didn't growl like I would expect for someone he didn't like.

If this boy wasn't going to capture me like the mercenaries outside, I didn't have time to worry about who he was. Instead, I peered through the gap I'd been pulled through: a small crevice barely wide enough for me to fit into sideways.

"Stay quiet," murmured that same boy, from behind me. "We can't let them hear us."

I wanted to ask, *But who are* you?

Loud footsteps kicked through the grass, breaking branches as the mercenaries outside walked only *inches* away from the gap. I didn't even dare breathe. Ember stayed pressed to my legs, quietly understanding the urgency of this moment. Only the faint sound of water dripping along the rocks echoed hauntingly in the narrow space.

"No one?" one of the mercenaries asked, so close that I could hear the soft, dangerous sound of his dagger sliding into a leather sheath.

"Just the four for this team, I guess," another mercenary replied. "Strange, though. They do usually keep to their five-person groups, and they got that replacement truck of workers today. Would've thought they'd shuttle in another Councilmember, too."

The first mercenary snorted. "Yeah, another Councilmember to capture, just like we demolished that little 'protected' campsite of theirs."

No. Had they truly found the camp? But—the protection bubble—all of the shielding spells…

Fear froze me as the two mercenaries strolled off, chuckling easily, as if they weren't talking about hurting people with such simple candor.

From behind me, a light suddenly glowed. I turned to see a boy pulling a bandana off a lantern, illuminating the small gap between the rocks that we stood in, no bigger than the washroom of my cottage back in Auteri. But that sudden light wasn't what had taken me by surprise.

My jaw dropped. *"Soma?"*

The once-pirate nervously shifted his eyes to the rocky ground. But the dark curls, the bandana over his forehead, the thick, raised scar on his jaw...it *was* Soma—the very boy who'd cruelly teased me back in Auteri for my weak magical powers, for being nothing close to a real witch. Rin, my guardian, had protected me from the worst of his taunts, but whenever she wasn't around, he'd laughed and laughed at me...until the Culling hit. During the storm, he'd decided to support me, instead of jeering like the other ex-pirates, and even got his crew to help fold paper shields, too.

Then I stared down at his gray-black clothes. My heart thudded. The same drab garb as the mercenaries who had captured my teammates.

"You...work for *Grottel*?" I burst out. At my feet, Ember growled, letting out an angry little cough of ash. This time, there was a trail of smoke, but we were too focused on the boy in front of us.

"Please...Eva, Ember, let me explain," he said, his thin lips twisting together, his eyes pleading, switching nervously between me and my wand and Ember, who had his hackles raised.

That took me by surprise. Soma had never bothered to acknowledge my flamefox before.

I crossed my arms over my chest, my hand ready on my wand. "I see your clothes, though.... Doesn't that explain for itself?"

"I... I give the gold to my parents.... My little brother's sick, and without the extra coin, he can't get medicine," he said, his jaw jutting out defensively. I remembered what Rin had told me about how he took care of his family. *He sends a chunk of his pay back home every moon, even if it isn't as much as when he marauded. I heard his father will even read the letters he sends, sometimes.*

"And Grottel had the deepest pockets," I murmured in shock. I stared at the boy who'd kept me safe from his fellow mercenaries. "But... why *help* me, then?"

"I owe you," he said plainly. "I owe you for saving my life, and the life of my crew when the Culling hit Auteri. This... it's dangerous, but I owed you more than anything I owe Grottel."

His eyes met mine, worried and nervous, but gleaming with surprisingly raw honesty.

"Thank you, Soma," I said softly. And, at my feet, Ember sat down, washing a paw, content with his response.

"There's...there's something else, too. To show I'm earnest about repaying my debt." He jerked his thumb over his shoulder. "Follow me?"

The uncertain way he said it—hopeful, but unsure if I'd ever trust him again—tore at me. I nodded. "To where?"

"Grottel's underground hideout is a maze of caverns and paths...and...I'll prove to you, I'm trying to repay what I owe you, honest." The ex-pirate turned on his booted heel, and slipped through another narrow crevice in the rock I would've never seen, if not for him.

"You don't owe me anything," I said, puzzled. But my heart pounded nervously as I followed him, the damp rock walls brushing against my cold skin. What if this was a trap?

"*Eva...*"

Again—that voice, faint as chimes. I stopped. "Did you hear that?"

Soma frowned, glancing around. "Hear what?"

I swallowed. How did he not hear the girl—if it was Maika—too?

But all was silent again. So I followed Soma and his lantern, swinging in the dark, its gentle glow chasing away the shadows, my hand tight around my wand. Ember trotted alongside me, his pointy ears twisting left and right.

The narrow path widened, opening to a gaping cavern

with a tall ceiling, far, far above. More water trickled here, softly dripping onto the loose, sandy ground. This spot was as wide as the town hall in Auteri, a stunning monument of nature, with curving rocks and gentle quietness in the air.

But that wasn't what had caught my breath. Far away, in the center, two small figures sat next to another lantern just like Soma's, leaning against each other and talking.

I cried out across the cavern, "Charlotte? Davy?"

My two best friends ran over, engulfing me in their arms. I breathed in deep; the faint scent of Auteri's salty waters still stuck to them. Even though we were in a dark cave with so much chaos surrounding us, being with them felt like home.

"We've *got* to go back to the camp," I blurted out. "My entire team of witches and wizards, they got captured by Grottel. We need to take a truck back to—"

Charlotte and Davy looked at each other, exchanging a worried glance that sent a spike of dread through me, making my skin icy-cold.

"What is it?" I asked, rubbing my hands on my arms, trying to soothe the sudden goosebumps. Ember crawled into my arms and coughed again, trying to breathe out a fire to keep me warm. His ears drooped as ash spluttered out, but I hugged him tightly to me; just his heat was more than enough.

"That's how Soma found us...." Charlotte breathed

in deep, trying to summon up the right words. "We'd gotten to camp, thinking we could surprise you. But you'd already left...."

"And?"

"Around an hour after we'd arrived, when all the non-magical workers were sitting down for lunch, we got attacked."

"Attacked?" I breathed out in shock. The mercenaries had mentioned they'd managed to break the shield, but I hadn't wanted to trust their word. "But the protection spells...*no*...Ralvern...all the other workers."

Davy's light brown eyes were as dark as a storm. "Grand Master Grottel strolled in with a flick of his wand, breaking that bubble shield. And he cursed everyone who tried to put up a fight, putting them under some sleeping spell. We had no choice but to go with him, led by ropes to his hideout."

I gripped their hands. "Then—how—"

"Soma found us," Davy said, shooting the once-pirate a thankful smile. Soma abashedly rubbed his forehead, tugging his messy curls. "When he saw us, he gave us these clothes so we'd blend in with the other mercenaries. Helped us get out."

I spun around to look at Soma. "But why—"

He looked at me, eyes shifting. "It's..." His mouth opened and closed, as he searched for words. "It's...You made me think of things that I could do, when you saved

Auteri, okay? And when I saw your two best friends...
You saved my crew. I wanted to save your crew, too."

My heart lodged in my throat. I reached out my hand.
"You should be part of my crew, too."

Soma's lips twitched up in the faintest smile. "I'm...
I'm not good enough...." He glanced at Charlotte and
Davy, pleading for them to explain what he couldn't
voice. "There's more."

Davy dropped his head. "Ralvern tried escaping at
the same time, but Grottel saw him. He got put under
that sleep-trance spell, too."

"The rest of the workers, they're down in Grottel's
caverns," Charlotte whispered, her eyes wide. "We can't
just leave them here."

"That guy, Grottel, he's not going to let his captives
get out easily. Not with all the mercenaries he's hired to
keep an eye on them." Soma spat on the ground. "You all
need to *run* for your lives. I didn't save you three to have
you come crawling back in for trouble."

"Stop that!" Charlotte hissed. "We don't want any
traces that anyone was here!"

"Oh." Soma looked confused for a second, then
rubbed a hand through his messy curls. "I've...I've never
done anything secretive like this before."

"And I'll never forget that you did this for me, for
us...for *Rivelle*. Thank you, Soma," I said.

The pirate's ears turned bright red. "It's nothing.

Nothing, really. Why d'you gotta be so nice like that? Geez."

I blinked at him in confusion, but Davy cleared his throat, pointing at the dusty ground. "Char's right. We need to erase our marks; they're going to give us away." His eyes gleamed. "But...wait. Eva, why can't we see *your* footsteps? Are you a ghost?"

I stared down at the dirt. Soma, Charlotte, and Davy's footsteps marked the soft, dusty dirt of the crevice, but my footsteps and Ember's were nowhere to be seen.

"Oh!" I pulled out my wand. "One of the Master Wizards placed a spell on me so my footprints wouldn't show. I'll do the same to all of you."

Charlotte nodded, and Davy threw himself on the ground and waggled his feet. "Curse me first!"

"I do *not* want to curse you!" I spluttered, as Davy grinned.

"It was worth a shot," he said, scratching Ember behind his ears. "I've always hoped that Eva might turn me into a nightdragon. I'd be *fierce*."

"Why you'd want to be a nightdragon is beyond me," Charlotte sighed.

"*Eva...*"

I jerked upright, staring around the cavern. "Did... did one of you call my name?"

Charlotte and Davy frowned, and Soma shook his

head nervously. "No...Hopefully no one's looking for me right now. I'm supposed to be on my break."

I blinked, and tried to smile. "Sorry, it must've been the waters trickling down; it just sounded funny for a moment."

Charlotte and Davy exchanged glances, but then Davy said, "So? Go on, curse me!"

I let out a laugh, and Davy grinned. My two friends held still as I tapped their boots and chanted, "*You won't be helpless, you'll be stepless.*"

A gentle shimmer, like a handful of moonlight, cascaded down from my wand and onto their feet.

"I guess I didn't turn into a nightdragon," Davy said, checking his arms as if they might have expanded into the black, scaly wings of the legendary beasts. "But I *feel* like a fairy from Arcia."

We were far from that magical land on the other side of the seven realms. But I hoped Charlotte, Davy, and I would be able to go there someday, after all of this.

I turned to the ex-pirate. "Ready?"

Soma blanched, shaking his head. "Sorry, Eva. I'll pass. Anyway, the other mercenaries will expect me to have footprints, right?"

I blinked. "You're...you're going back to them?" For some reason, I'd hoped the ex-pirate would stay with us, maybe even guide us through the cavern to find Grottel's conduit. "But..."

The scar on his jaw twisted slightly as he gave me a half smile. "I still need the money, Eva, even if I don't believe in this work."

I was here because I wanted to help my mother, with all my heart. And Soma was here to help his family in any way he could. Even if my chest ached at the thought of him going back to the cold-blooded mercenaries, it was his choice.

I met Soma's sad eyes. "After this, after all this is over, we'll work together to find a place where you don't have to work for the highest bidder, where it's a job that you'll enjoy, so you don't have to do this."

He breathed in sharply. "Really?"

"Really," I repeated back.

His lip tipped up slightly in a smile. "That sounds like a dream come true." Then he jolted up, gave me and my friends a quick nod. "I've got to go, though. I've been away from my post too long as it is."

Then he looked at me sadly.

"What is it?" I asked.

The boy looked down, scuffing his raggedy boot against the sandy ground. Soma took a deep breath, and whispered, "I can't stay with you all...but also, if we meet in front of Grottel, I can't help you. I *have* to pretend that I don't like you, Eva."

Charlotte bristled. "How can you do that? After all she's done for you?"

Soma flinched from her words. But I gently rested my hand on Soma's shoulder. "I understand," I whispered. "But no matter what, you're part of my crew, too."

Soma's face looked shadowed in the darkness of the cave. "I don't deserve that." He glanced over at my friends. "And Charlotte, Davy. I'm sorry I can't do better, but stay safe. You've *got* to get out."

I couldn't promise that we'd even try to escape, no matter how much Soma's eyes pleaded for me to get away. I couldn't respond.

With a shake of his head, the ex-pirate turned away and slipped through the gap in the wall of the cavern, leading down into Grottel's hideout.

Charlotte glared after him, her forehead knotted with wrinkles. "I still don't trust that pirate."

Davy grimaced. "I don't trust Soma, but he did get us out."

My shoulders drooped. "Soma doesn't *want* to hurt people. But he's got to take care of his family...even if they don't take care of him."

Charlotte's eyes clouded. Then she turned to me. "So what do we do next?"

I swallowed. "No one else is going to be able to get here in time to stop Grottel. Not if he's going to act tonight. And I'm sure he's got guards watching for communications; it's not like I can send out a bird-letter to the Council."

The memory of what Grottel had said pierced me. *By midnight, it'll all be over. Finally, I'll have the power I need for the conduit. And then, at last, all will be right for the realm.*

I reached out, grasping Charlotte's and Davy's hands in mine. "This is going to be dangerous. But...I want to try to save all the innocent people here."

"You're saying that like we won't be joining you," Davy said, his raised eyebrow disappearing under his messy curls. "Hello, I crossed the Sakuya Mountains for you. I volunteered to spend my entire day chopping fire-wood for the camp to get back to being by your side. *No one* who knows me wants to see me with an axe, least of all me and my currently attached ten fingers."

Charlotte's gray eyes met mine steadily. "What's the plan? We're in, and you're not going without us."

My heart swelled as I turned to look at the crevice where Soma had disappeared, now swathed in darkness. Where, deep within these caves, we might be able to find Grottel's conduit. Maybe, hopefully, we'd find Davy's mother and Charlotte's parents. If we could figure out a plan to sneak into Grottel's hideout and shatter the conduit, we could stop the Grand Master from wrecking the realm, once and for all.

"And why'd you think you were hearing someone calling your name?" Davy asked, narrowing his eyes.

I swallowed. He'd brushed over it easily while Soma

had been around, but his curious, knitted eyebrows told me that he hadn't forgotten. "I...well, I think someone who Grottel trapped is trying to send me a message."

"What?" Charlotte exclaimed.

Quickly, I explained how I'd seen Maika, the girl in the water with the sad, lost look to her eyes, the way she'd whispered, *Save me*.

Davy blanched. "A girl in water...I think it's obvious Grottel's doing something strange here. We've got to help."

But Charlotte frowned. "We've still got to be careful. We don't know anything about her...and why did she choose to reach out to Eva?"

I'd wondered about that, too. But even though we talked through ideas, none of us could figure out how the girl had managed to find me or what we could do—other than sneak into Grottel's hideout and try to find her.

So, over the flickering lantern, Charlotte, Davy, and I put our heads together to make a plan. Ember snuffled at my pocket until I pulled out a wrapped package of kaki-mochi, crispy fried rice crackers.

As we chomped on the crackers, the sweet-salty taste filling my belly like a bowl of hot rice, Charlotte and Davy told me about the parts of the caverns they'd seen.

"There's one big room," Davy explained. "And there are little tunnels that go to other parts of Grottel's hideout. It's like a huge maze."

"Are there a lot of mercenaries?" I asked, biting my lip.

"Maybe five dozen?" Charlotte guessed.

Three of us, and a flamefox, trying to outwit five dozen mercenaries and a Grand Master, to sneak in and break the one thing they were all protecting. The odds were *not* in our favor.

But I thought of Mother, gray-faced and sickly after Grottel had cursed her. Or Ralvern and the other camp workers, who'd been so kind to me. And Charlotte and Davy's families, who *needed* our help.

Ember coughed out again, another mouthful of ash; it sounded like he'd had too many of the dry rice crackers.

I looked around. "Oh, curses. I don't have water." Could I summon up a bowl to collect water from the walls, maybe? Would that be enough? Even my throat felt parched from the rice crackers.

"Soma gave this to us." Davy brought over a small leather drawstring bag resting against the wall of the cavern. The gentle waters trickling down the rocks had splattered the fabric, but when he pulled it open, the cloth-wrapped food and a slightly dented canteen were safe and dry. I cupped my hands as he poured out some water, and Ember eagerly lapped it up with his soft, pink tongue.

"Where'd Soma get these supplies from?" I asked, surprised. I hadn't seen any of the mercenaries with bags like these.

"I think those were his own rations," Charlotte said softly, and my chest tightened. If, somehow, we managed to get out of this place, I *had* to find a better job for Soma, something that he could be proud of.

"Here, let's eat some of this," Davy said, pulling out a package wrapped in brightly dyed blue cloth, with geometric patterns all over. He peeked at the inside. "It looks like steamed vegetable buns. They're cold, but smell tasty."

Charlotte, Davy, Ember, and I divided the two buns between the four of us, relishing the savory, thinly sliced shiitake mushrooms mingling with shreds of steamed bamboo shoots.

"The mercenaries kept talking about a pit," Davy said through his mouthful of food. "If there's anywhere for the conduit-thingy, I think that's where it is."

"A pit?" I asked.

Charlotte nodded. "They were all too scared to get close. Grottel got mad at one of the mercenaries and sent him down there. Apparently, everyone who goes near it doesn't leave."

Davy grimaced. "But how are we going to get inside?"

"That's right." Charlotte gestured at my clothes. "You'll stand out, immediately, Eva. Your blouse is the right color, but…"

I spun my wand. *"Gray as a cloudy day, invert my skirt."*

My black skirt shimmered, losing the faint bronze sheen at the hem that I'd adored so much, and fused into my leggings, turning into loose, gray-black pants, soft as clouds. And like Charlotte had said, my gray blouse would blend in just fine.

Davy shook his head in awe. "This is the first time I can truly say that someone's pants are *magical*. Are they stainproof, too? Do you have as many pockets as me? I've got twenty-two."

"Plans. Focus on plans," Charlotte reminded him.

I looked between the two of them. "Okay. So, our plan is this: Pretend to be mercenaries. Get down into Grottel's pit. Find the conduit. Break it. Escape with your parents and everyone else trapped underground. All in one piece."

"Simple," Davy said. "Or, at least, it sounds simple enough."

"We have to avoid Grottel, for sure, though," Charlotte said, polishing her short dagger. Her face was pale in the faint lamplight. "He may not know either of us, but he definitely knows Eva."

"No big deal," Davy said, nodding firmly. "Avoid the evil Grand Master, the most powerful wizard in the entire realm, and his group of well-paid, well-equipped, and poorly mannered fighters. To get to this conduit-thingy they're protecting. No. Big. Deal."

Charlotte rolled her eyes at him.

"Ready?" I stood up, glancing nervously at the tunnel that led to the main cavern. My voice sounded thin and weak.

Despite all their jokes, my friends stepped to my side.

"Ready," they said in unison.

I took a deep breath, my eyes meeting Davy's and then Charlotte's, and then glanced down at Ember pressing tightly against my boot and reminding me that he would be with me every step of the way, too.

My heart clenched. I was lucky to have the best companions I could've ever met at my side.

We turned toward the crevice in the wall, where Soma had disappeared. The tunnel that led to Grottel and the mercenaries.

"Let's fight," I whispered. "Let's fight for our parents, and for our realm. Let's stop Grottel."

CHAPTER 20

ꟼNTO THE ℬELLY OF A ꟼNIGHTDRAGON

From my left, Charlotte held up the lantern, carefully helping us pick out our path to the main cavern; onyx-black rocks, like the fins of dragonsharks, pierced through the sand. Every droplet of water down the walls made me grip my hand tighter around my wand as I imagined stumbling upon mercenaries with their sharp blades out. When I glanced over at the lantern, I noticed the oil looked low.

I shuddered, imagining being lost in the tunnels, swathed in pitch-black. "Let me cast a spell for more light—"

"Wait," Davy interjected. "Take a few steps forward."

I craned my neck to look deeper into the cave, and then I gasped.

It looked like the stars had fallen from the sky. Tiny blue-green lights flickered from the ceiling. Gossamer wisps hung from each budding glow, like chandeliers in the queen's greatest hall.

I dropped into a reverent silence, staring all around. Ember danced here and there, trying to catch the slowly moving lights. I felt transfixed by the glow, like I could stay here all my life, looking up, and never have to remember what lay outside the cave—or deeper inside.

Reluctantly, I drew my eyes away. "What are they?"

"Hotaru spiders," Davy explained. "Soma told me their light attracts bugs, and then they trap their prey in their netting."

I shivered, once again transfixed by the lights. The glows flickered and moved, like swirling constellations in the most vibrant of night skies.

"Come on." Charlotte tugged my sleeve. "We don't have all the time in the world."

I nodded, and we continued down the tunnel, our faces illuminated blue-green. Every once in a while, I peeked up in wonder.

As the walls narrowed, we had to start walking single file. Then, eventually, we had to crawl.

"It'll be just around here," Charlotte said from the lead. "Be quiet now. We'll have to check that there's no one watching when we get out."

"Do you feel it?" Davy whispered from behind me.

"There's something weird about this place, right? It feels like we're getting sucked into the belly of a nightdragon."

A shiver rolled down my neck at the thought of night-dragons, the terrifying, fire-breathing creatures that nested in the dark abyss between Rivelle and Constancia, keeping anyone from going close—or if they did get too close, keeping them from ever getting away.

I murmured, "Stay alert. Even though we're dressed like mercenaries, we're still going to stick out since we're not used to the cavern like the rest of them."

As we crawled, trickling water got louder. Then the path ended in another crevice like the one Soma had first pulled me through. But footsteps and a muffled conversation echoed beyond the opening. We all froze, sweat prickling on my skin, and Charlotte quickly extinguished her lantern.

In the darkness, with just the hotaru spiders spinning webs above us, the light of the crevice shone brightly. As the footsteps receded, Charlotte peered around the corner. "All clear."

The yawning gap swallowed us up and spit us into a small side chamber. I looked at where we'd come from; with all the rippling, edged rocks, it was tough to see our route, even though I knew it had to be there.

We quickly brushed ourselves off, Ember shaking the dirt from his fur with annoyance. Davy squinted at me and pulled a gray cap from his pocket, motioning for me to swap it with my pointy witch's hat.

Then Charlotte looked down at Ember, her eyes wide. "Eva...none of the mercenaries have flamefoxes. It'll be a dead giveaway."

I looked down at my flamefox, and Ember stared up with his big, dark eyes. I couldn't leave him to hide in the crevice like I'd placed my hat; my heart felt like it was being torn from my chest just at the thought.

Just then, the pounding of boots on the sandy ground echoed through the tunnel.

Davy and Charlotte stared at me.

"Someone's coming," Charlotte hissed. At my feet, Ember whimpered, trying to hide behind my legs.

"Here," Davy said, pulling open the bag Soma had given him and shoving the contents into the pockets of his gray trousers. "Can he fit in here?"

My shoulders eased with relief as Ember readily jumped in. I slung the strap over my chest, feeling the heavy weight of my flamefox in the pouch against my hip. Carefully, I eased the drawstring so that it was closed enough that no one could see in, but my flamefox could breathe.

Then the stomping footsteps rounded the corner.

My heartbeat pounded in my ears as I took in the gray-black drab clothes, the lean yet muscled shoulders, and the mean sneer on his face. I knew this man already.

It was the very same man who'd captured my teammates.

The tall mercenary stared at us in the side chamber, and growled, "What're you doing here?"

Davy stepped forward, a sheepish look on his face as he scratched his forehead. "We thought we heard a weird sound over here, sir, so we checked it out."

I couldn't breathe as the man's gaze traveled over me. Did he know the faces of the Councilmembers? Might he know me?

Or, worse, did he know that we didn't belong among the mercenaries?

But, after a long, petrifying silence, the tall man jerked his head in a nod. "Too many of us to keep count. What a ragtag operation. Get back into the main room. Don't let *that* guy see you loitering."

Davy chirped, "Yessir!"

The man stared at us one more time. "What, you think I'll escort you like you're the queen or something? *Git!*"

The three of us, with Ember tucked safely in my pouch, hurried down a path to the left.

The man groaned. "Are you kind of incompetent or completely incompetent? That's the wrong way—it goes to the clearing, you numbskulls! Grottel didn't send you out to sweep the lands, did he?" Then he snorted. "Not that there's anyone out there, anymore, magical or non-magical. Between us and Grottel, we got 'em all."

"Right, sir, right," Davy said, laughing airily, as if it was a simple mistake. "This is nothing like being out in the open air. I get lost down here. Creepy depths, you know?"

The man shrugged, seemingly acknowledging that. "Just get out of my sight before you cause more trouble."

Quickly, before we said something the man thought was weird, the three of us hurried the opposite way, to the right.

Glass lanterns flickered in small nooks chipped into the walls. I was surprised to see a non-magical light source for Grottel's so-called hideout. But he was probably gathering magic for bigger things, like the Culling, or to keep for himself.

We turned the corner, and the path opened up to a vast cavern the size of three of Auteri's town halls. Water trickled down the walls, and in the middle, a river sliced through the rocks. For an instant, it reminded me of the stream back home, but that wove through the garden under the warm sun instead of a cave crawling with glowing hotaru spiders.

Davy quietly explained the layout of the cavern. "This is the main area. Those small tunnels go to storage rooms or sleeping rooms, I think."

It was like a small underground village, or even a campsite like the Council's. Long oak tables were scattered throughout, with a few mercenaries stirring pots set over crackling fires, the smoke curling up into the heights of the cave. Another two dozen mercenaries filled the vast cavern, some at work carrying crates between the tunnels, others simply lounging about.

Charlotte's hand snaked out, wrapping around my wrist. "Don't scream...but..."

Her warning saved me from revealing my shock too much.

No matter the similarities between this place and the Council's camp...

We hadn't had mercenaries dragging through roped witches and wizards. Heads down, the very Elite and Master Witches and Wizards that I'd believed could save the realm from Grottel's Culling were stumbling through the sandy ground, their hands bound and their faces ashen, their eyes strangely lost. It looked to be the effects of Grottel's strong spell, making them as agreeable and entranced as cattle going off to get slaughtered.

But worst of all, they were led by...

Soma.

My eyes widened as the scar on the ex-pirate's jaw twisted when he saw me, Charlotte, and Davy. The boy jerked his head away, and pulled at the line of Council-members, seemingly cold.

I don't deserve to be part of your crew, Soma had said. My heart burned for all that he'd had to do to take care of his family, but to not make himself feel worthy.

"Enjoy the pit!" one of the chefs snickered. He slung a ladleful of burning hot soup, and a Master Wizard yelped with pained shock as it hit his legs, steaming through cloth. "Good riddance for what you've done to *us*!"

Most mercenaries had been pirates freely roaming the sea until the queen and the merchants' guild had asked the Council to crack down on them. Because of that, there had always been a rift between the once-pirates and the Council.

"Keep breathing," Charlotte murmured. "Breathe in, breathe out."

I took a gasp of air. But this...this felt so cruel, so awful. Tears blurred my eyes as I watched my comrades stumble over the sandy ground.

My heart felt hollow as Soma pulled them around the corner, to the biggest tunnel leading away from the cavern.

"Good riddance to the Council!" the chef jeered, and nearly all of the mercenaries in the cavern clapped gleefully.

Grottel had caught too many people in his twisted, awful web. And I *had* to shine light through this darkness somehow. I had to mend this rift between the mercenaries and the Council.

I stumbled forward. "We'll 'help' Soma. That's our way in."

Pulling down my cap, I hurried through the cavern, Davy stifling his gasp of surprise as he and Charlotte rushed to catch up.

I reached the opening of the tunnel—

And a figure stepped in front of us, dark and foreboding. "You're not allowed in here."

It was a slight girl, around our age, with long brown-black braids that went down to her waist and sharp eyes, clever as a snowcat's. My heart lurched as I shifted my head down, the brim of my cap shielding my eyes. She was part of Soma's crew from Auteri and had made fun of my shields mercilessly, just like many of the other pirates. Her eyes widened as she caught a glimpse of Charlotte and Davy, from behind me. "You're not—"

She tugged at my cap, and I let out a gasp, wrenching it back down over my eyes.

"*No*," the girl hissed with shock. Her eyes gleamed. "Wait until Grottel—"

"Akari…," Soma whispered from behind her, a plea entwined into his words. He'd dropped the rope of witches and wizards, who stood numbly in their trance. He strode toward us, his face pale.

My heart leaped.

She stilled, turning to look at her friend. "You *knew*?"

"*Akari*," he repeated, his voice ragged. "We owe them a debt. Let them pass."

"Now you'll owe *me* a debt," she snickered, her eyes coolly assessing Soma, who jerked his head into a reluctant nod. With a flick of her long braids, she strode back to the main tunnel, grinning like a cat.

He watched her retreat. "I can't promise she'll keep this to herself," he hissed, his voice rising. "I told you, I can't *ever* do this for you again."

"Do *what* again?" a cold, harsh voice growled, sending shocks up my spine.

Slowly, I shifted my head down more.

A man strode out from the depths of the tunnel, carelessly passing by the entranced witches and wizards. I couldn't even breathe, like each step of his was pulling the air out of my lungs.

I stood firm on my feet, hoping desperately he hadn't seen my face or heard my voice. Because if he had, I'd be trussed up like the rest of the witches and wizards. Especially if the person looming above me was...

The wizard lowered the edge of his cloak, revealing a face still swathed in shadows, darkness crawling over his skin. From the corner of my eyes, I could see exactly who it was.

Grand Master Hayato Grottel.

Grottel glowered, his hooded eyes burning deeply.

CHAPTER 21

A Ghost from the Past

Grottel turned to stare at Charlotte, Davy, Soma… and me, my face hidden by the gray cap.

"What are all of you doing here?" he growled. "Why aren't you at your posts?"

I gulped. How were we supposed to answer that?

Charlotte stepped forward, her voice smooth. "We were escorting those witches and wizards, sir." She gestured at the rope-chained group behind Grottel. "Some of them were causing us trouble."

"We'll get back to it," Davy chirped, "Grand Master, sir."

"Why are there *four* of you?" Grottel sneered. "I recognize you"—he turned to Soma—"but who's this last one?"

His boots crunched sharply on the sand as he turned toward me. My heartbeat pounded in my ears.

Could I somehow charm my face to someone he wouldn't know? Could he recognize my voice, too?

At my side, Ember shifted uneasily in the pouch. If I tried to run—would Grottel strike me down, in the way he'd always intended, to take away my magic? Would I end up just like Mother, the person I was trying to help?

"I asked you a question," he growled.

I searched for words, for a spell . . . for *anything*. Sweat beaded on my forehead, running through my hair tucked behind my ears.

"She's . . . she's shy!" Soma blurted out.

"Shy?" Grottel seemed only more suspicious. He took another step forward, stretching his wand out to flick off my cap—

"Grand Master!" A call echoed from down the tunnel. "Grand Master, sir!"

Grottel paused, his voice stiff with annoyance. "Tamura, you had better have a good reason for bothering me, when I said *no one* was supposed to interfere with my work tonight."

"It's . . . it's urgent, sir. I think." It was the tall, bearded mercenary, the one who'd captured my team and who we'd first bumped into in the hideout. I peeked out from under the brim of my cap. Now, in front of Grottel, he was a stammering, sweaty mess. Then again, all of us— Charlotte, Davy, and Soma, too—had a sheen of nervous sweat over our faces.

Then, from my side, Ember shifted in the pouch, his wet nose poking out of the opening. He stuck his head out, a growl vibrating through his body, and my heart jolted as Grottel turned toward me.

Davy shifted in front of me and started coughing. "Excuse me. Sorry. The dust." Grottel shot him an annoyed glare but refocused on the mercenary.

But I'd seen what had caught Ember's attention—the blade dangling from Tamura's waist. I could recognize the three strips of braided metal on the hilt.

Ettie's dagger.

I remembered the joy on her face as she'd shown it off to me. How she'd named it—Barty. She treasured it. And now to have it taken away by my enemy...

Anger swelled up in me. Grottel, Tamura, the rest of the mercenaries...I *had* to stop them.

"You *think* it's urgent, or it *is*?" Grottel snapped. "Can't you tell I'm in the middle of—"

"There's something strange outside, something magical!" Tamura blurted out. Then he paled. "Sorry to interrupt you, sir, but we all don't know how to fight it."

"Magical?" Grottel hissed.

The tall mercenary nodded, nervously tugging on his beard. "It looked just like the fog from earlier....That was a strange fog. But now...now there are shadows walking through....They look like witches and wizards, with their pointy hats and all, flashes of spells, and some of them with companion animals, too."

Grottel snapped, "You promised me on your bounty that you swept the land for stragglers."

"We did! The entire forest is on lockdown, with groups patrolling. Your sentry trees are silent, no one's come in since that truck this morning, and no bird-letters got out. We even captured everyone in the camp. I don't know how they got in!"

"So get them," Grottel snarled.

"We…we can't, not without you!" the mercenary squeaked, terribly shrunken under the force of Grottel's glare. "They've got some strange sort of magic!"

The Grand Master let out a noise of disgust, and began striding down the tunnel, the mercenary tripping over his feet to follow.

Charlotte, Davy, Soma, and I nearly melted to the ground in relief as the Grand Master and the mercenary turned the corner.

But the ex-pirate quickly squared his shoulders, glancing over at the line of entranced witches and wizards. "I have to finish this job. You *shouldn't* have come down here. I wanted you three to escape, not get wrapped up in this."

I bit my lip. I couldn't argue back; Soma had put so much on the line to help me.

"Where are you taking them?" I asked instead. The

boy only shook his head, his eyes dark, as if he didn't quite have the words to explain.

Charlotte, Davy, and I trailed after Soma as he walked down the narrowing path, tugging the witches and wizards along. The Councilmembers followed him in their trance, their bound hands pulling them forward. I knew their names, could recognize their power by their Elite- and Master-marked tunics. How could I fight against Grottel when they hadn't been able to?

The lights on the walls flickered as we walked deeper through the water-drenched, curving tunnel. Then the boy stopped, turning into an alcove made of rough white marble with threads of black stone.

I stared. It wasn't an alcove. It was a *cage*. Long iron bars covered the entrance, but when Soma pushed the witches and wizards in, they walked *through* the poles.

"It's used to hold them," he said softly. "Witches and wizards can get in, but they can't get out."

"What about non-magicals?" Davy asked, prodding a bar. His finger went straight through, too.

"None of us have been foolish enough to test it," Soma said sharply, and Davy withdrew his hand. "If any of the mercenaries have gotten caught in one of Grottel's cages, then they haven't come back to tell the tale."

I gulped. "Where do they go from here?"

Soma's eyes flickered darkly in the dim lantern light. "I don't know. We're only told to drop them off in this cage. Whenever we come back, they're gone. Grottel takes them onward." He pointed further down the path, where lanterns continued to light the tunnel.

I took a step forward.

"That's foolish," Soma whispered. "He's got protections in the deeper areas of the cavern. It's a death wish to go further. I'm not sharp-minded, but I know *that*. Escape while you can, Eva."

I shook my head, my eyes sad. "I can't leave these witches and wizards to Grottel, nor any of the other people he's trapped, magical or not. Go back to the cavern, Soma. Pretend we've never met."

Soma scanned Charlotte and Davy, but they stayed resolutely at my side, unwilling to budge. And even Ember poked his head out, jumping out of the pouch to stand next to me.

"Don't get caught, please," Soma whispered, his voice strained. Then he turned on his heel, quickly walking back toward the cavern, his shoulders hunched.

Charlotte, Davy, and I looked between the cage and the path leading further into the depths of the earth. I'd expected magical traps....I just hoped my powers would be enough to get us to the conduit—especially before Grottel came back.

I glanced at my friends and down at my flamefox. "Let's go."

Charlotte and Davy nodded, without a trace of hesitation, and followed me onward, into the cave.

The deeper we walked through the caves, the cooler the air became. Fewer hotaru spiders lit our way; even their prey didn't dare get close to Grottel's conduit. The path wound down and down, the water dripping along the walls running stronger than ever. But a soft sound kept tickling my ears, like a faraway call that I couldn't quite hear clearly.

"Do you two hear something?" I asked. But Charlotte and Davy shook their heads.

"Just the water dripping," Davy said. "I swear, if we ever make it out of here, I'll have that sound pounded into my head. Drip, drip, drip, drip…"

Then we stumbled to a stop. The path split into two. The right kept following the trail of lights, the left was nearly all shadows and unlit. Cool air circled around us, riffling my cap playfully.

"Which way do we go?" Davy asked.

"Clearly, the right," Charlotte said. "The right feels like a good path."

"I like the left," Davy interjected. "A better adventure."

They turned to me. I frowned, trying to think of a spell that would work, without taking too much magic. "There's got to be some way to figure out… something to guide us."

"*Eva…*"

I jolted up. The voice. "That's *her*!"

Davy squeaked. "Um, am I really seeing this…"

I followed his pointed finger. Instead of the onyx-black rippling walls, a girl stared out of the watery rock between the paths, her dark eyes clashing with her pale skin. The faint ripples of her white dress fluttered, looking like it was spun by threads from the hotaru spiders, and the dress swirled, pushed by a wind I couldn't feel. Her feet, hovering inches above the ground, were bare. She was so tiny, maybe a few years younger than me, but her eyes held a deep sadness that made her seem far more aged.

Ember yapped and pounced forward, his paw scratching at the mirage of the girl.

But only the water rippled. The girl stayed completely steady, like she hadn't felt my flamefox.

Her dark, sad eyes met mine. *"I've been waiting for you, Eva."* Her high, soft voice echoed against the walls, delicate as chimes. *"Go to the left. But there're others afoot, keep alert. Please…save me, before he comes back."*

And with a flash, she disappeared.

"I…I wasn't just imagining that, right?" I said, my throat dry.

Charlotte and Davy were nearly gray.

"I wish you were," Davy croaked. "You weren't joking about your new friend, after all."

We turned to stare at the fork in the path; the right was brighter, guided by light. But the path to the left was thrown into inky shadows, warning us of the darkness to come.

"She needs my help," I whispered. "I can't ignore that."

"*If* we can trust her. *If* she isn't a trap," Charlotte said, voicing my worries.

"I know. But if this was really Grottel's trap, we wouldn't have a chance; you've seen his powers. And if the left is where Grottel's storing the conduit...then that's where I have to go."

Charlotte's hand, her calluses skimming across my softer skin, met mine. She squeezed my hand tightly. "Then we'll be with you, every step of the way."

With that, we turned to the left, and using Charlotte's lantern to guide us, we plunged into the dark tunnel.

The sound of water got louder, and suddenly Charlotte raised up the lantern. "This...it's something different."

It was an alcove, with the same roughly hewn white marble that had marked the cage holding the witches and wizards.

We strode under the arch and then stopped short.

The air was musty and thick with dust. Through grimy lanterns, flickering from the walls, I realized figures stood all around, their eyes glittering as they stared down at us.

I bit down a scream. Charlotte shoved me behind her as she pulled her short dagger out of her pocket.

My heart nearly shot out of my chest. I tried to summon up a spell, but what could I do in the face of so many people?

"Wait, wait, *look*," Davy hissed.

I peered closer, and my stomach lurched. The figures around me were statues, not living people. Yet there was something morbidly lifelike about their smooth stone skin, the humanlike hair coming out of their scalps, the dusty dresses like they'd just finished playing out in the Twisted Forest. I was in a place that was once a gallery— or a tomb.

Because they were all the same girl, with different clothes and expressions. But all with long, slightly messy dark hair, fluttering around their shoulders, and the same vacant look. Her cheeks were speckled with faint freckles, like someone had dusted the constellations on her face.

Charlotte breathed in sharply. "That's the girl...the same girl that was in the water."

"No...," Davy whispered in shock.

Maika. I stared at the statues all around us. I didn't want to believe that, either. Because that meant the girl *was* trapped by Grottel.

I was peeling Grand Master Grottel's layers away, seeing what his magic was really like. What rogue magic could become.

And it left a bitter taste in my mouth, so strong that I felt like I'd never be able to wash it away.

I felt eyes on my back and froze. When I lifted the lantern, a statue a few paces away stared down at me. I would have sworn that none of the other statues were this close when we'd first slipped into the room. Somehow, her glass eyes stared down, meeting my eyes perfectly. She looked to be much shorter than me, but on the square pedestal, she towered over me. I couldn't breathe. In her chest, where her heart should've been, an opening had been hacked into her blouse and a clock clicked, slowly counting out time. But her arm was thrown out, her index finger pointing at a door opposite the entrance we'd come through.

I crept closer, and pushed on the door.

Locked.

Maybe I could create a spell. But if it alerted Grottel...

I turned to look at the girl pointing toward the door.

Taking a step forward, I felt the eyes of the statues follow me. The hairs on my neck prickled. When I turned around, the girls were frozen, with those same vacant eyes and endlessly ticking clock-hearts.

"Is that where I need to go?" I whispered. "Does Grottel go this way?"

Did this girl know what Grottel was doing with the Culling? Was that why she'd begged for me to save her? Who *was* she, really?

"Um, is it just me, or do they move when I'm not looking at them?" Davy said nervously.

"It's not just you," I said grimly. Charlotte nodded in agreement, her dagger out and ready.

Now all the statues' fingers pointed toward the door

leading further into the darkness, into the depth of the tunnels.

I wanted to get away, fast.

A hotaru spider bigger than my hand scuttled up along the rocks, its thin legs barely holding up its plump body, and Davy stifled a yelp. But there was something else more distracting than a locked door or the statues around us or the flickering, gigantic spiders crawling on the walls.

Ember had his head turned toward the tunnel we'd come through, his pointy ears shifting.

"What is it?" I whispered. "Is someone coming through?"

Charlotte cocked her head to the side, listening, too. "I think...yes. Ember's right."

I pulled Charlotte and Davy close to my sides, behind one of the marble statues. Charlotte pulled a thick cloth from her pocket and wrapped it around the lantern, throwing us into darkness.

My heartbeat pounded so loud it felt like it echoed against the statues and the walls. Davy pressed against my right side and Charlotte held my left hand tightly in hers; Ember stuck close to my boots. My friends' presence warmed and comforted me, despite the dizzying darkness.

Tendrils of light flickered through the chamber as someone approached.

Then a lean figure in all black strode inside. A small

bobbling light illuminated his path, like he'd managed to capture a bit of the sun and pull it underground. He stopped suddenly as he caught sight of the statues of the girl, and sucked in a sharp breath of surprise.

I was in just as much shock.

"No...," the boy was whispering as he skirted through the figurines. "It can't be...not for this...He wouldn't...*never.*"

There was a familiar haughtiness that made me grind my teeth instantly, but there was a touch of disbelief in it.

A vulnerability I'd never heard before.

I moved forward, not believing what I was seeing or hearing. Charlotte and Davy tried pulling me back...but we wouldn't be able to move forward if this intruder was in the way.

Quickly, I motioned out a plan in silent gestures. They widened their eyes but nodded, creeping away and through the maze of statues, to surround the boy.

And when I caught flickers of shadows from the sides, I knew they were in place.

I stepped forward, uncovering the lantern, unleashing a flare of light. With my other hand, I held my wand steady as I could, pointed straight at the intruder.

"Conroy Nytta," I said, my voice even and cold. "Explain what you're doing here."

CHAPTER 22

ᵀHE ᶜAVERN OF THE ᴸOST

Fear shot through my veins as I stared down Conroy, my rival and Grottel's nephew. His usual crisp all-black clothes were a mess, torn at the hems, his tanned skin smudged with dirt.

Our wands crisscrossed in the air: his pointing at my neck, my wand straight at his heart.

"Lower your wand," I hissed. "You're outnumbered."

Conroy's eyes widened, as Charlotte leaned over from behind him, her dagger tickling his neck. Davy had somehow acquired a length of the rope that the mercenaries had used to subdue the witches and wizards and was snapping it, looking like he was itching to use it on my rival. And Ember growled, not ready to let him out of his sight.

"Quiet!" Conroy snarled, low and sharp. "Are there

more of you? How are you sure Uncle Hayato or the mercenaries didn't see you?"

"Why would we tell you that?" I gripped my fingers around my wand, wondering if I should be trying to curse him into the next realm. "Aren't you patrolling for your uncle?"

"If I was, I wouldn't be trying to find my way through this place, like you," Conroy hissed.

"Prove it," Charlotte growled.

Conroy looked around at the three of us. "Because if…if my uncle's really causing the Culling…I want to stop him. I want him to be innocent. I don't want him to be hurting the realm, not like this. My uncle that I—I thought I knew…he'd never do this."

"Well, he cursed my mother's magic out of her, and I'd never thought the once-head of Council would do that, either," I snapped.

His eyes flashed. "I promise," he said. "I promise I'm not here as a patrol. Here, take this if it'll prove to you that I'm not under his command." He offered up his wand in his open hand, and I stared at him in shock.

Conroy Nytta, biggest pain-in-the-realm, freely giving up his magic?

I snatched his wand, and the floating globe he'd charmed to light his way extinguished. Ember growled in confusion.

"Okay, can you call off your bodyguards?" Conroy grumbled, eyeing the knife Charlotte still held at his neck.

"Well, I'm not convinced," Charlotte said. "Make us believe you."

"Okay, how about this," Conroy said, sighing. "We've only got half an hour or so before my uncle returns. Our time is limited if you're trying to go any further. And you need me, because I know my uncle. I know how to break through his protections."

"What do you mean, only half an hour?" I frowned.

"I set up some distractions outside, next to the entrance. Used my weather magic to summon up clouds in the shape of witches and wizards. I'd bottled up some lightning to make it seem like they were casting spells, that sort of thing," he said casually, as if that wasn't an *extraordinary* amount of magic. He squinted at me in all gray-black. "I didn't think of dressing like a mercenary. That's clever."

When that bearded mercenary, Tamura, had alerted Grottel to the disturbances outside, I hadn't made the connection. But...everything Tamura had described— the fog, the flashes of spells, the strange shadowy figures—it had to require a strong magic user, and it definitely could've been Conroy's weather magic.

"But first," I said, turning to look at Conroy. "I'm not going anywhere unless you explain what's going on."

His eyes slid to the ground. "I...I don't know what Uncle Hayato's doing here."

I clenched my skirt in my fists, shaking my head. "What do you mean? Grand Master Grottel is causing the Culling to try to gather all the power in the realm for himself."

"No." Conroy shook his head. "My uncle isn't like that. He wouldn't want to bring about the end of the realm just because he wants power. He's so strong already. Either he's not really the one behind the Culling, or there's a real reason for it all."

"How can he have any excuse for destroying so much?" I whispered.

"He's already wrecked city after city, damaging so much of Rivelle's farmlands," Charlotte added. My eyes stung as I remembered the terrifying storm that had hit Auteri. The way Kelpern had turned into a rotting town of the lost. All the cities I'd desperately fought to save in the past moon.

Anger burned in my veins. "And Grottel tried to curse me—but hit Mother instead. Tell me how there's an excuse for that."

"That's why there's got to be a reason," Conroy said, his voice small. I stared at him, at his pinched eyebrows, his downcast eyes. As far as I could tell, he truly believed that Grottel had good intentions...but how could anyone mean well with something as horrible as the Culling?

I reached my hand out. "Okay. Temporary alliance. We find out what your uncle is doing, and you promise, on your life, not to put me or my friends in danger."

Charlotte and Davy stared at me incredulously.

"Eva, this is Grottel's *nephew*," Davy reminded me.

I knew that. I knew this was a risk, but if Conroy was willing to help, I *needed* him to get to the conduit in time, before Grottel came back and finished his spells.

Conroy crossed his arms. "That doesn't sound like a fair deal for me."

"I'll do the same for you," I said. "I'll do my best to make sure you don't get hurt." Then I paused. "And... if there's a way to help my mother get her magic back, I want you to help me."

His eyes darkened, perhaps remembering that moment when my mother had fallen onto the cold tiles, too. It replayed in my mind, day after day, night after night, as I tried to think of what I could've done differently, what I had done wrong.

Then he nodded and stuck his slender hand into mine. "Fine."

I turned to look at my friends. "We need to work together to get answers, okay?"

Charlotte and Davy glanced at each other, but then they reluctantly nodded.

"Our priorities are helping the people who are stuck," I said. "Including Maika."

Conroy frowned, his eyebrows knitting.

"This girl," I said, gesturing at the frozen statues around us. "Her name's Maika, and Grottel's trapped her—"

The sound of bubbling water grew stronger from beyond the next door, and we glanced at one another with surprise.

"That's Maika, I think," I said. "She's probably trying to signal us, to see where we are. She's trapped here, and we have to help her get out, but she seems to have some sort of water affinity, so she signals me through water."

Conroy looked skeptically around the room at the statues. "I don't think—"

"My terms," I said shortly. "If Maika's there, somewhere below, and she wants to get out, we *help* her get out."

He shook his head. "Fine. But I doubt she's there."

We couldn't go back without rescuing the girl. If she was being hurt by all of this, if she was asking for my help, I couldn't leave her here. Though I didn't know why, I had a feeling that the girl was the key to all of this. I shivered from head to toe.

I could only hope that we'd be able to find Maika and the conduit without getting caught. We turned to face the next door, our shoulders squared.

Conroy tried to push it open, but the marble wouldn't

budge. He traced the outline of the keyhole with his finger, frowning. With a flash of his wand, he muttered, "*Windkey*."

A swirl of warm air flowed through the cavern, speckled gray from bits of the wet, sandy ground. I took a step away as the gust grew in ferocity, battering our clothes.

"Are you going to just *break* the door down?" Davy said. He jangled the ring of keys in his pocket. "I could try my recent invention. Multiple keys, different shapes and—"

Conroy shook his head in a grunt, focusing his wand on the keyhole. Flicking his wand, the air funneled down, the sand and air spraying at the door, and then—

Click!

The door swung open.

"I'm on your side," he said to our shocked faces, and strode forward into the next room.

Charlotte, Davy, and I exchanged glances, our thoughts mirrored in each other's eyes.

For now, at least, it did seem he was on our team.

CHAPTER 23
WATER AND FIRE

The next chamber was faintly lit by silver-cast lanterns hanging from the walls, illuminating an archway at the top of a steep, narrow incline. But there was nowhere to walk. Water flowed down the hill in a rush, disappearing below the stone we stood on. The air was thick and heavy, almost a little smoky, like a fire had just been extinguished.

"How're we supposed to get to that door?" Davy asked.

"We can climb through the water. It's low enough." Conroy stepped forward, but I flung my arm out.

"Wait. Something feels strange." I tugged a loose thread from the hem of my shirt and dropped it in the water.

The thread wriggled, and then burst into flames in a sudden blast.

We stared at one another.

"Rogue magic," I whispered.

Then Ember whimpered, his dark eyes fixated on the lanterns.

I reared back, Charlotte barely catching me as I lost my step. Flamefox fur glowed inside the glass. This place was too horrible.

I shuddered. Charlotte picked Ember up and secured him in her arms. She knelt, staring at the water, Ember sniffing curiously. "I think—yes, I see it. There're rocks in the middle, barely visible above the waterline. If we stick to that path, we should be fine."

"Just don't fall," Davy said grimly. "And don't splash."

Carefully, we walked up the stones in the center of the narrow chamber, the water rippling around us. Before me, it looked like Conroy walked on water.

Finally, breathing huge sighs of relief, we stumbled onto the rock platform at the top.

"I thought I'd become toast with one step," I muttered.

"Not toast, really," Davy commented, wiping sweat off his forehead. "Maybe soup."

Charlotte gurgled. "Um. Look."

I jerked my head up. Where there were the markings

of an archway, water filled the door, pouring down with the same slightly burning scent of the water we'd just traveled over. A girl stood in the gushing waterfall, her dark eyes staring straight back at me, crystal clear as if she actually stood right in front of me.

Conroy wobbled backward, but Davy caught him.

Maika's mouth bubbled, but words didn't come out. I couldn't hear anything.

But the water moved, and she stayed, staring.

I croaked, "What are you trying to say?"

The girl waved her hand, beckoning us toward her.

Conroy pushed in front of us, but she shook her head, and motioned toward me.

"*Eva.*" Her voice was soft; we strained to hear every word, like a drop of water in the middle of a vast, empty cavern. "*Please, help me.*"

I stepped closer.

"How...how do we know this isn't a trap?" Charlotte said, echoing my very thoughts.

I closed my fingers around my wand. "Davy, the lantern, please?"

He held up the light. Sure enough, she was just an image, dancing on the water droplets.

"Maika's not a trap," I said, wishing I knew for certain that this was true. "She's just as stuck as anyone else who's caught under Grottel's spells."

Conroy made a noise of protest, but even he seemed subdued under the gaze of the girl.

"She may not be a trap," Davy muttered, "but she may be the bait."

"Shh," I murmured. "She's trying to say something to me."

Close up, I realized her dress was woven lace, not spiderwebs. But there was something ethereal about her, too. The way she looked at me, with a smile that seemed to know me, all my faults, all the times I never seemed to cast charms right, and she accepted me all the same, like she'd chosen me to help her *because* of that.

"We can't walk through this burning water; it's filling the doorway," I said. "If you want us to find you, we need some way to get—"

Maika shook her head. *"I can't. I'm stuck here. My magic isn't strong enough, not yet."*

"Here," Conroy said. "Let me use a spell. I should get us inside, easy."

Charlotte rolled her eyes at me, but we stepped back on the platform to give him room.

"*Windbeam*," Conroy chanted, arcing his wand up in the same shape of the alcoves Grottel favored so much throughout his hideout. A splash of light circled through the water, and a gentle breeze whirled by me, fluttering my clothes.

"We can go through," Conroy said, both his hands on his wand as he controlled his spell.

Davy raised a skeptical eyebrow. "Maybe we should test it." He jostled through his pockets, pulled out a strip of paper, and waved it through the gap that Conroy had created.

A small spray of water that escaped Conroy's spell splashed down, and Davy's paper roared into a red-orange flame, like a torch. He dropped the paper, stamping out the fire. Davy shook his head. "We're going to get burnt."

"Just move fast," Conroy snapped tersely. "I'll reinforce my spell as we go through."

"I'd like to walk in one piece, thanks," Charlotte shot back. "Not as a flamegirl, obviously."

"Okay, okay." I waved my hands at my bickering friends. "Let's see if I can do something, too."

"Oh, you have magic?" Conroy shot at me.

I narrowed my eyes at him and said to Charlotte and Davy, "Remind me again why we don't just push him into the water?"

Ember growled reproachfully.

"Because he might raise an alarm and alert his dear uncle if we just tie him up and leave him here," Charlotte sighed, wistfully. "And unlike his uncle, we're not cold-blooded killers."

Davy rummaged through his pockets again and said with hope, "I've still got my rope, though."

My rival grunted, eyeing the looks on my friends' faces, and then muttered, "Sorry. Fine. Do your magic."

Did Conroy just…*apologize*? I wanted to paint that look of apology into a piece of art and put it on the wall of my cottage.

But I rolled up my sleeves. There wasn't time to bicker, not with so many lives—including Maika's—on the line.

"*A passage of safety to continue on, give us a clear path to walk upon*," I chanted, swirling my wand.

One of Conroy's eyebrows raised, ever so slightly in surprise, as my spell shimmered through the tunnel he'd made, reinforcing the wind. By the look on his face, he hadn't believed I *could* do something. But when Davy waved another strip of paper in the water, it stayed unlit.

"You need *us*," Charlotte reminded Conroy, who muttered mutinously under his breath.

"I can't hold on to this magic for long." I gnashed my teeth together, feeling the power leach out of my body. Even with Conroy's spell blasting away most of the water, this was more consuming than I thought. "So, run!"

Together, the four of us sprinted through the windy tunnel, Conroy and I holding our spells up. The water churned around us, and for a moment, it felt like I was getting tossed around in the waves of the Culling that hit Auteri, my lungs filling with water instead of air—

Suddenly, from the front, Charlotte let out a scream.

I breathed in sharply, the bitterly cold air harsh on my lungs—

Because there was only a thin platform for us on the other side. Charlotte barely managed to stop in time, to avoid falling into the darkness beyond the crumbling ledge, clutching a whimpering Ember to her chest. Davy windmilled his arms, and grabbed me and Conroy, pulling us back safely on the thin line of rock, barely as big as Davy if he were to lie down.

Conroy and I panted, our hands on our legs, trying to catch our breath from the sprint—but also from the pull of magic that had seeped from both of us.

We turned to look back at where we'd come, but the water roared fiercer than ever, burning droplets flinging viciously. I winced, seeing spots where the spray had burned into my clothes and onto my skin, stinging with pain.

Overhead, a fierce waterfall arced over a gap in the rocks. I blinked. So that's how Grottel had hidden this place. . . . No one would've suspected something under the strong currents.

And below us, below the ledge . . . it was a pit, a cylinder of smooth black rocks, too slippery to climb. It went so far down that we couldn't see the bottom.

"Eva, please . . . I haven't much time until Master gets back."

We spun around to face the water roaring through the alcove again.

The faint image of the girl stared out at us. Swallowing, I asked, "Maika, where do we go from here?"

Maika turned her head to the side and pointed downward, toward the pit. *"You made it through.... Now the platform...will bring you to me."*

"What?" Davy glanced down at the thin ledge that we stood on. "Is this a magic carpet from Arcia or something?"

Then the ground pitched us forward, and we all screamed. We tumbled down, freezing air sharp on our faces as we fell, fell, fell....

Just as I thought I was done for, I tumbled into an inky pit of water, the force knocking out the breath from my lungs. I felt like sinking to the bottom. The currents pushed me away from the center of the pool. I wasn't strong enough, not for this. How could I even think I was strong enough to face Grottel?

I have to fight. I have to keep fighting for my mother, for my friends. I kicked and pushed up to the surface, my body burning from air and brackish water mixing in my throat.

Coughing, I treaded water. Around me, Charlotte, Davy, Conroy, and Ember broke the surface, and relief washed over me.

I swam to a rocky ridge, clinging to the sharp edges. We'd fallen from two or three stories, deep into the pit.

"Eva." A thin, light voice spoke out of the pitch-black air.

A hand clasped my arm, and I let out a scream.

"I'm helping you," the voice said, and then I was getting pulled forward, onto a flat platform.

On solid ground, finally, I tried to breathe, but coughed out a mouthful of the brackish water. Where was I?

I looked around, my eyes adjusting. I was on a circular rock island in the center of the pit of water, and the very girl who had beckoned me through the caves stood steadily, with her hands clasped. Though I swore she was in front of me, there was something faint about her that made her seem ethereal, or maybe not really there at all.

She tipped her head to the side, and curtseyed in her beautiful, fragile lace dress.

Maika.

"Hello, Eva," she said. "Please save me."

My head spun, and then everything swept away into darkness.

CHAPTER 24

THE NEST OF A MONSTER

Lights winked above me. The night sky?

No.

I was still inside the cave, resting on blankets piled onto a raised section in the middle of the rock island, illuminated by hotaru spiders crawling along the walls. Far, far above, I saw the rim of the pit. The waterfall arced overhead, creating a roof of sorts. Faint rays of moonlight shone through the roaring waters. It felt like I'd fallen far through the earth and lay deep in the center of the world.

The ticking sounds drummed louder, thrumming in my bones. Memories of the girl rushed back, and I jolted upright, my head spinning.

"Be careful, Eva." That voice—light as chimes.

I turned my head, my throat dry.

Maika sat next to me, her hands clasped in her lap.

She had thin, stringy midnight-black hair and pale skin, as if she'd fallen down from the nighttime sky and the moon above. Her eyes gleamed bright as the hotaru spiders' iridescent glow. She was made of flesh and blood, not a mirage...but there was something faint about her, even as I stared at her, an arm's length away, that made her seem strange, almost unreal.

A crease pinched her forehead. "I've been waiting for you."

"Who are you?" I whispered.

"Me? I'm just Maika." She nervously glanced at something behind her. "I've been waiting for you." Her eyes lit up. "It was so difficult to speak to you, but I knew I had to, and look at us now, together! You'll be able to get me out, right?"

"Yes," I whispered, and her eyes glowed with excitement. "But..."

I slid my feet to the side. Around me, Conroy, Charlotte, and Davy groaned, slowly recovering from the fall into the pit. Ember shook out his fur, a slight steam emanating from his heated body.

"Be careful," she said. "The second hand is moving along quite quickly toward us."

The second hand?

I sucked in a cold breath. We weren't on a rock island.

Davy rubbed his eyes and gasped. "We're...we're on a *clock*."

Time surrounded us in hours and minutes, with each creaking turn of the hands. The bed lay in the center, carved out of a dark stone. A thick slab of metal pointed north, at the midnight position, and a shorter hand marked eleven o'clock, submerged in a half foot of water.

Maika stepped gracefully over the second hand as it ticked toward her. She did it in a familiar way, with her hands in the pockets of her dress. "This is how I sent you messages, Eva. I created potions to help me scry and find you."

"Why me?" I asked. "Out of all the witches and wizards in the realm..."

"I saw that you used potions, like me. And I saw what you did for that town by the sea," she said simply. "I thought you might understand how to help. And, thankfully, you came closer to the forest, so I started sending you messages."

The mirage in the water...so it really had been her. It hadn't been a trap, after all.

The second hand moved toward me so suddenly that I stumbled over it.

"Don't get in its way!" Maika said nervously. "It bothers Master if the clock isn't wound, or if someone toys with the hands, or..."

Master? Did she mean Grottel? She chattered out a handful of other concerns, but I was transfixed by the water. At each of the twelve points where a number would usually be placed, pools of water shimmered, each with a different iridescent glow.

"How…how did you get here?" Charlotte whispered, staring in shock around the dark pit.

The girl wrung her hands nervously. "I don't remember. I think I used to have a brother. One day, I woke up, and Master had found me." Her voice hung with a heavy sadness. "He couldn't figure out where I'd come from, but people tried to take me away. Scary people. Strange people. So he brought me here, for safety."

Conroy exhaled loudly, murmuring in disbelief, "I still don't believe Uncle Hayato would do this…."

"I tried to scry for my brother, but when I look, I can only see clouds and mist." Maika turned to me, eyes unfocused. "He's not gone, is he? Master promised he's searching for him."

"Searching?" Conroy echoed, and Maika turned to face him, frowning.

"You remind me of my brother somehow," she whispered. "But I think he's younger than you; he's quite a bit younger than me."

Conroy blanched. "I'm not your brother."

Maika's face fell, and I quickly said, "We'll help you find your brother, promise. But first, can you show me… there should be others….My friends here"—I motioned at Charlotte and Davy—"are looking for their family.

Might you know where they could be? And other witches and wizards, too, Grottel must've brought many more in recently. We need to help them."

"Oh." Maika frowned, her forehead wrinkling ever so slightly. "But there are so many of them.... Those who are left."

Those who are left? Bile rose in my throat. At my side, Charlotte and Davy were pale, like her words had bleached all the color from their lives. The clock ticked louder, pounding in my ears, feeling like it was shaking the walls. Darkness pressed down my shoulders, heavier and heavier, until my muscles ached.

"Please," I breathed out. "Show me them."

"It might alert Master," she said. "I don't know why, but he always seems to know when I go in there."

"Please, Maika," I said. I had to know. I needed to search for any way to help my mother. Any way to find the conduit and break Grottel's hold over the realm. And I wanted answers for Charlotte and Davy. I wanted to find their parents, so they could reunite with the people they'd been hoping to find for years.

Maika nervously ran her hands through her long hair. But, finally, she nodded, and I breathed out in relief. The girl pulled the clock hands as they churned around, nudging them to point to midnight.

The clock gears screeched as it ticked slower, slower, the water rippling from an unseen source....

At last, the clock stopped shuddering, and the ground lay steady below us. At the midnight spot, Maika pulled up a panel I hadn't noticed, with a brass handle that glinted in the moonlight. "Follow me. It's always so dark in here, but Master says it helps preserve things."

A thick fog poured out of the hole, obscuring whatever lay below. The four of us stared warily, Ember whining as he let out another cough, dry and ashy, as if his fire might be able to chase away the sudden cold that was billowing out.

"Careful on the stairs." Maika hitched up the hem of her dress and felt for a step with one of her bare feet. "Come, now. You're not afraid, are you?"

The gap yawned open like a nightdragon's mouth, the broken stairs sharp as teeth.

Uneasily, Conroy, Charlotte, Davy, and I looked at one another.

My fingernails dug into my palms as I stepped forward. "Of course not."

CHAPTER 25
ᴛHE ᴛOMB OF THE ʟIVING

Maika disappeared into the shadowy depths below. I waited one, two seconds to see if she'd scream and suddenly be eaten by a monster, but all I could hear was the shuffle of her bare feet on stone.

Conroy muttered, "Great, let's just walk into complete darkness. I love this idea."

My heart clenched. We needed to see what lay below, even though fear seemed to freeze me in one spot. When I looked around, Conroy hadn't moved, either, as if seeing what was below would finally cement the truth of what Grottel had done. And Charlotte and Davy, though some color had returned to their cheeks, were warily staring at the pit of darkness....I couldn't blame them. What if they found their parents? Or...what if they didn't?

Here, I had to lead.

Slowly, as I stepped down the stairs, faint green-hued lights flickered on at the edges of the long room carved out of the rocks. The air was cold, like plunging into freezing water, as I stumbled off the last step. My eyes adjusted to the darkness, and it felt like my body had turned into ice.

Long, rectangular stones, like raised beds, were laid in rows that went on and on and on. Forms rested on the platforms. And I thought they were statues, like in that room in the chamber above, until I saw their chests move up and down.

Alive.

The chill of the cavern slithered deep into my bones. I couldn't breathe. Charlotte and Davy gasped from behind me. It felt like my body couldn't stand on its own. Ember dug his paws into the ground, pressing against my legs, keeping me upright.

"What—what's going on here?" Conroy stared in horror, and finally, I believed that he hadn't known what Grottel had really been up to. He and I didn't get along, but it didn't mean I wanted him to be like Grottel.

Davy asked, "How many people are hidden away here?"

Maika frowned. "There's quite a few...."

Too many to count.

Conroy was staring at Maika, lost in thought. It was

as if he was seeing her, yet also not seeing her at all. When I tapped his shoulder, he jolted up. "What?"

"Are you okay?" I asked.

"I just…Uncle Hayato…he's…he's like a father to me. I can't believe he never told me about this." His voice cracked. "He's the 'Master' that Maika's talking about, isn't he?"

I swallowed. "Maybe…maybe he didn't tell you because he wanted to protect you."

Conroy looked at me, and for the first time in forever, it felt like we were seeing eye to eye. "But…why would he do this? *Why did it come to this?* He's bringing himself to ruin."

"I don't understand it, either," I said. "The statues in that room were of Maika, like Grottel had tried to find ways to put her back together, like she was some sort of broken puzzle…but…*why*?"

Conroy's brow furrowed, in a strange display of anguish. "Let's get Maika and all these people out of here." Then his voice softened, like he was talking to himself. "I want…I want Uncle Hayato to answer for this."

I didn't have any words to respond; I couldn't just magic up an answer to ease away his pain. Instead, I reached out, placing my hand on his stiff, cold shoulder for the briefest of moments, trying to remind him that he wasn't alone in this.

"I'm wondering," I mused, watching Maika shuffle

to a shelf carved out of the rock, filled with potions, her fingers moving here and there like greeting close friends. "Why are you the only one awake?"

The girl spun around, her lips tugging down. "Master has me watch over them, to make sure they stay in their sleep. My potions help, he says." She gestured at the liquid swirling in the glass vials.

Grottel had sneered at my potions, even when my elixirs had helped fight the Culling. Had he been scared because I'd begun learning the same magic as Maika? That I might be able to counter whatever designs he had to gather magic for his conduit?

"I think...Grottel's testing the conduit's magic on Maika somehow," Davy said, frowning. "That's the only thing that makes sense. And, like Maika said, he's using her to take care of the rest of them."

I nodded tersely, turning to the closest person, a woman just above the age of my mother, her hands crossed over her chest. Gently, I shook her shoulder. "Hello? Hello? Wake up!"

Maika dragged me away, her long nails cutting into my skin. "Stop! We're not supposed to wake them up."

"But if you're going to escape, are you going to just leave them here?" I spun to face her, my heart aching. "These are people, Maika. They had lives, they had hopes and dreams! Until your Master dragged them here."

She shifted, turning her head to the side. "I know...

you're right...." Her eyes filled with sadness. "It's not just me...it's not at all..." Then her voice rose. "But I didn't have a *choice*! I'm stuck here."

"They have people they love, too, Maika! Families they want to be reunited with, just like how you want to see your brother again."

She flinched. At my side, Charlotte, Davy, and Conroy were silent with shock, as if they couldn't even form words to comprehend what they were seeing around us.

"Master said they were safe," Maika cried. "He said they were happier this way, that I was taking away the misery from their lives! He said they felt like I had, when I'd been lost without my brother! And after they leave, they feel better!"

Leave...By that, did Grottel mean...after they were *dead*? After Grottel had used rogue magic to suck their powers out and siphon them into his conduit?

Maika's eyes flashed white and her hands shook. Tears leaked from her wide eyes, shocked and confused.

She had only tried to survive here.

I held my arms out. "Maika," I whispered, gently. The girl barreled into me, and I held her sobbing body. "Maika..."

"That's why I chose you!" Maika cried into my shoulder. "I'm not dumb! I knew. I knew something wasn't right, not with all those strange storms he kept starting up. He said they were happy! But I searched for you. I knew you could help! But...it isn't my fault! Don't blame me!"

"I'm so sorry," I whispered. "I know you never asked for this."

All Maika had wanted was to be reunited with her brother.

All she had ever wanted had been taken away.

"How do I wake them up?" I whispered.

Maika tugged nervously at the ends of her hair. "I—I don't know. They've always been asleep, and Master always brings more when it's time for them to go."

I shifted, staring out at the sea of people, the hundreds of victims locked in this cruel, half-alive state.

"Master uses his magic so they don't feel hunger, anything," Maika said, looking up hopefully. Her eyes glittered with tears. "Master said I'm helping them, so we can collect their powers, magical or not, and use it to make things right."

I swallowed. "That's good, Maika. I'm glad you're helping them. Can you show me how you collect their powers? And where their powers go to?"

She nodded, moving to the nearest sleeping figure. With a gentle hand, she pushed away the man's long, overgrown hair from his eyes.

There was a kindness to his face; he looked like he'd just fallen asleep for a nap by a bubbling stream, with a book still propped up on his chest, a canteen of barley tea nearby...

Sadness radiated from Maika's eyes. "They're happy—happier than me, really." With one pale finger, she traced the marble stand the man rested on. "This is ensorcelled to take just a bit of his strength, see?"

As the man breathed out, the silver flecks in the rock flashed ever so faintly.

"The more capacity they have for magic, the better," she said. "The stronger the light. Though nearly all people have a touch of potential for becoming a witch or wizard, really. It's just stronger in some people."

From behind me, Charlotte mused, "So, sort of like the way some people can run faster or are better at drawing?"

Maika nodded. "Exactly, exactly! It's a talent, of sorts."

Then Conroy asked, his voice faint, "Then your Master gathers these powers to...to..."

"Where does this all go?" I asked, finishing the question that Conroy didn't seem to be able to voice.

"To the clock," Maika said, blinking innocently at us. "Their beds pull out their powers, and siphon it above, so the clock can keep spinning, can keep moving along. Master doesn't ever want the clock to stop."

The conduit...Davy and Charlotte stared at me.

Conroy had his hand on his forehead, shielding his eyes as if he couldn't bear to see what surrounded him.

We'd *stood* on the conduit, and seen it with our own eyes.

"All of this," Maika added, waving her hands around the chamber, the countless rows of bodies, entranced to sleep. My heart shot up in my throat as I recognized witches and wizards who'd gone missing while investigating the tower; they, too, were under Grottel's curse, their marble bases slowly pulling their powers away and up into the clock.

No—the clock was just the face of it. . . . Grottel's conduit was like a monster. . . .

And we were *in* it.

Just then, a rumble echoed from the chamber overhead.

Shouts echoed through the pit, sharp as a rock-crow's screech. Then something pounded against stone, sounding like the cavern above was getting rattled like a baby's toy.

"Oh, no," Conroy whispered in horror.

"Do I. . ." I glanced up at the ceiling. "Do I want to know what that is?"

We all turned to Maika.

The girl's lips turned down as she blinked worriedly. "I think . . . Master knows you're here."

CHAPTER 26
ᴛʜᴇ ᴅᴇᴄɪꜱɪᴏɴ

arricade the door!" I cried. Charlotte, Davy, and
Conroy spun around and rushed for the opening,
Conroy with his wand extended. I raced behind them,
trying to catch up.

But we weren't fast enough.

Shadows fell onto the stairs, faintly illuminated in the
moonlight. Charlotte tried to yank the door back down,
but hands pulled her away instead, whisking her out of
sight.

I let out a terrified scream. "No, Charlotte! Davy, get
away!"

But Davy was still trying to grab at the door. He
yelled, "I can't let them get my mother! Not again!"

Then figures in drab gray-black started advancing
down the stairs, and Davy let out a shout of surprise.

With the way the moonlight cast long shadows, the mercenaries looked like gigantic hotaru spiders with scuttling legs, breaking in.

I shouted, "Run, Davy!" I couldn't cast a spell to push the mercenaries away, not without the chance of hurting my friends, too. Still, I raised my wand, trying to aim at the intruders, despite the drain from the earlier enchantment to tunnel through the burning water. "Step away or I'll curse you!"

Their eyes widened at the threat of my wand. Davy darted forward in their moment of hesitation, grabbing the door and pulling it down—

I shouted, "*For all I hold dear, let the pathway be clear!*" Light blasted from the tip of my wand, my heart trembling, shoving the mercenaries back. I had to save my friends, I had to.

From a little closer ahead, Conroy shouted, "*Windbeam!*"

A furious voice roared from the overhead chamber, "Don't let them close that door!"

Despite our spells, the mercenaries pushed forward again, pressing into the light, shoulders bent like they were walking into a fierce wind.

Between my and Conroy's spells and Davy's strength... it wasn't enough. They wrenched the door back up—

And then—the mercenaries grabbed Davy, too. He shouted, pummeling at them with his fists, but—

He, too, disappeared, whisked away above.

I let out a scream as the mercenaries threw open the door and advanced below. Tamura, the bearded mercenary, led the charge. His beady eyes narrowed as they caught sight of Conroy, and Maika shivering behind me, her tears leaking through my shirt.

"Don't come any closer!" Conroy shouted.

"We don't listen to you, little boy," Tamura sneered. "You don't pay us."

Conroy shouted, *"Windshield!"* The shadowy figures blew backward from the gust of wind—but not before Tamura grabbed him by the wrist, pulling Conroy with him.

I screamed out, *"Let the path stay blocked! For all who are here, stay safe without fear!"*

Light shot out as stones rumbled over the gap, shifting and rolling onto the stairs. Rocks settled into place, like a set of locks clicking shut, and faint, perturbed shouts from above signaled that my spell had worked.

But I was too late. My friends were *gone*.

I crumbled to the ground, the chipped rocks scraping my knees and red blossoming on the gray cloth. Tears burned in my eyes.

Always, *always*, my magic had been too slow, too late.

Charlotte, Davy, even Conroy had been taken by the mercenaries, all because I didn't have enough magic, all because I hadn't been able to cast fast enough.

Silence reigned within the cavern, as I felt the loss of my only allies. Ember whimpered at my side.

"We're stuck," Maika whispered. "We're never going to make it out."

"My plan was to destroy the conduit before Grottel appeared," I whispered, fear lancing through my chest, and Ember circled around my legs, whining worriedly.

Boom. A loud, shaking sound ricocheted through the cavern, dust sifting down onto the sleeping bodies.

A man's voice sneered directly in my left ear, "You should just give up now."

I screamed, stumbling backward, Maika catching me. She clutched at her head. "Why? Why is Master's voice in my mind?"

Ember let out a sharp whine, pawing over his ears to shut out the voice. But it was only us and the still-asleep bodies.

"Isn't it dark in there?" the voice continued, slithering and sinister, so seemingly close to us that my hairs rose.

"It's a spell," I gasped out. "Grottel isn't inside here, no matter what he tries to say."

"What if I know better than you what'll happen next if you don't give up?" Grand Master Grottel continued.

"A voice to be heard, heed my word." I tapped my throat and shouted back, "Leave us be. You're not getting in."

My magically amplified voice soared around the chamber, echoing strangely. *In, in, in.*

"Oh, is that so?"

The lanterns flickered on the walls, sending us into flashes of pitch-darkness, and Maika let out a cry of fright. "Please, no. Not the darkness! Please, Master!"

My heartbeat pounded in my ears.

"If you try to break in, Maika and I will run!" I shouted.

There was a sudden silence, as if Grottel was taken aback.

Somehow, *somehow*, I knew the girl was essential for Grottel to unlock the power of this conduit. He hadn't chosen just anyone; it *had* to be Maika for some reason. Or...perhaps...my throat felt like it was burning with acid at this thought—was she part of the conduit, too? Maybe her magic with the elixirs made her the *key* for the conduit?

Grottel growled so loud that Maika let out a cry. Then he snapped, "No time for your foolishness. Take away this spell blocking the door, or I'll do that for you. And you'll severely regret it."

"Oh, yeah?" I called back, with far more bravado than I felt. But he didn't have to know that my legs felt like water. "We're not giving in to your demands."

"So be it," Grottel snapped. "You had your chance."

The lights went out again, plunging us into utter darkness.

I reached out, and a soft, trembling hand clasped mine.

"Maika?"

"Eva?"

Our sighs of relief echoed through the chamber. Then there was a strange shuffling sound around us, like boots scraping against rock.

"Is that you, Maika?" I whispered.

"N-no," Maika whimpered. "What is that?"

At my feet, Ember pressed against my legs, shivering. He let out another ashy cough, and I could almost hear him say, *I'm sorry, Eva. I wish I could light up for you. I'm not a very good flamefox, am I?*

"You're still the best flamefox around, no matter what," I murmured, distractedly. The shuffling sounds were getting louder. My skin pricked ominously.

"So, little witch," Grottel sneered from above. "Are you enjoying your time down there?"

I raised my wand, *"Bright as my flamefox, let me see, the world all around me."*

Maika and I screamed.

All around, the bodies had moved. Some sat, some stood, some were lying on the floor. When I lifted the light toward them, they stopped. But without the beaming glow, the bodies moved closer and closer.

The younger girl let out a shriek. I spun around, illuminating the light toward her.

The figure on the pedestal closest to Maika had reached over and grabbed her wrist in its hand. Nails pressed against Maika's skin, clawing at the girl, the body's eyes opened but unseeing.

I yanked her hand out from the figure's grip, and she clung to me, sobbing. "No, no, please. All these people... no, it wasn't my fault, no..."

Ember circled worriedly, growling at things I couldn't see in the darkness. Maika clutched to my legs, with her eyes shut, tears leaking from the corners. I tried to calm her. "Maika, you're safe now. I won't let that happen again."

She took in a shuddering breath, but she still kept her eyes shut. "I knew you'd save me. I knew you would. But I didn't think it would be like this...."

"Would you like for me to make the bodies dance for you?" Grottel's sneer echoed through the chamber, seemingly coming from all of the pitch-black corners at once.

The bodies jerked around, scuffling closer and closer, and Maika let out another petrified scream. "No, no, please, no!"

"Stop!" I shouted up at the ceiling. "Grottel, stop!" I had to distract him, stop him from casting this cruel, awful spell. "Stop and tell us the terms!"

There was a moment of silence, then—

"We'll trade," Grottel declared. "The girl for your little friends."

I shook my head, even if he couldn't see me. There was no way I'd let Maika get into his clutches. But a hand tugged at my sleeve.

"They'll get in anyway." Maika widened her eyes frantically as the pounding got louder. "Let me go to Master, please. Open the door?"

"No, we can't—"

"But he—he's going to hurt your friends!" Maika cried out, pushing away from me. She screeched and stumbled back from a body. I caught her, just as she was about to slam into a marble pedestal. "Please, please, let me go to Master."

"I can't," I whispered. "Grottel shouldn't be allowed to decide your future. You should."

Grottel snapped, "You have two minutes to choose. But I won't wait a moment longer."

I met Maika's eyes.

"We can't go after them, not without us all getting caught," I whispered. "We have to destroy the conduit somehow." I looked up. Could I break the clock from down here?

A steady *plop*, *plop*, *plop* distracted me. I held my hand out and water pooled in my palms. Then I looked up.

Fissures ran through the ceiling, like lightning had slashed through the sky. And through the cracks, water poured down steadily and grew stronger and stronger, like the start of a storm.

"Curses." Horror filled my veins. "Grottel's breaking through the ceiling. But we're under all the water. We're going to get flooded in."

Maika whimpered from where she huddled against a marble pedestal. The water sloshed up to my ankles; it was swelling fast, higher and higher.

"C'mon, please." I knelt in front of Maika. My body was still sore and magic-drained, but the tiredness began to wash away as determination beat through my veins. "Can you help me? Together, I think we can get out safe."

"Not if he's there. That's impossible." She balled her hands into fists, covering her eyes.

I gathered the younger girl's hands in mine, soothing away her trembles. "Maika, this is where we fight. We're not giving up without a battle, because we're not letting Grottel get away with this. We're not letting anyone else get hurt."

"But..." Her hands were still limp in mine as I pulled her upright. "But...how?"

"You're a witch, like me."

"All...all I do is potions, really." Maika shifted in the calf-deep water nervously, her dress dragging behind her. "I can't do any of the nifty things you do, those spells and all."

I frowned. "Why not?"

"I'm not clever like you."

Shaking my head, I swallowed deep. I knew how that felt all too well. "Maika, you're just as clever as me. Some of my strongest magic is from potions. No matter what form your magic comes in, potions or charms or something in between, all that matters is what you *do* with your strengths. And we can't give up, not with people depending on us." She followed my gaze toward where my friends were captured above.

"But what can I do?"

"Potions..." I would've paced to think, but the still-standing bodies waited around us like a living graveyard. A shiver ran down my spine. "What kind of potions do you have, Maika?"

She gestured at a shelf next to the stairs. "Just a few types. For things like cuts or bruises, in case some of the people here need my care. But...Grottel did show me how to bottle some of their thoughts, into the essence of a daydream or a good memory. And there were a few bad eggs, like nightmares or fears that I bottled, too, by mistake. I have some of those vials."

I grinned at her, even though weariness tugged at me. "Perfect. You've already made what we need for this fight. Lean in close. Here's the plan."

Maika and I tucked our heads together, with Ember keeping an eye on the bodies.

"We have each other," I began softly, "and we can do this. Even if it seems impossible."

"Really?" she whispered.

I nodded firmly. "Together, we're full of impossible possibilities."

※

Maika clung to my arm as we strode through the standing graveyard of bodies, my wand providing just enough light. The figures stayed frozen, but their eyes followed our every step. I wanted to escape to my cottage and crawl under the blankets with Ember and forget about this day.

We huddled by the stone door as Maika gathered her potions. "This one's filled with sorrow; this one will bring forth memories of pain....Here's joy..."

Like we'd planned, Maika and I slid the vials into our pockets.

"Your time is up," Grottel growled. "So, have you made the *right* decision?"

Ember nosed at my hand, and I smoothed down his ruffled, wet fur. He leaned into my hand and looked up at me, eyes wide and worried.

I swallowed. "Stay safe, Ember. That's all I want."

He glared back. *I'm a flamefox. I can fight by your side, too.*

Maika tugged at my sleeve. "We can do this?"

"We can do this." To my surprise, my voice was calm and steady. "We've got our plan, our potions, and our people. We'll be able to break the conduit and make it out of here."

"What's outside, beyond the waterfall?" Maika asked.

Tears burned in my eyes as I unraveled the spell on the rocks. "The most amazing realm ever, Maika. There are so many people I want you to meet. My mother will love to be friends with you, and she knows a lot about magic, too."

"She sounds lovely," Maika said.

My heart thumped as I thought of how I'd be able to get Mother's magic back, if I could only somehow outwit Grottel and break the conduit.

If...if...

There were a thousand ways this wouldn't work.

But Mother had said...that even in the face of the seemingly impossible...

There were still impossible possibilities.

And I would prove it to myself, that I could become a possibility, too.

The rocks tumbled down, and a hint of the fading moonlight shone through the gap, casting a faint glow on my face.

A new day had begun, but the fight had just started.

CHAPTER 27
ꟻIGHTING FOR THE ℒIGHT

Maika squeezed my hand, her skin just as cold as mine. Just as we'd planned, she called out loudly, "Master, I'm going to step out. Please don't hurt me."

From outside, Grottel growled. "Fine. But Novice Evergreen better not have her wand, or I'll curse her before she can mutter a word."

A shudder ran through my spine. I smiled grimly at her. He clearly wasn't taking any chances. Neither were we.

Maika tugged me out, holding my wand high in the air. "No wand for the witch, Master!" she called cheerily, so believably that, for a second, worry flickered in my heart. But she glanced over her shoulder and the corner of her lips tugged up slightly. It was still going according to plan.

Faint moonlight illuminated the pit, filtering through

the waterfall above. Dark, hooded figures surrounded us, standing at the edge of the island, maybe twenty paces away, and then forming a bigger circle around the edges of the drained pit.

We'd finally met Grottel, face-to-face, and his band of mercenaries.

Fear zipped through my spine as I noted the mercenaries' daggers steady in their hands. They were well accustomed to fighting. Already, they'd taken out far more powerful witches and wizards. Beating a lowly Novice like me would be easy.

The water that had surrounded the clock had seeped to the chamber below, and the mercenaries stepped forward, among the damp, rocky stones, guarding any possible path leading above and out.

No matter how well we'd planned to break the conduit, Grottel was no easy opponent.

But—hopefully—we had a plan that would work.

Ten or so paces away, Grottel stood at the edge of the clock, his wand pointed at us.

Next to him, my friends—including Conroy—were slumped, on their knees. Mercenaries guarded them, striding around like dragonsharks ready for their next meal. Charlotte looked up, her face filled with hope, but a mercenary pushed her head down.

I recognized the scar twisting the mercenary's jaw, those rumpled curls.

Soma's eyes quickly dropped away from me, returning to his patrol around my captured friends.

Traitor. Traitor. Traitor. Soma, even if you'd warned me of this... I'd hoped you'd be my ally.

Glaring at the pirate, I squeezed Maika's hand reassuringly and murmured, "We can do this. We're an impossible possibility, I promise." Ember pawed at my boot, letting out another ashy cough. I couldn't wait to be back in our cottage, reading through another magical tome on our bed and feeding my flamefox strips of mackerel jerky. But to get to that, I'd have to fight.

"So." Grottel crossed his arms, his hand still tightly closed around his wand. "Come over here, Maika. Come back, and we'll let Novice Evergreen's little friends go free."

At my side, Maika wavered, plucking at the hem of her dress. But I didn't want the girl to spend another ten years in this pit. I shook my head. "Sorry, Grottel, but we've got our terms, too."

He scoffed and with a flick of his hand, the first circle of mercenaries advanced toward us.

"No." Maika pointed my wand out at them. "Don't make me cast a spell, don't make me—"

Grottel paled. "Wait, Maika. Put down the wand, please."

There was a strange hollowness to his voice, like one action from her might shatter everything for him.

I frowned.

Did he...actually care about her?

Slowly, it felt like one piece of the puzzle was fitting into place.

"How about this," I said. "You don't want anyone"—I glanced pointedly at Maika, and I heard Grottel's hiss as he followed my gaze—"to get hurt, so you'll listen."

"Evergreen, you think your magic can help," he spat out. "Your pitiful spells. Ha. I'll decline."

"Eva, watch out!" Charlotte shrieked.

Grottel had started muttering something too far away to hear, but his wand was pointed up at the waterfall. Water rushed down, all around us, billowing into a thick fog. My heart thumped uneasily as I blinked, trying to see what was happening.

Then through the heavy mist, the spray froze, forming into a sharp-pointed icicle—

Aimed directly at me.

I took a step backward, but Maika and I were surrounded by mercenaries. There was nowhere to run.

Maika screamed out, "No! Don't hurt her!"

But Grottel didn't care; his wand flashed down, and the icicle shot straight at me, on course to slam me off the island—

Fighting Grottel is impossible—

Maika still clutched my wand; there was nothing I could do, no spell I could create in time—

A small, tiny, fierce burst of light pounced in front of me, letting out an ear-splitting cry, and—

Fire.

Ember roared out, a pillar of flames shooting from his mouth and straight into the air, melting the icicle just inches before us.

As the mist cleared, my flamefox let out a fierce growl at Grottel, as if to say, *Don't you dare hurt* my *witch.*

Slowly, even though I wanted to fall down to the ground, even though my wobbly legs felt like they were barely keeping me upright, I raised my head up, my gaze burning into Grottel's. "If you won't even listen to our terms, I'm sorry, but we'll have to decline."

Grottel growled. "Not a chance—"

He hadn't given me a warning. So he wasn't worth one, either.

"Fight!" I shouted, and just as we'd planned, Maika tossed me my wand. I hurtled two potions toward the closest mercenary as I roared, "Take that!"

The glass exploded at the feet of the mercenary and a noxious, black-green potion flowed out in a fog of ropy, slithering swirls, like a snapping shadowsnake from the pits of the abyss. The black-green fog enveloped him as he shrieked. "It hurts! It hurts all over!"

As he opened his mouth, mist slithered out, dark and heavy, like it'd turned into smog.

"One dose of a nightmare." My eyes narrowed. "Though this isn't all. I'll *ensure* the queen doses out proper penalties."

From behind me, Maika cried out, "And this is for keeping me locked here, all these years!" She tossed two vials at Grottel.

With a roar of shock, the Grand Master disappeared behind a screen of scarlet smoke.

I threw one vial at the mercenaries guarding my friends. "Don't you dare mess with the people I love, or you'll have to deal with me!"

Glass exploded into fuchsia fumes that skittered up their legs in plump clouds shaped like rats. One man stumbled to the side, screaming, "Get it off me, I hate rats! Oh, I hate rats!"

Davy, Charlotte, and Conroy broke out of the ring of mercenaries surrounding them and raced toward me.

"What do we do?" Charlotte shouted, over the pained shrieks of Grottel and the mercenaries.

"We have to break the conduit—this clock!" I called out. "Conroy, can you help?"

My rival paled, looking at the clock below us, with its metal hands that continued to churn through the chaos. "Eva, this is far too dangerous....There are things you don't understand....We should wait for Elite Dowel and the Council—"

"What do you mean?" I shouted. "This is our *one* chance!"

I pointed my wand down at the ticking clock, summoning up the spell I'd thought of in the chamber below. I recalled how Maika had called for my help, trusting that *I* would be able to save her. I channeled memories of the times Charlotte and Davy had fought for me, fought to stay at my side.

I couldn't let Maika or my friends end up like my mother, sacrificing everything for me.

I had to fight. Mother had reminded me to believe in impossible possibilities, moments after being cursed. Even if it seemed impossible, I had to persevere.

The tip of my wand glowed as I chanted, *"Believe in what is real, what only time can reveal. Believe in impossible possibilities to break what should not exist; fight on, and continue to resist."*

I swung my wand, the light arcing like a sword, cleaving downward.

Boom. A crack split in the thick rock, through the midnight spot. From behind me, Maika let out a shriek of surprise. But I had to focus on the conduit; she had enough potions to keep herself safe for now. I needed to break this clock clean through; I had to smash the rock that was imbued with magic, and release all the powers back into the realm, to the people they had been taken from. I aimed my wand down again. *"Believe in what is—"*

Conroy cried out, "No, Eva, wait, you don't understand—"

He lunged forward, trying to grab my wand out of my hand. Shock and disappointment zipped through my veins.

My rival had shown his true colors, after all.

"Just consider yourself lucky that I won't curse you into the next realm." I threw down one last glass vial next to him, and it shattered into pieces, pouring out oily-black flames. "Enjoy your worst nightmares."

"*Wind—*" Conroy let out a shout of pain as the potion's vapors stole into his mouth, cutting off his air. The potion was too fast for his counterspell.

Conroy stumbled to his knees, letting out a shriek. He clutched his arms around his head, curling on the ground. "No, please. Maika didn't mean to, she only meant—"

"*Eliminate the past!*" a voice roared from behind us, enraged. Diamond light shot through the sky, and Conroy's body flew up into the air as the black flames evaporated. "*Slow.*" Ever so softly, Conroy's still-shaking form landed on the clock.

Why...why was *Maika* in his worst nightmare?

Through the fumes of the fight, a tall, dark figure strode through. Grottel's hooded eyes glinted at Maika, who clutched my arm from behind me. I glanced over my shoulder, and with shock, I realized she looked *transparent*, like she was starting to fade away. But—I stared down at the cracked conduit—*how*? And *why*?

Grottel growled, "Maika, I will *never* let you go. And your friends will now have to stay here with you."

CHAPTER 28
THE FINAL CURSE

Grand Master Hayato Grottel stood at the midnight spot of the clock. His wand flashed at the cracked marble, where water seeped to the chamber below. *"Seal, now."*

His powerful spell, a sharp demand, cracked like thunder, and the stone that made up the pit began folding upward, sealing itself, and then the currents diverted from the arcing waterfall above to pour down the sides, refilling the pool. The mercenaries who had been standing in the pit crawled onto the island if they could. Or, they merely washed away in the currents, but the Grand Master didn't spare them a second glance.

Grottel's magic was so strong that it was terrifying.

His dark eyes focused on Maika, behind me. "It's time for the conduit to rise, fully. Maika, come here."

With a flick of his wand, Charlotte, Davy, and I were

thrown against one another, and ropes knotted around our hands and ankles.

I cried out, tugging against the burning threads, but I was stuck. My wand lay five feet away, where Conroy had pushed it out of my hand.

Grottel sneered down at me as he strode toward Maika. "Good riddance, Evergreen. It's time, now, for the final Culling. I'll let you watch—not that you'll survive its strength."

I didn't know how I'd ever thought that I could fight against him. Helplessness seeped into my bones, icier than the spray of the water.

Still, the key to all of this was missing: *Why was Grottel causing this destruction?*

Another flash of Grottel's wand spun the clock hands to point at midnight. He snapped his wand as he shouted, *"To the edges of Rivelle Realm, through waterways and air. Cull what you find; bring all power and life here."*

The clock trembled from the intensity of his enchantment, the stone oozing noxious black fumes as the water churned around us, rising in that same tainted color.

This...this was the start of a *Culling.*

The water swirled and swirled, a deceptively gentle mist, as it rose to flow through the streams and rivers, to sink into the very land and people it would reap its bounty from.

All for...all for *what?* So Grottel could be the most powerful wizard in a broken realm? *Why?*

"Maika," Grottel said, holding his hand out. "It's time, finally."

Her eyes widened, her translucent body shuddering as she stared in fear at the water all around us. "But it's so frightening…"

"It will help you," he said in the gentlest, most careful tone I'd ever heard from him. "It won't hurt. It never did before, right? It's made you stronger, so much stronger."

From his side, Conroy looked up at Grottel with pain furrowing his eyebrows. I didn't understand.

Something was missing. There had to be some link between Grottel and Maika, but…

The statues of Maika in the cavern, each carefully crafted, with clockwork pieces clicking like a beating heart. Time, time…Maika needed more time….

Grottel's careful watch over Maika, like she was far more precious than anything else in the realm.

The way Conroy had stared in disbelief when we'd entered the chamber of slumbering bodies. "Why did it come to this?" he'd said.

"Eliminate the past." Grottel's spell to remove Conroy's nightmares about Maika….How could Maika be in Conroy's past?

Unless…Could it be…

"Father!" I exclaimed. Charlotte stared between me and Grottel in confusion. "No, *her* father."

Everyone, even the bedraggled mercenaries, turned to the focus of my gaze.

Maika blinked, with her hooded eyes just like her father's, the pointed chin I'd once despised so much on Grottel. "My...my father?"

"'*A rogue witch had, with one wayward spell, decimated an entire town*,'" I said hoarsely, quoting *Sorcery of the Lost Ones*, the book on rogue magic that my mother had researched and one of the last tomes Kaya had procured for her store....It'd been such a rare book, so hard to find...almost like someone was trying to hide the truth. "I thought the witch had died...."

I stared at Maika, and the way light seemed to flow through her, just a bit, making her pale skin a tinge translucent, her dark hair ethereal and unreal. The way that breaking the conduit had made her even more washed out, as if she wasn't quite fully here.

"And..." I turned to look at Conroy and then Grottel. "She did die, didn't she? After she took out a whole town? The village next to the tower?"

The tower...the way it looked like it'd fallen into itself. And the few thatch cottages next to the lake, looking strangely small in the wide clearing...because the village had been wrecked, and never been rebuilt.

The ghost stories Mother had told me, of lost souls wandering through the Twisted Forest of the North... had those all been experiments done by Grottel? All to save his daughter? Or souls lost during that first unintentional Culling?

Maika backed away from us all, toward the edge of the rock island. "No...no."

Grottel's forehead was slick with sweat. "Maika..."

The girl shook her head wildly. "No. Say it isn't true. I thought I'd lost my memories, not...Not died. I remember I had a brother. He was so kind...We were such good friends. That *had* to be real!"

"I don't think you ever had a brother," I said. "But you had a cousin, right, Conroy?"

My rival looked sick to his stomach, with his lips tugging down sharply. "Wait, Eva, please..."

Grottel rasped, "This was all for you, Maika. I have done everything for you—"

"I never asked for this." Maika's voice swirled through the pit like wisps of vapor, not strong enough to stand up against the roar of the waterfall above. "All I ever wanted was to be reunited with my brother, my *family* who loved me. But even that was a lie."

"I nurtured you, Maika. I gave you everything I could. So you could live." Roughly, Grottel gestured at the clock below us. "You don't have all the time in the world. I've been doing everything I can to give you life, before you run out. Let me transfer the powers in the conduit to you, before it's too late. You need this to survive, Maika."

She shook her head, her stringy hair limp on her face,

guilt twisting her features. "No. You are not my father. My real father would've loved me enough to tell me the truth. My real father would've let me be free of the cage you've made for me. My real father would not have cursed me from having a real life."

Grottel hissed, eyes wild with denial. "I will help you, whether you want my help or not. Your mother never let me help, until it was too late for her. Without this, without us feeding you life, you will die, too. Come here, Maika. Give me your hand, so I can transfer the powers to you."

The girl backed away, until she was at the edge of the island, rocking over the mists that swirled ominously. "No. That's wrong. I don't need you. I never needed you."

The mists started blowing around, like we were in the center of a tornado, the air whipping cold and sharp against my skin. The mercenaries still clutching to the clock shouted out, begging for help.

Grottel choked. "Wait, Maika. Step away from the Culling. Step away—"

Maika raised a wand high into the air, and Grottel's face bleached of all color.

"My wand," Conroy breathed out in horror. "No, Maika, please."

I could feel their love for her, even as the wind swirled more and more fiercely around us with its burning spray.

Maika took another step backward, shaking her head

in revulsion, as recognition of the horrible truth filled her eyes with sadness.

"I'm the only one who can stop this, aren't I?" she said, sorrow permeating her voice. "You said you would help me find my brother, but I never had one. And this chaos you're causing, this Culling...it's hurting all these people, and hurting the realm, isn't it? So if...so if I'm no longer here, there's no reason for the Culling again, is there? There's no reason to hurt anyone again...Father."

Grottel's eyes widened, and the pain mixing with joy was heartbreaking to see in his face. He did love her, so terribly much.

He would do anything for her, in the same way my mother willingly sacrificed her magic for me. My eyes stung, and I wasn't sure if it was from the mist or from the terrifying, horrible scene unfolding in front of me.

"Maika!" I cried out. "No. There's got to be some other way. Please, come back here, *please*!"

Suddenly, my hands were free; Charlotte started using her dagger on Davy's ties. I stumbled forward to snatch up my wand, pushing against the screeching, fierce wind. *"A reason to believe, please let her see."* A shimmer of bronze light, burning with impossible possibilities, the same color as my rank, burst from my wand, engulfing Maika.

Then it shimmered, shooting out toward the water all around us.

And visions flashed against the water. Somehow, impossible as it was, I'd managed to use my magic to pull wisps of memories, to remind Maika why she should stay.

A dark-haired girl and boy laugh as they charm their rice balls to race across the table, even as a man with hooded eyes scolds them.

My head jerked back. It was Maika and Conroy... but my rival was a few years younger than his cousin. And Grottel... Grottel looked *happy.*

Then Grottel comforts them when their rice balls fall to the ground, crumbling to pieces, and makes fresh ones, chasing away their tears.

Late nights when Conroy and Maika can't sleep, and they're snuggled up in their beds in the nursery. Grottel brings in stacks of books and reads from cover to cover, until the two of them are snoozing easily, and Grottel's voice is hoarse, and sometimes he falls asleep on the hard tile floor of the tower.

Days out on the lake next to the tower, Maika and Conroy playing in the shallows, under the hot summer sun, with plenty of sweet waterberries, until their cheeks are freckled and noses burnt.

Practicing magic, even though Conroy can easily summon a rainstorm, Maika keeps trying simple spells and when she just manages to levitate a scroll, Conroy and Grottel cheer like she's saved the realm.

"Stay!" I cried out to Maika. "See this, all around

you? Please, don't step into the waters! There's got to be another way! You *are* loved, Maika! Your family is here for you!"

Maika stared at the memories all around her and then at Conroy and Grottel, etching every angle of their faces in her heart.

Then she smiled, eyes oddly bright. "Father...I don't want you to do this anymore. I will end this, now. So you will never have to do this again, so you will never have to hurt another person, another family, for my sake."

Grottel's voice was low and raw. "No, please—"

She began to chant, gripping Conroy's wand to her chest, "*Undo the price of the lives I chose to take; to end the Culling, I willingly forsake.*"

"NO!" Grottel shouted. "No, Maika, no!"

The girl stepped backward, off the island, into the frothing waters that leaped and grabbed at her with sinister waves. The water burned at her, sizzling into her skin, like liquid fire. She seemed to float there, in a split second that stretched out in time, her white lace dress fluttering around her like wings, her hair swirling in the mist as she smiled, eyes bright with tears.

Grand Master Grottel screamed, leaping forward. His hands scrambled to clasp hers.

But this meant—my heart leaped into my throat—he was moving too fast; he couldn't stop himself in time.

Shock turned my veins into ice.

He *didn't* plan on saving himself.

Grottel grabbed Maika, shoving her onto the island, and the waves of the Culling opened wide, hungrily welcoming him in—

Midair, he turned, his eyes searching for her. His eyes relaxed in relief as he saw me and Conroy clutching Maika, holding her back on the rock island, as her hand reached out for him, screaming for Grottel to return.

And, somehow, the memories switched to his, as if he wanted to tell her one last bedtime story.

Grottel holding a young Maika up in the air, his eyes beaming as she's successfully created a potion to turn black hair into green, and he smiles even though his hair is now the color of a poisonous swamp.

And then—*A midsummer day, Grottel trying to slowly ease Maika's wand out of her hand, shaking his head, and she pulls away, her mouth saying no, no, please, let me keep my magic.... And his eyes say it all: If I could give up my magic for you, if I could give up everything for you, daughter, I would.*

And Conroy behind them, frozen as Maika casts a spell for freedom—

But it somehow twists, changing into a storm, gathering and gathering into a tornado, knocking bricks off the tower and the nearby homes in the village, and roaring until there is only sand and dirt and—

When the dust filters away, it's just Grottel and

Maika, him holding her broken body, crying and crying, but his eyes burning with the determination to do anything to save her.

Anything.

Grottel raised his wand, high in the air, and his lips moved. At first, fear rippled through my bones. Was he—was he cursing us, in his final moment?

Bursting from his wand, a diamond-bright globe surrounded all of us on the rock island. Outside, the water frothed and foamed, but not a single acidic drop touched us inside.

Hayato Grottel had created a shield...to protect his daughter, his nephew...but all of us, too.

His final sacrifice.

This was a promise of his everlasting love for his daughter: The curse Maika had placed on herself had been traded for Grottel's sacrifice.

His eyes closed as the waters claimed him, pulling him into the foaming waves. Maika darted forward, slamming her fist on the shield as she screamed. But no matter how her nails scrabbled at the surface, she couldn't break through. And Conroy shouted spell after spell, his face soaked with tears and mist, but his enchantments bounced off uselessly, holding him at bay.

Then all around, the pit rumbled.

The clock cracked, shattering into a million marble shards.

Suddenly, all noise faded away as a sharp glow seared my eyes, burning ever so bright.

That was the last thing I remembered: the silence, the absence of all sound, and that eternally bright, pure diamond light.

CHAPTER 29

ℐMPOSSIBLE 𝒫OSSIBILITIES

Water lapped gently against a shore, bubbling and tinkling as it flowed to faraway places. As I slowly awoke, with Ember curled up around my shoulders, my eyes drank in the strange new sights around me.

Grottel's sacrifice and final spell had blown out the entire pit, taking away the cage Maika had always wanted to escape from.

Under the rays of the soft, golden-yellow sunrise, I looked around at the people picking through the new valley that had formed. Some of the mercenaries were slinking away; others—including Soma—were sitting in a daze, frozen in shock. The waterfall had turned into a stream, rippling next to me, through this valley and cascading down, heading out to the Northern Sea. Fresh dirt, cold and gritty under my fingers, covered the ground. Even the tower had crumbled into a pile of stones, wiping away its once-ominous presence.

In the center of this new valley, the doorway still led to the cave below, but the figures who'd been woken by Grottel's curse had lain down, locked back in their slumber. My chest tightened. I'd have to wake them somehow.

As I got to my feet, two figures hurried up to me.

"Eva, you're awake!" Charlotte cried out. Davy's shoulders relaxed behind her, his eyes crinkling with relief. Ember circled around them, his tail waving so fast it looked like it was flickering.

"What happened?" I asked. Was it really as I'd remembered—

Charlotte shook her head in disbelief. "Grottel...he sacrificed himself for Maika...and it was like the Culling was here, in the pit."

A voice broke the quiet.

"He hurt the realm. So, so much," Maika said, stepping forward from behind my best friends. "I couldn't let him continue."

We all looked at the gently bubbling stream, carrying the last words and the last breath of Grand Master Hayato Grottel.

"It's not your fault," I said fiercely. I thought of Mother, and the way she had clutched my hand after she'd been cursed, saying that it had been her choice. "He chose."

I hadn't—no, I couldn't understand back then.

But now, I said, "Hayato Grottel chose this because he loves you, but it was his choice. He was the one who wouldn't let you go, ever, because of how much he cared about you."

With that, like an uncurling breeze of fresh air, a heavy weight shifted off my back. The rightness of my words settled deep in my heart, a balm to the pain I felt when I thought of Mother. When she'd stepped in the way of the curse meant for me, she hadn't made an easy choice to understand. But, through watching Maika and Grottel, I had come to accept what had been done, because there was no way to change it now and, most of all, because it had been Mother's choice.

Impossible possibilities, like Mother had said after being cursed. Maika and I, Char and Davy, even Conroy...we were the impossible possibilities of the future, the chance to change things for the better.

"But...why?" she said. "He destroyed so much for me, and I never wanted that."

That was true. Hayato Grottel had committed unspeakable evils, all for Maika. He was no hero, not by any means.

"I think...I think...people who care for us, like my mother, or your father...they want us to continue on, because they believe in our ability to change the future for the better," I whispered.

Slowly, tears trickled from her eyes. She glanced

away, gazing at the chaos around us, as if seeing Grottel
in every crack and crevice. "I want to change things and
try to make amends for what he's done."

I extended my hand out to Maika. "Come on," I said
softly. "We can do that. Let's change this place, and take
care of the people here. Let's change the future."

Maika was still translucent, but her skin was smooth
against mine as she firmly took my hand, her eyes shining
brighter than the sunlight above, glowing with life.

We turned to the cavern, blood pounding in my ears.
We would change Rivelle Realm for the better, with every
next step.

Just a few hours later, a brilliantly bright light shone from
above, a sharp pure white that burned into a deep red,
like flames coming down from the sky. And a voice rang
out, "Announcing Her Royal Highness, Queen Alliana
Sakamaki, our chosen ruler of Rivelle Realm."

I'd sent a letter as soon as I'd woken, but I hadn't
thought that the queen would come so quickly. I stood
from where I'd been stirring a potion to give the once-
entranced people some strength, and brushed off my
knees. There was a hollowness to my every motion; I was
sapping my pool of magic that was already so weak to
begin with.

All around, people huddled on the rocks in small

groups, or some simply laid out, drinking in rays of sunlight. The Councilmembers we'd been able to revive—like Masters Arata and Roone, and the Elite triplets—had been bustling around, taking care of the more severely injured. Some of the mercenaries were even helping, too. I'd even seen Elite Kaya Ikko, the bookseller, recovering with her hands around a mug of steaming tea, and Ralvern, the campsite worker and Hikaru's brother, cutting wood for fires. But now they stared like me, hands cupped over their eyes, as a dozen passenger broomsticks floated down, each carrying a flier and a second rider.

A tall woman stepped off the first broomstick, where she'd ridden sidesaddle, and a handful of attendants from other broomsticks hopped off and began smoothing out the queen's wind-ruffled gown. Her clothes were silvery like the strands of gray streaking through her hair, and the hems were tipped in scarlet.

Elite Norya Dowel, the interim head of the Council, had flown her in. Norya dismounted, leaning her broomstick against the broken shards of the clock. Queen Alliana strode forward, a steely look in her eyes, with Norya following in her wake. The queen stopped in front of me, placing her long, thin fingers across her arms. "Novice Evalithimus Evergreen."

"You received my letter quickly," I said with surprise, as I sank into a bow.

The queen pulled a wrinkled piece of parchment out

from within her sleeve. "A mercenary delivered this to me. A message from a boy named Soma Enokida?"

I gasped, looking over at the handful of mercenaries who'd chosen to stick around and help out. A familiar face was helping feed a weary wizard who was recuperating from his slumber. Soma...Soma *had* helped, after all.

"I read the letter, but—what has happened?" Her eyes skimmed the recovering people, gaping at her, clearly undernourished and weakened.

From behind Queen Alliana, familiar brown eyes met mine. Princess Stella, the Regional Advisor to Auteri. The princess nodded at me, and then she broke off to help a recovering woman drink a cup of water, kneeling at her side.

I raised my head, eyes heavy with sorrow. "Rogue magic, all cast by Grand Master Hayato Grottel." Slowly, stiltedly, I explained Grottel's interference with the realm. The cavern full of entranced bodies, how he'd sucked the powers from their memories and souls through the Culling, and channeled it into his conduit. How he'd taken life after life all for his own gain, all for—

"All for me, though I never asked him to." Maika stepped out of the cavern, where she'd been administering strengthening potions to more injured people who lay on marble beds, too weak to step out into the sunshine. Her thin dark hair floated over her shoulders, and her white dress looked as delicate as hotaru spiderwebs. She floated forward like a phantom out of the tales of the North, and now I knew there were some truths to those ghost stories. "I will make amends for the evil he's caused. I promise."

From behind the queen, Norya let out a gasp. "Grand Master Grottel's daughter," she whispered, her voice hoarse. "I remember when you were just a tiny girl.... You haven't aged. Yet...I thought you had..."

Died. She stared around sadly, as if she could find the missing word there. Norya's brow wrinkled, turning toward me. "Did Grand Master Grottel escape?"

I couldn't meet anyone's eyes. "He...he perished, sacrificing himself so that Maika could live."

Norya jerked back in surprise. Some of the other witches and wizards muttered, shaking their heads with shock.

"I'm very thankful for what you have done for our realm, Novice Evergreen," Queen Alliana said. She reached out, taking my hand in hers, her warm fingers gripping me strongly. "You and your friends have fought well, and Rivelle Realm would not be the same without you."

A sudden shout came from below. I spun around and raced into the cavern, with the queen close at my heels.

At the far, far end of the cavern, Charlotte crumbled to the ground.

"What is it?" I rushed to my friend's side as she pounded a fist on the floor, and I held her tight as she wept into my blouse, drenching me in her quiet tears.

"I'm sorry, Eva," Charlotte whispered. "You've got

so many people to help and here I am, worrying about the past—"

"No, no," I said fiercely. "There's nowhere else I need to be right now. What's the matter?"

"My parents...they're not here after all," she whispered. "I looked and looked....I asked every person in these chambers....None of them. None know of my family."

Foreboding filled my veins, but I swallowed it down. Surely...*no*. "I can try casting a spell?"

Her gray eyes searched mine, shimmering with a faint sheen of hope, and she nodded. "Do you need a lock of my hair again? Or—anything—whatever you need—"

I shook my head, even though my magic felt so faint from overuse. "The enchantments Grottel used to mask the Culling should be gone now....Let me try a spell."

Slowly, I slid my hand around hers, holding her tight. I didn't know if this would work....Still, I *had* to try.

"*A search for a friend close to my heart, show her parents so they will never be apart,*" I chanted, raising my wand up.

The point glowed, pulsating with light. Suddenly, my wand pulled me and I tripped forward, taking Charlotte with me.

We hurried to the far end of the chamber, and when I saw what was ahead, I tried to slow down, but my wand insistently tugged me forward, draining my magic.

Charlotte and I stumbled to a stop in front of the wall of glass vials, swirling in a multitude of colors. My wand tapped against a tiny bottle of sky-blue, and then the light from the tip of my wand burned out.

"W—what?" Charlotte's voice trembled as she stepped closer, picking up the elixir, and turning it around.

In spidery-thin letters on the label, there was one word: *Love.*

That was it. Her parents *had* been here, once upon a time, until Grottel and his rogue magic had twisted lives, reducing them down to...to *this.*

Charlotte's body shook as she threw her arms around my shoulders, clutching the vial close in her hand, and sobbed. She cried and cried twelve, maybe thirteen years of tears, and I didn't let go. I couldn't let go.

My bones ached from the weight of my friend's sorrow, but this was all that I could do now, until I could somehow help her smile again.

☙☙

At the far end of the valley, Davy sat with his feet dangling off a rock, staring in shock at the woman sitting next to him.

His mother.

Utter joy mingled with complete disbelief.

Their hands were clasped as they chattered in that excited, Davy-like way that I knew so well.

Charlotte and I walked slowly to the other side of the fires, so we wouldn't interrupt their reunion, and I supported her with my arms.

This...this should've been a victory, to free Maika. To free those stuck in the cavern. A chance for Charlotte to find her family. But my chest ached.

I wanted to take away her grief, but no potion or spell would ever truly heal my friend. Not pain like this.

Charlotte sat next to one of the fires boiling up fresh water, away from everyone else, and Ember jumped into her lap. She held him close, his head pressed in the crook between her neck and shoulder, trying to give her comfort.

I stepped away as Queen Alliana walked toward her.

Surprise broke through Charlotte's haze of sorrow as the queen sat down, rubbing Ember behind his pointy ears. My friend moved to bow, but Queen Alliana motioned for her to stay seated, and spoke to her, her voice gentle as the bubbling stream.

My heart swelled, watching some of the darkness in Charlotte's eyes fade. Even if ever so slightly, the queen's words seemed to absorb some of her pain.

"You? Without family?" Charlotte said, her voice rising in disbelief.

"A stepmother who would never care for me," the queen said grimly. But her eyes brightened. "But I had a dear friend in Nela, Novice Evergreen's mother, and that made all the difference."

"But that didn't…that didn't give you a family," Charlotte said.

The queen shook her head. "A true friend is like family." She motioned to me, my wand tight in my hand, standing guard over my dear friend, and Charlotte looked up, a faint echo of her past smile on her lips.

Charlotte had reminded me, time and time again, that I was never alone. And I wanted to be at her side, too.

"Once I was free of my stepmother's claims on me, I had Rivelle's Academy to devote myself to," Queen Alliana said. "Now the entire realm is my family. You should consider it. I see a spark of myself in you, Charlotte of Auteri. Perhaps, one day, you could become Charlotte of Rivelle."

Charlotte was speechless as the queen placed one gentle hand on her shoulder, rose, giving her one last smile, and continued on her way.

I let Charlotte and Ember stay there, next to the fire, as I went to check on someone who I hadn't met since waking.

Every witch and wizard who'd come along with the queen was working on awakening those in the chamber, whether making potions or using spells to take away their enchanted slumber, or feeding and watering those in need, nursing them back to health.

I found my once-rival working with a handful of Elites to clear up broken marble beds and glass vials.

Conroy was sweeping up some of the shards with his magic. "*Windchurn.*"

Tinkling glass neatly jumped up and slid into the Elite's canvas bag.

"You're all good now," the Elite said, dismissing him. "Go on, take a rest."

Conroy's shoulders slumped as the other witches and wizards continued through the cavern, cleansing the cave of Grottel's dark touch.

But Conroy stayed, his eyes searching the now-vacant marble pedestals, the broken shelves, the empty doorway. As if Hayato Grottel might come striding in again.

I cleared my throat, and Conroy jolted upright. His dark eyebrows were tight, like angry ink slashes.

His shoulders dropped when he saw it was me.

"He's gone, isn't he?" Conroy's voice was a whisper, but it felt as sharp as knives to my ears. "Forever. I couldn't do enough, no matter how hard I tried."

"Conroy, it isn't your fault," I whispered.

"I didn't want to believe it. I tried to pretend that what he did wasn't evil...or that it had to be someone else making him do these awful things." He shook his head. "But he'd been working on this long before Maika's accident."

"W-what do you mean?" I asked.

Conroy gestured at the alcove hewn into the cavern wall, at a stack of scrolls I hadn't noticed before. "There's years and years of research here. It's been going on since my aunt...Maika's mother...since she died. But I can't say he didn't do evil things anymore, can I? It wasn't just the Culling. This was more than a decade of research and planning, from beyond when the first Culling started."

My heart sank. "So that's why Charlotte's parents were here..." To Conroy's questioning gaze, I explained, "They'd disappeared long before the first Culling, so I thought that maybe my spell looking for them had misfired, that they were safe somewhere in the seven realms...."

Conroy shook his head. "I should've seen a sign of what my uncle was doing. I should've stopped him. I should've...I should've done *something.*"

I wished I could charm away my rival's pain. But I couldn't erase the irreversible, awful truth of what Grottel had done. "It was his choice, Conroy. No one pushed him to this other than himself. You *can't* take the blame for this."

Conroy breathed in deep. He looked around, as if trying to find a sliver of redemption in the wreckage around us. "Maika's still here, though. That's...that's something, right?" Then his voice cracked. "She...she reminded me of you, you know. With your potions, and all that...and I think that's why Un—Uncle Hayato found it hard to see you, too."

I opened my mouth, closed it. Conroy had always

been dismissive of my lack of magic, and then of my potions, but I'd never known exactly why, until now....

"Uncle Hayato..." Conroy gripped his wand tightly, as his hand shook. "He was the one who first saw me cast magic, you know, on the day I was born. I always looked up to him so much....And now he's *gone*."

His voice cracked on that last word.

None of us were meant to be alone. I had my parents, Charlotte, Davy, and Ember. We were all meant to lean on each other, especially in times of need.

Grottel had thought he was alone for far too long, even though he'd had Conroy at his side.

And I wouldn't *ever* let that desperate loneliness happen to Conroy, even if I considered him my rival.

But there were no words I could really use to console Conroy. He needed actions, something to do, something to work toward.

"Let's work together, to fix the realm," I whispered.

Conroy paused, his face shadowed and his shoulders stiff. Our rivalry was ages old, even though it felt different, now.

"We can fix the realm and become Adepts, Elites, even *Masters* together." I held out my hand. "C'mon, let's shake on it."

Though his eyes were still sad, his rough hand slid into mine. "Deal." Then he paused. "Though I'll be a Grand Master first."

I raised an eyebrow at him. "I highly doubt that."

A trace of a smile tugged up the corners of his lips, ever so faint. And as he turned away, he murmured something so gentle that it could've just been wind swirling through the cavern. "Thank you, Eva."

But I was sure he'd said it.

᎒᎒

The fading sunset burned on the horizon, shiny and golden red like a flamefox racing across the skyline. Magnificent as it was, it revealed no secrets as to how to fix the realm in one day.

It would take time, but I would reunite each person who had been claimed by the Culling back with their families and friends, as much as I could.

"I swear on my magic," I whispered, out to the bubbling stream and the moss-coated trees in the distance, the witnesses to my oath. I looked around me, at my friends trying to mend their lives, trying to figure out their next steps. "Every day, I'll fight for the realm to be whole again. Even if it feels like nothing but an impossible possibility, I believe it'll happen. One day at a time, I'll make it happen."

PART FOUR

THE
BURNING
FLAME

EPILOGUE

ᎢHE ᎽEAR-ᎬND ᎱEAST

FOUR MOONS LATER

My cottage glows in the sunset, the wood slats shining gold through misty winter clouds. I touch down at my landing spot a few steps from the door, smiling at Mother's fresh footsteps and broom marks in the dusty ground. Though my mother doesn't have enough magic yet for the same spells as before, she's promised me that she feels her powers come back day by day, and she's begun to fly all around the realm on the Council's missions again.

Ember bounds out of my knapsack and circles around my boots, stretching out after our long ride from the farmlands, which I've been assigned to in addition to Auteri, after the Culling finally abated. Conroy likes to grumble and say that *he* wanted the farmlands, but for now it's my duty.

Before I go inside, I look over my shoulder at the rippling waters. The Constancia Sea is as steady as ever. The occasional rainstorm or flurry of winds hits the coast, but it's been nothing like the Culling.

I hope, with all my heart, that nothing like the Culling will ever hurt our land again.

Finally, Rivelle Realm is peaceful.

Loud chatter floats out of the windows glinting in the sunset, beckoning me out of the frosty air. My cottage is as cozy as ever, not much more than a small one-room home, but right now it's extra special because everyone has gathered to celebrate the Year-End with a feast.

"I'm home!" I call, hurrying into the warmth.

My family and friends from Auteri and all around the realm turn to welcome me, eyes bright. They merrily shout, "Happy Year-End!"

The tiny cottage has been decorated from the floorboards to the ceiling in bright red and festive gold streamers, to celebrate Rivelle's end-of-year traditions, every corner crammed with the cheery colors. It all starts today, on the last day of the year, and continues through the new year, a way for us to reflect over the times that have passed and to look forward to what's to come.

"Eva!" my parents call. They jump up from their seats around the rickety wood table stretched out to fill the small cottage; it's much longer than I remember it. Mother must've used one of her charms. Father engulfs me in a hug. I breathe in deep, drinking in his scent of freshly baked bread and feeling his scruffy chin scratch my forehead. I've been getting taller, slowly but surely. Someday, I'll reach Mother's height...and maybe even her Grand Master level, too. At least, that's my goal.

"My turn, my turn," Mother says impatiently, and we laugh. She squeezes me in a quick hug before spinning me around to greet everyone else who's here.

"Took you long enough to get back. Almost thought the rockcrows carried you away. Or maybe that you got eaten by a nightdragon," Davy teases from where he's setting out a tray of croissants in front of his mother and father, who wave cheerily. Father's been teaching Davy how to bake, and when he's not adventuring around the realm or spending time with his parents, my friend often stays over to learn all of my father's baking secrets. According to Davy, a good meal is a special magic of its own. I think he's been listening to Ember's stomach too much, really.

Someone rushes over, throwing their arms around me, and I breathe in peppermint and rich leather.

"I've missed you, Char." I grin at my friend. "We're going to Okayama together tomorrow, right?"

"I'm...I'm ready," Charlotte says, taking in a deep breath. "I think." She bites her lip, tucking a loose strand back into her braid. Even though my best friend is usually as unflappable as the queen, she's so nervous about her new goal: joining Rivelle's Academy to try to become one of the Regional Advisors. And, I hope, vying to become Queen Alliana's successor.

Charlotte, as protective and full of belief as she is toward me, doesn't believe in herself yet.

But until she does, I'll do what she did for me and believe in her. After all, even if we're not bound by blood, Charlotte and I will always have each other.

"You're more than ready," I reply, and Charlotte's cheeks burn as she motions me to one of the wood chairs, also wrapped in red and gold streamers. Even though, as Auteri's town witch, this is technically my cottage, Charlotte and Davy visit so much that I think of it as their cottage, too.

Rin tweaks the brim of my hat when I sit down next to her, and Yuri and Edmund, the sugar artists at Seafoam Sweets, wave at me from the far end of the table, where they're wearing matching red-and-gold scarves. Kaya's sitting with them, chatting about their favorite cookbooks, magical and non-magical alike, and Soma's close at her side. To my surprise, the ex-pirate has taken a liking to working in her shop, helping her with everything from filing to searching for the perfect book-match for shoppers.

"Ah, it's so good to see you," I say, squeezing Rin in a hug.

My once-guardian laughs. "You've only been out on your Council's quest a few days this time, but it does feel like forever, doesn't it? I've missed seeing you, too."

From the other side of the table, Maika waves, her hand fluttering like a moth, almost translucent in the lamplight. "Good to see you, Eva."

"Any updates?" I ask, studying the way that Maika is slightly fainter than when I saw her last; she's still not fully corporeal, not yet.

"Your mother's wonderful," Maika says, softly, her voice gentle as the sea breeze ruffling my hair. "Her research has been insightful."

My chest clenches. Grottel's shielding spell saved us from the wrath of the Culling, but it kept Maika locked in her ghostly form, so she continues to fade away, day by day. But between me and Mother, we're determined to find a way to help Maika—without raising another Culling.

"Don't talk too much. You should save your strength," Conroy worriedly chides next to her, but she only laughs a light, tinkling sound, sweeter than wind chimes.

"If I don't talk, if I don't live, then I'm truly a ghost," she says, smiling gently, and Conroy relaxes with a nod and finally shoots me a faint smile. Neither of us has forgotten our rivalry, and we're both working harder than ever to get ready for our Adept ranking quests—whatever they may be like. Mother's been hinting that they're not quite what I might expect.

Within seconds of Davy setting down a platter of roasted mackerel, Ember whines loudly from where he's weaving around my legs, hungrily sniffing at the deliciously scented air. Charlotte's managed to tie a red-and-gold bowtie around his neck, but he wrinkles his nose at it, probably thinking he's already far too charming to need any ribbons.

"I think Ember's saying it's time to eat," Mother says.

I grin. "I think he's *always* saying that."

"Char and I worked all day on our Year-End feast!" Davy says. "Now all we need is to bring the rest of the plates to the table." The counter next to the stove is nearly collapsing under the weight of dishes. He turns to Mother, eyes wide with hope. He adores watching Mother's magic at work, even for the simplest of spells. He thinks she's legendary—and I wholeheartedly agree.

But Mother turns to look across the table at me, questioningly.

"I'll charm over the food," I offer. She smiles widely, her eyes bright with pride. Father reaches his arm around her and she leans into his touch, and my heart flutters as everyone turns to me expectantly.

I'm surrounded by my closest friends and family, and if I'm going to cast my magic for anyone, I want it to be for them.

I look around the table. Seeing everyone's eyes shining

back makes my heart feel like it's overflowing. I breathe in deep, raise my wand, and chant, *"For those I hold dear, a feast for all here."*

It's a simple spell, with not enough words to express how much I truly love everyone who has supported me through these past moons—or years—of me trying to become a witch.

There are never enough words to truly explain how much I love my friends and family. But then, that's what the enchantment of a spell is about, right? Even though there are just a few words, magic pulls my emotions and channels it into something that shows those I love exactly how much I care for them.

Ember dances around my feet as the dishes float over, decorated with mouthwatering fresh herbs or piled high with sweet baked confections.

"A wonderful spell, well said," my mother says, and I beam back at her as I guide the plates over with my wand.

Soon enough, the table is groaning under the feast that my friends have prepared.

"Cheers to the Year-End!" I raise my cup. "Cheers to the future, and to all of our possibilities."

"Cheers to the Year-End!" everyone echoes, clinking glasses full of redbud cider. Eagerly, they tuck in to the meal, starting with Davy stealing a contomelon roll from under his mother's grasp, but then setting it on her plate with a laugh. On my other side, Ember butters up

Charlotte by rubbing against her legs, so she'll sneak him a few bites of her mackerel.

I look around at my circle of friends and family, who I love with all my heart. I can almost see their amazing futures stretching out ahead of them. All of their wonderful possibilities, just around the corner.

And me?

I'm just a girl who believes in impossible possibilities.

And, a girl with a pinch of magic.

I look down at the table and smile at my friends and family surrounding me…and my rival across the table, too. Conroy raises an eyebrow, as if he knows exactly what I'm thinking: When it's time for me and Conroy to fight for our Adept rank, I bet he'll claim he's going to become the first Grand Master.

But some day, I'll be the head of the Council. And, of course, a Grand Master. *First.*

Acknowledgments

Thank you, dear reader, for joining Eva and Ember on their adventures. This story exists because of your support. Ember is sending you lots of flamefox hugs in thanks!

To Sarah Landis, thank you for your brilliant work as my fearless and wise agent.

Alvina Ling, thank you for your dedication to making Eva's story shine.

Ruqayyah Daud, thank you for always taking the best care of Eva and Ember.

Thank you to the magical team at Hachette and Little, Brown Books for Young Readers: Megan Tingley, Jackie Engel, Tom Guerin, Siena Koncsol, Janelle DeLuise, Hannah Koerner, Karina Granda, Sarah Van Bonn, Jen Graham, Andy Ball, Nyamekye Waliyaya, Emilie Polster, Stefanie Hoffman, Savannah Kennelly, Mara Brashem, Bill Grace, Rick Cobban, Christie Michel, Victoria Stapleton, Marisa Russell, Paula Benjamin-Barner, Shawn Foster, Michelle Campbell, Danielle Cantarella, the sales team, the publicity team, and many, many more.

Shan Jiang, I am absolutely in awe of your talent and

dedication to creating the intricate, beautiful artwork that brings Eva to life and makes her glow with a spark in her eye!

A huge thank-you to the booksellers, teachers, librarians, and bloggers supporting Eva, who always seem to have a special kind of magic of connecting readers with the right book at just the right time.

Thank you to Mom and Dad, and my extended family, for cheering me along on this journey.

A special thanks to Fonda Lee for your mentorship that prepared me for the journey leading to publication.

Thank you so much to the wonderful authors who blurbed *Eva Evergreen*—Temre Beltz, Kat Cho, Sean Easley, Debbi Michiko Florence, and Elizabeth Lim. Your kind words warm my heart like flamefox fire.

Sending endless thanks to Alyssa Colman, Bridgette Johnson, Chelsea Ichaso, CW & Xiaolong, Eunice Kim, Grace Shim, Graci Kim, Jessica Kim, June Tan, Karina Evans, Laura Kadner, Melissa Seymour, Meredith Tate, Michelle Fohlin, Natasha Buran, Robyn Field, Ron Walters, Sarah Harrington, Sarah Suk, Susan Lee, Suzanne Park, Tara Tsai, MGical Misfits, Team Landis, my Vancouver family, WFC, Ken, Leon, and Julie-chan.

Mimi—thank you, dear friend.

To Conan, thank you, always, for our fry-day drives.

For our dearest Emily—this story is for you. Thank

you for brightening each day and inspiring us with your strength. You make our lives magical.

Thank you to Eugene for encouraging me during the toughest of days, for our wonderful adventures together, and for believing in me—and us—always.